FAMILY
SECRETS

FAMILY SECRETS

Deathbed Confessions of a Mob Boss

Kennedy had to go

JOHN GRECO

FAMILY SECRETS
DEATHBED CONFESSIONS OF A MOB BOSS

Certain characters in this work are historical figures, and certain events portrayed did take place. However, this is a work of fiction. All of the other characters, names, and events as well as all places, incidents, organizations, and dialogue in this novel are either the products of the author's imagination or are used fictitiously.

iUniverse books may be ordered through booksellers or by contacting:

iUniverse
1663 Liberty Drive
Bloomington, IN 47403
www.iuniverse.com
1-800-Authors (1-800-288-4677)

ISBN: 978-1-4917-9199-8 (sc)
ISBN: 978-1-4917-9200-1 (hc)
ISBN: 978-1-4917-9198-1 (e)

Library of Congress Control Number: 2016904216

Print information available on the last page.

iUniverse rev. date: 04/25/2016

CONTENTS

Dedication vii

Preface..xi

Chapter 1   Frankie Makes An Offer....................................1

Chapter 2   Decisions Are Made...9

Chapter 3   Party At The Big House...................................19

Chapter 4   On A Mission 46

Chapter 5   The Kennedy Ordeal......................................53

Chapter 6   People Sometimes Disappear 64

Chapter 7   Business As Usual..74

Chapter 8   Change Of Plans...89

Chapter 9   Time To Expand..101

Chapter 10 Rise To Power 113

Chapter 11 Cleaning House...127

Chapter 12 Keep It Quiet..135

Chapter 13 The Secret Meeting 148

Chapter 14 The Kill Shot...157

Chapter 15 Run Fast – Run Far 164

About the Author 171

DEDICATION

Writing this book was not an easy task for me, and it took years to finish. I have vivid memories of the day I was in Catholic school watching the presidential motorcade driving down Elm St, the President being shot live on TV and the announcers crying as they reported the sad news that our beloved President was dead. The entire country was in mourning for weeks while government agencies tried desperately to piece the puzzle together. The best they could find was with the Warren Commission's report blaming one lone nut for shooting the President, getting off three shots within six seconds.

There was much more the people did not learn until 20 years later – i.e., the conspiracy theory involving major players in the world of finance, big oil, government agencies, and other countries. Stopping John Kennedy at any cost was their top priority.

The real truth will never be known.

I dedicate this book to my father who was much like the character Michael Delagatta portrayed in this fictional novel; kind hearted and gentle, but not as vicious. He is the rock on which I stand!

Those who knew him know precisely what I mean. Loved by all, feared by many.

Special thanks to:

Aunt Dee. Thank you for helping in so many ways with this fictional novel.

My lifelong friend Eddie T. (Money) and his loving wife Kathryn for always being there and showing my family and me the better parts of life. For pushing me hard every month to write the book. And the closer I got, pushing even more for me to finish it.

My wife and counselor for putting up with my crazy years and enduring for over forty years.

My blood family including cousins and friends for always being close and supporting me through good times and bad.

Special thanks to all those Brooklyn boys in the 60's who showed me how to grow up fast and hard in the streets of New York and survive it all. You guy's taught me how to stay alive and endure all that life throws at you and stand Italian strong.

PREFACE

Back in the early 1900s, thousands of immigrants made their way to the, shores of the United States of America. They came with the purpose of living a better life and providing for their families. America was called the land of milk and honey. Most found it harsh and much tougher than what they were told in their native countries.

Italians were among the many diverse ethnicities fleeing to the New World for freedom and prosperity. New York was the drop-off point for most. Ellis Island was the gatekeeper to the interior sections of America.

Vincent and Josephine Delagatta were among the Italian immigrants to settle in Brooklyn, New York. Michael was one of five brothers born in the New World.

Competition for jobs was high and most had to find any means possible for staying alive and providing for their families. Some turned into thieves and robbers while others worked hard and saved. Either way, it was not an easy life. Living in the New World was harder than most thought.

During this time, small pockets of young gangs started to band together, and the American Mafia was born. In the beginning, it was a rag-tag operation until one man decided to make the organization run like a business. That man was Lucky Luciano. He was branded with the nickname Lucky, because after being shot several times and left for dead, he lived. After taking out his enemies, he formed the Commission, consisting of devoted Italian members who were loyal to this new organization. It took decades to build an empire of illegal money making rackets within several dozen states. Prohibition was the most lucrative money-maker, along with loan sharking, prostitution and several other ventures. The Commission functioned like a well-oiled machine, with bosses, captains, and workers. It was decided that five of the original members would be the bosses of the groups they controlled within the organization.

They were known as the Commission members. They agreed that for decisions to be made, they had to come from and be approved by the Commission only. The decisions were final and anyone who did not follow orders was terminated. It was later decided that a member of the Commission would be made the counselor and spokesman for the entire Commission. Because the bosses were busy running the daily operations in different states, they needed someone to act as the voice that spoke for all of the bosses.

The counselor would be a separate entity from the five family bosses, with his own crew and members who worked for him only. They could be loaned out to the other bosses if needed, but they were independent of the five families and loyal to their boss. The counselor was the go-to person for a variety of needs such as paid politicians, police department employees and government officials who were in the pockets of the mob. Along with many other duties, the counselor was responsible for setting up special meetings, new contacts, bribing judges and setting up fake corporations along with other official duties needed by the families and their associates.

Vincenzo De Napoletti was chosen to be the Commission's counselor, as he was one of the original members and the only person having the education and expertise needed that would be required in the future. He was known in his younger years as the Ice Man for a variety of reasons. One being the fact that to support himself in America as a young boy, he sold ice blocks on the streets of Pitkin Avenue in Brooklyn, New York and became a part of the original crew along with Lucky and several others. Well respected, the brother, of Josephine, who in later years, would take a special liking to his nephew Michael. Some say it's because Michael reminded Vincenzo of himself in his younger days. Vincenzo became a powerful man in the early sixties. In addition to his own lucrative ventures, Vincenzo had dozens of government, political and prominent people on his payroll, which was funded by the families' combined income. The families were the strongest during the late fifties and sixties. Mistakes were bound to be made. Vincenzo and the Commission would have to make tough decisions and take swift action for the mistakes some members made, and some would lose their life because of it.

John Kennedy was the son of Joe Kennedy. Joe wanted his son to be President of the United States. John ran for the presidency as a favor to his father. The Commission decided to rig the votes and get John elected to the highest office as President. They assumed that by helping Joe get his son elected, they would have better control and that John, also known as Jack, would find favor and turn a blind eye to the family organization and, its profitable illegal operations. Everything was fine until Jack appointed his brother Bobby to the position of Attorney General. All hell broke loose when Bobby started going after organized crime and the bosses. Unacceptable to the Commission and its members, they tried to persuade Jack and his father to do something about it and to tell Bobby to back off, but Bobby was intent on destroying the band of what he called "hoodlums and thugs."

Michael, being the nephew of Vincenzo, was expected to rise to the position of Capo and eventually take Vincenzo's place upon his death with the blessings and approval of the Commission. Michael was given the task of organizing and overseeing the intended assassination of either Jack or Bobby based on the decision of the Commission and its final orders. Both Vincenzo and Michael were against killing either Jack or Bobby and tried to negotiate with both Joe Kennedy and the bosses of the most powerful organization in the world. The Commission made the decision that John Kennedy had to go. In their view, "cut off the head and the body dies with it." There were dozens of people and even countries that wanted Jack dead, including government agencies within the United States. Vincenzo and his closest associates were ordered to do something to stop the destruction of the Mafia and what they ultimately did would put all their live in danger.

Although this is a work of fiction, it should be noted that a percentage of the outcomes and actions are real and documented facts. I will not say or point out what is fact and what is fiction. It is up to you to find the real history and come to your own conclusions as to what really happened and why. To this day, many have been blamed, and it remains the biggest mystery in U.S. history as to who was involved and who shot John Kennedy. The Warren Commission report is the only government information released, and over fifty years later, the truth is still unknown to the World!

Every effort was made to use fictional names; however, there are eight billion people in the world. If the name of any character in this story is the same as or resembles someone you may know, it is purely coincidental

CHAPTER 1

FRANKIE MAKES AN OFFER

Brooklyn, New York 1958. Michael Delagatta was an above-average man, 6'4", 255 lbs., jet-black hair, round face with dark brown eyes, muscular build with abnormally large hands. His pinky finger was size 14. As an auto mechanic, he was used to working with his hands. He was married to Jackie, a 5'3", 102 lb. Italian/Irish woman with fire-red hair and a temper to match. Her personality and tempestuous style are what drew Michael to fall in love with this feisty woman.

They were Catholic and had three children. Michael had four brothers (Harry, Salvator, Jimmy, and Louie) and an adopted brother named Tony Garamondi, who was nicknamed Tony G. Tony's family died in a tragic house fire when Tony was a young boy and Vincent, Michael's father, took Tony G. into his home as an adopted son. Vincent and Josephine, Michael's parents, immigrated to America with twelve dollars between them and spoke only Italian. Because Vincent didn't speak much English and it was hard to find work he chose a profession he knew well. Vincent was what you would call a professional gambler, and he was a master of his craft. Poker was his choice for providing for his large family in the New World.

Survival of the family depended upon the money the boys made shining shoes on the streets of Brooklyn and surrounding areas for ten cents a shine, sometimes working the streets fifteen hours a day. The boys would give the money to their mother Josephine, knowing that their father would spend it gambling, killing the chances of

1

survival with such basic needs as food and clothing, among other things.

Michael started shining shoes at the age of eleven along with his brothers, who were older than him, except Louis, who was the baby and just turning seven at the time.

One day Michael was seen by his father shining the shoes of a sailor in uniform. The sailor gave Michael a quarter. Michael put it in his pocket just as his father came over and asked him how much the sailor gave him. Michael reached into his pocket and pulled out a dime and showed it to his father. His father asked him in his native language, "Is that all he gave you?" Michael was afraid to tell his father, yes, so he reached back in his pocket and gave Vincent the quarter he just received from the sailor. Vincent smacked him on the back of his head and said, "Next time you lie to me, you will go hungry for a week."

Michael and his brothers were afraid of their father as he had a short temper and would beat them for no reason. They all tried to stay away from him as much as they could. Vincent died in 1947 of a massive heart attack leaving the family to fend for themselves and support their mother who was the rock of the family.

In 1958, Michael was twenty-nine and working for Anthony Russell and Dominic Ramano. Michael was in charge of the auto repair department. One day his cousin Frankie Rutiglianno (aka, Frankie Ragu) showed up at the shop in a brand-new white Cadillac convertible. Michael went out to greet him with surprise on his face. "Where did you get this car?" Mike asked. Frankie smiled and said, "I've been saving money and bought this baby for cash. Come on, I'll treat you to lunch." Michael was shocked as he opened the passenger door and stepped in. "This fuckin' car new cost a fortune. How could you afford this car with a job like yours?" Frankie smiled and said "As a transporter. I make good money, and it's all cash, Mike." "More like a fuckin' car thief would be a better description" Mike replied. "We'll talk about it during lunch at Gino's Italian Restaurant," Frankie said. Michael had never been to Gino's. It was upscale and very expensive compared to other Italian restaurants in the Brooklyn neighborhood of East New York.

Pulling up to the restaurant, Frankie parked the car in front. "Come on let's talk and enjoy some good Italian food. I'll introduce you." Entering the front door, Michael was not sure if he should enter into such a fancy place. He was wearing his gas station uniform and smelled like grease. "Frankie, you sure it's ok for me to go in like this?" he said with a look of rejection on his face. "You're with me, and you don't have to worry 'bout it." Frankie was dressed with a nice blue button down shirt, black slacks, and shiny black shoes. Frankie was a good-looking man in his early twenties, curly brown hair and dark blue eyes that could woo ladies with just a look in their direction. The female hostess welcomed Frankie by name, "Frankie, would you like your usual seat?" "You know me doll, I have to sit with my back against the wall and my eyes on the front door. This is my cousin Michael. Look at the size of his fingers. You know what they say about a man with large fingers." The hostess looked straight into Mike's eyes while putting his hand in hers and smiled, "These are the largest fingers I have ever seen", as her eyes slowly looked down at his crotch. Mike, now blushing red showing his embarrassment, politely said "It's a pleasure to meet you," as he wrapped his hand around hers and smiled. The hostess walked Frankie and Mike to a back room which overlooked the front door from a distance and asked Frankie if he needed to talk to Gino. "Just tell Gino I am here and if he wants to come and see me, that's fine." With that, Gino walked into the room and greeted Frankie with a big hug and kiss on both cheeks of Frank's face. "Frankie, I want you to try some of my mother's homemade casada cake for dessert. It's the best." Frank smiled and introduced Gino to Michael. "This is my cousin Mike, and with any luck, you'll be seeing him more often." Gino reached for Michael's hand, and Gino's eyes opened wide as he looked down at Mike's hands. With a big grin, he said "Your hands are like sledgehammers. The size is amazing. And your nails look like half marbles. The biggest fuckin' hands I have ever seen." Frankie laughed "Thanks, Gino, you just gave Mike his official nickname, The Hammer. Gino meet the Hammer." Gino smiled. "Frankie, I would shit my pants if these hands came to me for my vig payment," Frankie replied, "Fix us something to eat, we're starving." Gino walked out of the room and Mike looked at Frankie with a puzzled face. "Frankie, how does he know what we want? We didn't even get a menu yet." Frankie sat back in his seat and smiled. "Gino will take care of that. Don't worry he knows what to send us."

Frankie leaned forward in Mike's direction and said, "Mike, what the hell are you doing working as a grease monkey? With your connections, you could be making a ton of fuckin' cash." Mike leaned back with a surprised look on his face. "Frankie, what the hell are you talking about, I don't have any connections." Frankie smiled replying, "You have more connections than I have and you don't even know it, do you? Your brothers all have jobs. Let's see, your oldest brother Harry is on a military base in Jersey. Jimmy works on the docks in Brooklyn. Sal works for the bank. Your adopted brother Tony works for the trucking company, and Louie just started a job in the insurance business. And let's not forget cousin Eddie T (aka, Money) who works with your uncle Vincenzo in the loan business and makes a shit-load of cash." Hell he can be a great asset and get you inside the family connection. You know, even though I started this job less than a year ago, I am just a soldier who steals expensive cars for cash, enough cash to buy that sweet little caddy out there, and I made enough cash in less than four months to buy it." Michael looked up to see Gino walking to the table with enough food to feed five people. "Enjoy," Gino said with a smile, "and leave fuckin' room for mama's dessert." Not another word was spoken as Frankie and Mike started to dig into the smorgasbord of food in front of them.

Mike wanted to know what Frankie wanted from him and how he would be involved. "So Frankie, what is it you want to talk to me about?" "I need a place where I can store cars and change the ID tags, and you have the perfect place in the yard. You can store them in the back lot, and no one will even know they are there." "I'll have to think about it," Mike said as he nervously reached for the napkin to wipe his mouth. "You got twenty seconds to think about it" Frankie replied with a grin on his face. The rest of the conversation was related to family, kids and memories of the past. After they had been done Frankie stood up and said to Mike, "OK, let's go. You gotta get back to work, and I need to pick up a car for big Sal." Frankie reached into his pocket and peeled out a wad of money rolled up in a rubber band holding it together. Frankie put a hundred-dollar bill on the table, and together they both walked out the front door. "Frankie, you didn't even get a bill. You know, that was a hundred large you left on the table, which was too much." Frankie looked at Mike as they walked out the front door. "If that wasn't enough, Gino will let me know."

Pulling up to the auto shop Frankie said: "Mike, think about what we talked about and let me know what you decide to do." Mike turned and looked at Frankie and smiled "Give me some time to think about it." Frankie drove off, and Mike went back to work.

Mike could not help but think about what his cousin Frankie had said to him. All that day his mind was racing with questions. My brothers? Connections? Cousin Eddie? How much money was Frankie making? Mike was clearly frustrated for the rest of the day and started getting depressed thinking about it. On Friday, Mike got his paycheck, and a look of disgust rolled over his face. Three hundred dollars for forty hours of backbreaking work just seemed too little and only enough to pay some bills. Mike did not live an extravagant life; in fact, he was like most Italian Americans living in the Brooklyn neighborhood, a good job and just getting by on what money he earned. Mike thought to himself, there had to be a better way, but what Frankie was doing was dangerous and illegal, was it worth the risk?

That month of May 1958, Mike struggled with himself over the private conversation he had with his cousin Frankie and the complications of changing his life's direction in an effort to make a boat full of cash and living an extravagant lifestyle. There were consequences and risks for getting involved with the life of crime, but the rewards were tempting and sweet. No more money problems, fancy restaurants, food on the table for the family and, let's not forget, a sweet ride, stylish dress clothes, and a diamond pinky ring. Mike's mind was dreaming big, and he wanted more than just three hundred bucks a week working for Anthony at his repair gas station on Fulton Street in Brooklyn. Mike struggled with himself for almost two weeks thinking about whether he should get involved in a life of crime.

June was Michael's birth month. He made a promise to himself that he would make his decision to give Frankie an answer on June 20th, Mike's birthday. He knew the family would be at his apartment because Jackie always had a birthday party for him and family and friends would all be there. Mike had two weeks to think about his future, and he alone had to make a decision without talking to or telling anyone, including his wife.

That same week he decided to ask his brother Harry, the oldest of the bunch, what he did at the military base in Jersey. Mike wanted to know why Frankie said Harry could be a connection. Knowing he was going to see Harry at his mother's, Mike stopped off at the pastry shop to get some Italian cookies and cannoli for the get-together. Brooklyn had some of the best Italian bakeries in the world and Savarese Italian Pastry Shoppe on New Utrecht Avenue was one of the best. Pulling up to the apartment house, the memories rushed through his head about when he was young and played stoop ball with the neighborhood kids and how easy life was at such a young age. He smiled and under his breath said, *those were the good ole days*. Looking down the street, he could see young kids playing stick ball and kids under the fire hydrant getting wet, thinking to himself *It was like yesterday, I was doing the same thing*. Mike rang the bell to the three-story apartment building, and he was let in with the buzzer that unlocked the door. "Mike is that you?" he heard from the second-floor landing, "Yes, ma, it's me" he answered out loud so she could hear him. In Italian, she said "Your brother Harry is here and Tony too. Come up." Mike knew that Harry would be there, but he did not know Tony G would be there too. "I'm coming ma," he said as he walked up the steps. Walking through the doorway, he gave his mother a great big kiss and she slapped him gently on the face "You no come see you mother for three weeks. Why you no love me no more?" Mike hugged her hard saying, "Mama, you the only girl I love, I die for you." They both smiled as their eyes met and kissed again. "Ma, I bought you some cookies. You make espresso, yes?" "Go see your brothers. They in the room on the couch. I make. Go." Mike walked into the little room with a smile and greeted Harry and Tony. He was not sure what he was going to say or ask his brother Harry, and with Tony there, he wasn't even sure if he could. Luckily Harry started the conversation. "Mike, what's on your mind? You got problems?" "No, no problems. Everything is fine. Work sucks, and I'm breakin' my ass for little money. Other than that, all is good." "How's your wife, Lucy?" "All good," Harry said as he reached for his cigarettes. "So what brings you here to Mom's, and why did you ask me to meet you here? You in trouble again?" Tony laughed saying "Michael never gets in trouble. He is the quiet one. But your brother Jimmy, on the other hand, well, that's another story, right?" Harry leaned back on the couch saying "I wouldn't want to be Jimmy. That poor fuck has the world on his shoulders with the dock workers and shit being stolen all the time."

Just then, Mike thought of something to say. "Who do you think is stealing the shit off the docks and how are they getting away with it?" Tony spoke up. "Come on Mike, you know the Galli boys are involved with that shit. Nobody gonna stop them. If they try, they swim at the end of the dock with the fish. Big money is running through the docks right now." Mike's brain went back to what Frankie had said; the only question was how to get Jimmy to let him get involved and would he? Jimmy could do one of two things, he thought. He could beat the shit out of me for asking, or he could let me get involved if he got a cut of the action. Mike wasn't sure what Jimmy would do. Looking back at his brother Harry, he said "Harry, do you think Jimmy is involved with that stuff at the docks?" Harry showed a confused look on his face as he looked at Tony and said, "I don't know, why don't you ask him yourself." "Maybe I will ask him," Mike said with a stern look "Maybe I will." "Ma is the coffee ready yet" Harry yelled out as he stood up to go into the kitchen where the smell of coffee beans perfumed the air. "Come on let's eat some of little brother's cookies." They all got up and went into the kitchen. The conversation was over for the moment. After everyone had consumed coffee and pastry, Tony got up and said he had to leave. He hugged everyone and said to Mike, "Nice to see you, Mike. See you around the neighborhood." Mike was feeling more confident that with Tony gone it would be easier to talk to Harry. Now he could pick Harry's brain. But he wasn't ready to discuss his conversation with Frankie from some three weeks earlier. For now, it had to stay a secret.

Josephine, their mother, was cleaning up the table when she said, "If you boys no mind, I'm going to go next door to Gina. She has some fresh clams her son picked up at the fish market this morning, and I make some pasta with white clam sauce. Your brother Louis love a my pasta and clams." "Ok ma," they both said as she took off her apron and started walking to the door. Mike now had a chance to ask Harry whatever he wanted. They were the only two in the apartment and timing was not going to get any better. "Harry, what do you do at the base?" Mike asked nervously. Harry responded "I'm in charge of equipment and tools. Why?" "So you are the man in charge of jeeps, trucks and tools for the whole base?" "Yeah, why you asking me this? You need something?" "No. I was just curious what you had access to and if sometimes stuff gets lost. You know, like Jimmy, stuff goes missing, and no one knows what happened to it." Harry smiled with a grin and said, "Yeah sometimes stuff gets lost, if that's what you're asking. There is so much shit there; no one even knows what we have." Mike sat back in the chair and smiled. He now understood what Frankie meant when he spoke about his brothers and connections.

Mike's decision to enter the bad-boys club was siding with saying yes to Frankie's offer. He now knew two of his brothers were in a position to hide losses from inventory they controlled, and if Mike and Frankie could talk them into losing stuff, they could all make a bunch of cash. "So, if I needed a truck or jeep, let's say, you could make that happen?" Mike asked Harry jokingly. "It's possible," Harry said as he stood up and was ready to leave. "Tools would be a lot easier, but, yeah, I could get you a truck or jeep. You would have to see Carmine to get forged papers for the vehicle. He's the best in the market for shit like that." "Wait," Mike said with a surprised look, "are you telling me Uncle Carmine can forge papers?" "What are you stupid?" Harry said in Italian, as he opened the door to leave. "Talk to you later, Michael. Say hello to Jackie and the kids." "I will. Take care." Mike replied. With that, Harry closed the door, and Mike's decision was almost made. Next week he was going to tell Frankie he wanted in. There were just a few more questions he needed to be answered, and he needed to confirm. Everything seemed to fit in place and money would be a problem no more for Mike and his family, so long as he did not get caught and everything went smooth

Chapter 2

DECISIONS ARE MADE

Michael left his mother's house feeling like his life was going to change, and everything was going to be better. He was also afraid of getting involved, as it was a commitment for life. Once a person joins the club, death is the only way out. His decision to take Frankie's offer was becoming a strong yes, but he had to know more about his cousin Frankie's reputation on the street. On the way back home to his two bedroom apartment building, he decided to pick up some flowers to surprise Jackie. He was feeling good about his decision to change his future. Yes, he had a lot to lose if he got caught, but the temptation and the offer was too good to say no. He already knew that his brothers would do anything for him and the family, and the timing was perfect. The Italian American club was just down the street from where he lived on Atlantic Avenue and Eastern Parkway, and he already knew some of the fellas who were involved. Mike use to play cards with some of them on the weekend. He wasn't as good as his father in poker but, he enjoyed the game and company, and the guys were fun to be around. They were fellow Italians, and some worked for the Gambono and other families that controlled the New York area, so what. They were good guys. If someone in the neighborhood needed help, they were there to support and protect the neighborhood from the blacks who occasionally came around to start fights with the street gangs. Back in the sixties, segregation was prevalent in parts of New York. The blacks stayed on their side, and the whites stayed on their side. Sometimes there were clashes and people got hurt, but for the most part, it was separated by the local young neighborhood gangs with names like the Fulton & Rockaway boys and the Prospect Park boys who patrolled the streets keeping blacks out.

Entering his apartment, Mike was upbeat, and Jackie noticed something was definitely different about his attitude. "Why are you so happy today," she asked with a hug and a kiss. "No reason, I went to see my mother and Harry was there with Tony." "And that made you happy" she responded. "Yes it did," Mike said as he gave her the flowers and moved to the living room turning on the TV. "Well, thank you for the flowers dear," she replied as she stood over, the stove making Italian tomato sauce, which her mother-in-law taught her how to make in the old Italian tradition. In most Italian homes Sundays were always spaghetti day in Brooklyn. It was cheap and filling and if done correctly, very satisfying and tasty. It was an Italian tradition. Even though Mike was watching TV, his mind was thinking about the upcoming meeting with Frankie, which was to take place in three days. "You having a party for my birthday this Wednesday." Mike asked out loud, expecting Jackie to answer. "Just a few family and friends for cake and coffee," she said. "Good I'm looking forward to it" Mike replied with a grin on his face as he continued to search the channels for something to watch. After dinner, Mike decided to stop by the club, just to see who was there and hear what was going on around the neighborhood. If he was lucky, he could get some input from the guys about his cousin Frankie and what they thought about him. Mike told his wife he was going to the club for a while to see the guys and would be back in a few hours. The club was close, so he walked down the block. On the way, he stopped off at the local candy store on the corner and saw the owner Albert. Albert was known in the neighborhood as the person to see if you wanted to play the numbers game, which was controlled by the local mob. Mike made a five dollar bet on 471. Albert took his money and wrote his name on a slip. Everyone in the neighborhood was playing the numbers. The odds were fifty to one. The winning numbers were chosen by the total attendance of the racetrack for that day and posted in the local papers. The winner of that number got fifty to one odds return, and the bookie of the numbers got twenty-five percent from the winner.

Mike proceeded to walk across the street to the local Italian-American club with fifty-six dollars in his pocket knowing that the money was not the reason he was going. He knew he would lose it on purpose to keep faith with the guys. He wanted to see if he could get more information on Frankie Ragu and if this was the lifestyle he wanted to get into. "Hey Mike, how are you paisan," he heard from the back of the room. "Oh, I didn't expect to see you here" as he started walking toward a friend he knew well. It was a local soldier named Anthony Mayo (aka Onions). Mike and Onions were childhood friends and did all kinds of things together when they were younger. They even painted a cop car while the officer was getting a haircut at Tony's Barber Shop. A tall skinny man, who was allergic to onions for some strange reason, therefore earning his nickname. "How you doin' Onions, good to see you," Mike said with a smile. "You here to play cards," Onions asked as he grabbed Mike's hand. "Yeah, you at a table," Mike asked. "Of course, come on I'll introduce you to some of the guys you may not know," Onions said as he led Mike to one of the six tables playing cards. In the far corner at one of the tables, he saw another friend he knew from the club. It was young Johnny G. (aka Dapper). John was always clean cut, well dressed and was an up and coming guy in the Gambono family. He was becoming a big earner for the family and Dapper in his style of dressing. Mike waved, and John acknowledged Mike with a hand gesture and an "Oh." Mike followed Onions to a table in the far corner of the room. Onions introduced Mike to five men at the table where he and Onions were about to sit and play five card stud. "Mike this is Tommy D. (aka Shine). Over there is Big Paul Varro. This is Jimmy B. (aka, Gentle Jim) and you know Sal (aka Cupcake). Everyone had a nickname of some sort. Shine, use to shine shoes when he was young. Big Paul was 200 pounds overweight and could always be seen eating something. Gentle Jim was a ladies man with a butcher personality when it came to business deals and people he didn't like. Sal was a delivery driver for Hostess cakes, and he hated the nickname as many would call him crumb cake, Twinkie, Devil dog, or any one of the other Hostess cake products. "Hello, guys. Ok if I sit here" Mike asked as he and Onions pulled out their chairs. "Sure" they all answered. Hope you got plenty of cash on you" Jimmy said as he started dealing cards. "Some," Mike said, "I'll make sure I lose it to you." "Nice very nice," Jimmy said with a smirk on his face. "I'll be happy to take it." "OK let's play," Onions said as he picked up his cards. After a few hands had passed, Mike asked openly, "Any you guys know Frankie Ragu?" "Yeah, he works for Big Sal's crew, why?" Big Paulie asked. "What kinda guy is he?" Mike asked as he looked at the faces of the players. "Ask Johnny over there, he works with him," Paulie said as he picked up his cards. "Can he be trusted?" Mike said out loud as he laid his cards down on the table. "He wants me to do him a favor, and I gotta know if he can be trusted." "Well, he hasn't gotten caught, and if he does get pinched and rats, he's dead, right" big Paulie said looking Mike straight on. "Besides, he has been doing this for about a year, and he's earning, so I guess he's ok." "He did some work for you didn't he?" Paulie asked as he looked at Gentle Jim. "Yeah, he did some little jobs for me. He was ok; then he tied up with Johnny and the crew stealing high-end cars to strip and ship. I haven't seen him around for a while, so I guess he's still workin'. You should ask Johnny. He could give you the scoop." "Thanks, guys, that's what I needed to know." Mike laid his last ten on the table and smiled, "I'm in" he said with a pair of tens in his hand. Jimmy raised his ten and Mike folded. "See Jimmy, I said I would give you my money, and you got it all." Mike stood up and said goodbye to all who were at the table and gave Onions a hug. "You comin' to the house Wednesday?" "Yeah," Onions said with a smile. "Thanks guys for the info. See you around the neighborhood." Mike said as he walked out the door of the club.

Mike got the answers he was looking for about his cousin Frankie. He also knew how some of the guys thought Frankie was OK, and he was stealing cars with the Big Al's crew, which included Johnny G. Mike knew that Johnny (Dapper) was no rat, and he never gave up any names when he got busted before. If he was working with Frankie, it must have been ok to trust Frankie. Mike walked home and said hello to all the old ladies who were lined up and down the sidewalk sitting in their chairs chatting with each other. In those days, the elders would sit outside in chairs and chat with each other about everything from recipes to who was doing what in the neighborhood. They also waited for the local bookie to walk the street and collect the numbers from those who played.

East New York was a self-contained local area with almost everything a person needed from food to funeral homes. On the corner of Atlantic Ave and Eastern Parkway was the local candy store/luncheonette. Next to that was the flower shop, hardware store, Pasquale's Italian food store, Carlucci's Italian Restaurant, Salvatori's bakery and Mullinaro's funeral home (which was owned by Carl Gambono). In fact, several funeral homes were owned by the Gambono family. They were used at times to lose or make a body disappear. It was a known fact that someone would put the body of an individual on the bottom and cover it with a false board to put the deceased on the top board.

No one knew there were two bodies in the coffin, and many a person disappeared this way. No body, no crime was the motto. Monday and Tuesday went by with nothing new and finally the day of reckoning came for Mike. It was his birthday, and he had made up his mind to give Frankie the answer that night at his birthday party. Mike's boss at the station gave him the afternoon off. "Mike go home and enjoy the rest of the day. Happy birthday" Anthony said with a smile. Anthony knew he would see Mike at the party and didn't want Mike to know about the surprise party Jackie was throwing for him. He was afraid that some of the co-workers might slip about the party. What Anthony didn't know was Mike already knew about the party. Mike decided to see his cousin Eddie T. (Money). He wanted Eddie's feelings about Frankie and if Frankie was trustworthy. Before he left work, he called Eddie to see if he could come over to talk to him. Eddie said okay to him coming over for a little while. Mike wanted to stay under the wire about being a soldier with one of the families, and he had to know Frankie could keep his mouth shut without bragging. If anyone knew Frankie, it was Money and besides Mike couldn't go home early. Eddie was well connected, but he was not a capo, meaning he didn't get his button yet, but he was a big earner and had been for several years. It was only a matter of time before he did get his button (capo) and Mike knew that. Eddie was a cross between a young Elvis and Garry Cooper in looks. He had blue eyes and jet black wavy hair that was always well groomed. He stood five eleven, average build with a hot temper if things didn't go his way. Eddie was excellent at staying under the wire and very few people even knew what he did for a living.

Eddie got his nickname Money because he was a loan shark. He owned a 30-foot fishing boat and went fishing every weekend. The name of his boat was Liquid Assets. Mike had been on the boat many times with friends and family and loved fishing with Eddie for shark and tuna offshore. Pulling up to Eddie's house Mike was nervous about meeting his cousin. It had been a while since he last saw him and he hoped Eddie was in a happy mood. If his cousin Eddie was in a bad mood, nothing was possible, and it would be a wasted trip for Mike. Eddie opened the door and to Mike's relief, Eddie was in a good mood. "Come in, it's good to see you, Mike," Eddie said with a smile. "You smell like fuckin' gas Mike; I hope you got no grease on your shoes." Mike was embarrassed, "I'm sorry Eddie, I got off work early and wanted to talk to you about Cousin Frankie" as he looked down at his shoes and stepped gingerly into the foyer. "You know what, let's go outside to the boat, I can hose it down if you get it dirty," Eddie said with a little disgust in his voice. They both walked back out the front door and turned around the corner of the house heading to the back yard toward the boat dock. "What're your questions about Frankie," Eddie said curiously. "I need to know if Frankie can be trusted. He's asked me if I would get involved with him in the car business and I think he wants me to use my brother's connections to get stuff and sell it to some of the guys in the club. I'm just not sure if I should, and I came here to ask you for your advice on what I should do" he said pleadingly as they climbed to the upper deck of the boat. Eddie sat in his captain's chair and laughed while Mike sat in the co-chair on the bridge of the boat. "So, you gonna get involved with this family of ours and Frankie wants to use your connections to advance himself and make more money. That little prick has big balls" Eddie said with a stern look on his face. Mike was somewhat confused. "You think he's using me?" he said. "You tell me. He comes to you and asks you to be a part of his crew and also wants your brothers to be a part of it too." "Frankie is a fuckin' soldier and he steals cars for a living, that's it." Eddie leaned over in his seat toward Mike and said sternly, "Mike, he needs you to move cars for him and change ID tags so he can sell them locally. The others go to the dock and are shipped out of the country, and he gets a cut. Now he wants to expand and involve you and your brothers for his benefit, not yours." Mike was surprised at what Eddie was telling him and never thought of it that way. "So what should I do? I need the money, and I am tired of bustin' my ass for Anthony for what, three hundred a week. It's bullshit, and I got a family to feed. I stopped by the club and spoke to some of the guys to get their opinion about Frankie. They thought he was ok and was an earner. I thought you would say the same thing" sadly looking Eddie straight on. "Mike, you're my cousin and so is Frankie. If you want to get involved, that's fine. If you want my advice on how to do it, I would be happy to tell you what to do to set it to your advantage and still keep control." Mike sat back in the chair. "Please tell me, I'm listening." Eddie reached into a draw near him and pulled out a cigar, lighting it he asked: "You want one?" "No thanks." "OK here is what you should do. First, Frankie makes a couple of hundred bucks for each car he moves to the dock. He makes more for the cars they sell. Tell him you want one hundred for each car he stores on the lot. And one hundred fifty for each car he wants you to change the ID tags for he has to pay Carmine for all the paperwork for the cars he wants to sell, and he has to move the cars on the lot in three days after they arrive and are stored on the lot. Tell him you will sell the stuff he needs from your brothers at a discounted price because he is family and you will only deal directly with him and no one else in all transactions. If he agrees, you make the deal. As, for Anthony, your boss, he owes me money so I will offer him a deal. I'll take twenty-five bucks off his loan for each car he allows on the lot, and you will give me that money instead. That gives you seventy-five bucks for the cars on the lot and one hundred twenty-five bucks for each car that goes into the shop for ID tags. That takes care of your bosses, and we all make some extra cash, happy, happy, right."

Eddie got up off the chair as to indicate the conversation was over. Mike smiled, "Eddie thank you. That is what I needed to hear; now I feel better about the whole thing." "You know you are getting into bed with some shady people and if you're OK with that, then who knows what the future holds," Eddie said as they stepped off the boat. "Yeah I'm OK with that, but if Frankie tries to pull some shit what should I do?" "You do what you have to do, even if he is family, tu capisce" (understand), Eddie said sternly as he hugged his cousin. Now I'll see you in a few days Michael and happy birthday if I don't see you." Mike thanked Eddie and proceeded to get in his car. Eddie walked to his front door and waved goodbye as Mike drove off. For Mike, it was not what he thought it would be, his cousin Eddie told him far more complex and educational information. Mike was impressed with his cousin's knowledge and advice. Now he was able to negotiate with Frankie on his terms and control the situation better than just being a pawn in the very dangerous game of chess. Mike arrived home right on time and was ready for the party to begin. Armed with the new information and the suggestions Eddie told him, he was willing to discuss his future with Frankie and Frankie either accepted or walked away. Mike was determined to be in control at all times while protecting himself and his family.

Mike walked into the apartment to the expected surprise party, and it was as planned. There were family and friends, and he acted surprised as he was expected to be with a smile on his face. "Oh, you shouldn't have", he said with a smirk on his face. "Thank you so much," Mike said as he hugged his wife and started to shake hands and kiss the ladies who were there. It all went as planned, food, drink and conversation for all. Mike saw that some of the fellas' from the club were there too and looking around he also saw that his boss, Money, and Tony G were in the corner talking to Ragu in a circle. "What's going on over here?" Mike said with a look of curiosity on his face. "You guys are talking about me?" he said as he shook hands. Frankie seemed nervous about something and Mike was not sure why. "Frankie, these guys roughing you up," Mike said with a smile on his face. "No, they're educating me," Frankie said looking like a child who was being reprimanded for something he did wrong. Mike knew it had something to do with the offer Frankie had made to him, and the boys were schooling him on doing the right thing. That was a great relief for Mike and would make it easy for him to negotiate a deal with Frankie. Mike's presences caused the conversation to break up and forced the guys to mingle with the other guests, leaving Mike and Frankie alone for a few minutes. Looking at Frankie Mike said, "We'll talk later OK." "Yeah, no problem," Frankie said as he moved into the kitchen for something to eat. Mike had to know what they were talking about, so he approached Tony G. "Tony, was that about me or something else?" Tony's reply was simple. "Mike, Eddie told me what was going on, and we decided to set Frankie straight before you two talked about a deal. We were looking out for your interest in getting involved; that's all." "So you know, and you are good with this?" Mike asked Tony. "Yeah it's okay with me," Tony said walking away to talk to someone else. Mike knew that Tony G and Money were involved with the family, and they must, have scared the shit out of Frankie, who was a foot soldier working for his capo and crew.

If Frankie fucked up, he would have to answer to either one of them and might even disappear if the boss approved it. Only made men and those higher than a soldier had the power to whack a soldier without permission, and it was a known fact to all those connected.

After the food had been served and guests were still waiting for dessert and coffee, Mike walked up to Frankie and said he wanted to talk outside in the back yard. Frankie obliged Mike, and they both walked out to the yard, just the two of them. "Frankie I have decided to take your offer; however, we have to lay some ground rules before I commit," Mike said with a stern face as they sat on the lawn chairs. "What are they," Frankie asked with a smile and smirk on his face. "You makin' me an offer now?", as he lit a cigar. "It's not an offer; it's an agreement between the two of us, like family. You know an oath. I will agree to help you with what you need from me and in return, you say nothing to anyone about this thing. Do You need to move cars? I need money to do this. "So what are you proposing Mike," Frankie asked. "I want one hundred a car to store in the lot, and you move it in three days, or it's twenty more every day it's there. I want one fifty for each car you want me to change the tag on cause I have to bring it in and out of the lot. If you got no problems with that, then it's a deal." Frankie was surprised, to say the least. He jumped out of his chair saying "you got balls, Mike. You set the terms, and I have to agree. Bullshit, I give you fifty a car and one hundred for ID's" Frankie snarled angrily, as if to be in control of the deal. Mike looked Frankie in the eyes and said "Well we have no deal Frank, I'm sorry" and Mike started to walk away from the conversation. "Fuckin' balls Mike. I thought you were here to help me and wanted money. I guess I was wrong" Frankie said as he was now walking behind Mike and was quite upset about the deal falling apart. "You're a prick, Mike," Frankie said as he moved along side of Mike. Mike turned quickly and with one hand grabbed Frankie by the neck and pushed him against the wall squeezing harder around Frankie's throat. "Watch your mouth," Mike said looking, Frankie, eye to eye. "You came to me. I didn't come to you. You want my help, and I am willing to offer, but I'm not going to be one of your little bitches. We both make money, and we keep quiet about it understand. If you ever insult me again for trying to help you, I'll break your scrawny little fuckin' neck" Mike growled angrily as he let Frankie go and watched him gasp for air. "This conversation is over Frankie. You have my offer now you think about it." Frankie was scared. He didn't think Mike would do what he did and suddenly realized Mike could have choked him to death with one hand that felt like a vise around his neck. He pulled himself together and said "I'm sorry Mike. That was a stupid thing I did. I was hoping we could be partners in this deal, and I fucked up, I'm sorry." "You can't be so fuckin' greedy Frank. You have to share if you want everyone to be happy." With a sense of sorrow, Mike said "I made an offer, it stands. Think about it, you know where to find me." Mike walked up the steps, and Frankie decided he would leave. "Mike I'm gonna leave okay." Mike never turned around and looked up the stairs he said "fine Frankie, see you soon."

Mike was visibly upset about what happened between him and Frankie, but he was not going to change his mind about the decision and offer he made. He had to stand his ground. Opening the door to the apartment, several people looked at Mike and saw he was not happy. Eddie walked over and softly said in Mike's ear "how did it go?" Mike softly said "not good" and kept walking to the dessert table for something sweet to eat. Eddie had to know what just happened. He and Tony were standing by the window that overlooked the backyard and were able to see the two talking but heard nothing they said. Eddie walked over to Tony. "You want to ask him what happened?" Tony looked at Eddie and politely said "Not now, maybe later. When he's in a mood to talk, he will." The conversation about the subject was over for now. In time, Mike would come around to ask for suggestions from his friends but for tonight it was over concerning a deal with Frankie, and Mike was unmistakably not in a good mood.

Night came and went, new day, new beginnings. Mike accepted the fact that nothing went the way he wanted with Frankie, and he would wait for him to make the next offer. For the time being, he would go to work at the station with hopes that something would change for the better.

CHAPTER 3

PARTY AT THE BIG HOUSE

Several days went by, and Mike was doing what he had been doing for the last few years, working to pay the bills and provide for his family. He decided to take the family for a weekend trip to Long Island to see his uncle Vincenzo De Napoletti, who lived in Massapequa Park among the wealthy mansion homeowners. His uncle was well connected and a loner of sorts. However, he loved Mike as his favorite nephew and was always happy to see him. Pulling up to the circular driveway lined with statues and water fountains, the kids were already excited in the back seats, while Michael was becoming notably nervous by the second the closer he got to the main entrance. The kids always loved going in the pool during the summer, and Vincenzo loved watching people enjoying the use of his beautiful home. Mike hadn't been there in a few months, and the family had been staying within the Brooklyn area due to a lack of funds and work. They stayed for the weekend and enjoyed each other's company. "I may be throwing a party in July for some friends and family. You and the family must come; that's an order Michael. I love watching pretty girls in bathing suits, and Jackie is no exception. Promise you will come and mingle with my guest and entertain me with your presence." Vincenzo said as he walked the family out the front door and gave the kids candy and hugs.

"I promise Uncle, we will be happy to come if you decide to have the party," Mike replied as he hugged Vincenzo and kissed his cheek.

The drive home took an hour, and the kids fell asleep in the back seat all the way home, tired from swimming all day.

One day at the end of June, he was visited by a person he didn't know, whose name he later learned was Donny Moldanato (aka Donny Boy). He was a young kid about nineteen or so with wavy brown hair, a slightly thick body and stood about five-feet-five-inches. "Are you Michael Delagatta," Donny asked looking up at Mike's eyes, who was a statue of great height compared to Donny. "Who the fuck are you?" Mike asked while looking down at this kid he thought was much younger. "My name is Donny, and I have a message for you. Eddie T. would like you to see him at his house this weekend on Friday night, seven thirty sharp." Mike looked at Donny like he was just smacked with a ball from left field. "Who told you to say this and how do you know Eddie?" Mike asked with a curious look on his face. For all he knew this kid could have been anyone and Mike wanted to know for sure.

"Mr. Mike, all I know is I was told to tell you this, and it comes straight from Eddie." "What's Eddie's nickname, and how do you know Eddie?" Mike asked. "Mr. Eddie Tumasso's nickname is Money, and I work for him running errands. He sent me here to give you that message. If you don't believe me, call him." Mike felt a calm come over him "OK you pass kid. Tell Money I'll be there" Mike said with laughter in his deep voice. Donny said goodbye, and when he reached his hand out to shake Mike's, he saw a hand four times the size of his and almost shit his pants. He initiated the handshake and was not ballsy enough to pull back. That would be an insult. Mike wrapped his huge right hand around the entire hand and wrist of Donny. All Donny could do is look at this claw vise closing around his right hand. "Please don't squeeze, too hard." Mike gave his hand a little squeeze and smiled, knowing full well he could literally crush every bone in Donny's hand. "See you kid," he said as he released his grip and walked back into the garage. Mike started thinking about Eddie telling him in his last conversation at the house before Mike's birthday that he would have a talk with Anthony and Dominic. This meeting with Donny stirred up his curiosity, so he walked up to the front of the shop and into Anthony's office. "Anthony, did my cousin Eddie talk to you about anything?" "Yeah, why?" Anthony asked. "No reason. A guy stopped by and told me to see Eddie this Friday, and

I wasn't sure why." "Have no idea why," Anthony said while moving papers around on his desk. Mike walked out and back to the garage to finish out his day.

Friday came, and Mike took a pair of dress clothes with him. He told his wife, Jackie, he would be home later than usual that night. "Going to see Eddie tonight. Be home late", he said walking out the door. "Say hello for me," Jackie said with a smile. Mike drove to Eddie's home in Belle Harbor, full of waterfront homes of immense sizes and affluent residents involved in politics, major corporations and celebrities. Money was in his late thirties and had been working for the family for several years loaning money and was involved with several other things going on within the family business. He was a big earner, and there was talk about him becoming a made man. To Eddie, it didn't matter. He wanted to stay under the radar of government investigations and indictments.

During the early sixties, the Feds were looking at the Mafia to figure out how they did business and what they were involved in, but they had very few agents working on the case. Besides, when John Kennedy announced he was running for President of the United States, all the families knew his father was a bootleg runner shipping alcohol during his early days and made a ton of money doing so. It was said that Joe Kennedy was good friends with Sam Giancolla, the boss of Chicago. The families also decided to help John Kennedy get into the White House, which was proposed by the Commission of families by rigging the ballot boxes in November and forcing the union members and their friends to vote for John. After all, with John in the White House, the families had a connection to the Commander in Chief of the entire United States. Anything Hoover was doing to break up the Mafia would come to a crashing halt, so it was in the best interest of all the families to get Jack elected. Anyway they could.

Mike pulled up in the circular driveway and noticed several parked cars. He saw Frankie's Caddy and his boss Anthony's Lincoln among them. Thinking to himself *"What the fuck is going on here?"* Mike's heart started to flutter with excitement and fear all at the same time. He was worried and not prepared for this type of meeting at all. Mike rang the doorbell, and Eddie's wife Kat opened the door. "Hi Mike, come in. The boys are downstairs in the game room. How's the wife and kids?" she asked as she escorted Mike to the lower stairway.

"They are fine. Jackie says hi", Mike said as he walked down the stairs to the huge game room. "I bet you shit your pants when you saw the cars outside, didn't you?" Eddie said laughing his ass off. "Very fuckin' funny," Mike said with a sigh of relief in his voice. "I thought you wanted to talk to me, not these guys." He shook the hands of the five people in the room. "Mike, you know Frankie, Anthony, and you met Donny a few days ago. This is Luigi Fontanno, but we call him Frenchy because his father is French. And he looks French, doesn't he? Over there behind the bar is Tommy De Salaro. He's my enforcer for those deadbeats that don't pay up on time. Now that we all know each other let's get down to business. I got things to do and have to leave here at nine sharp," Eddie said as he sat at the center table in the middle of the room. "Come on guys, sit, and let's get the show on the road." Everyone sat down and looked at each other as if they were sizing each other up. Mike sat between Frankie and Anthony feeling more comfortable being among fellas he knew. The others were strangers to Mike, but he had seen Frenchy in the local Italian clubs playing cards with some of the boys. He never saw Tommy De(Enforcer) and only noticed he was a large man who had too many desserts in his life and carried about three hundred pounds between his hips. He must have been a good enforcer, and he would have been a good match for even Mike to handle.

"OK, Mike, let me fill you in on some information, so you understand why everyone is here and how it involves you," Eddie said looking around the table to see the response from the others. "The deal with you and Frankie didn't happen as you both wanted, so I made an offer to both Frankie and Anthony about this thing Frankie wanted you involved with. Frankie has agreed to give you one hundred for each car that goes through the lot and stays for four days or less. He will also give you one hundred fifty for all the cars you have to pop and replace the ID tags on. Anthony has OK'd this and in return, he gets vig knocked off his loan with me. Frankie also gets vig knocked off the top of what he owes me for making the deal and the amount he gets off is based on the cars he gives you to fix or hide, so you keep tabs on the total each week and give the info to Donny when he comes to you. You Ok with this deal?" Eddie asked Mike as others looked in his direction. "Yeah, I'm OK with this, but I do have some questions. Frankie pays me directly at the end of the week for the cars, right?" "Yeah," Eddie said as he looked at Frankie with a stern look. "Frankie, you OK with this, and you too Anthony," Mike asked as he looked at each one of them to get the answer. "Yeah, were OK with it," they said in unison. "OK, I'll do it. But if the heat comes on me, I'm out," Mike said looking at Eddie to get his approval. "Don't worry about the locals. I'll take care of that when and if it happens," Eddie said as he looked over at Tommy (Enforcer). Tommy smiled and said "We shouldn't have any problem with that department. I know most of them." Eddie looked around the table and smiled. "So we have a deal, yes?" "I guess we have a deal," Frankie said as he started to stand up from the table. "Oh, who the fuck told you to get up?" Eddie shouted appearing to be upset. "Nah, I'm just kidding. Go, get the hell out and make us money. Mike has to buy shoes for the children." Eddie said with a smile as he stood up and put his arm around Mike's shoulders. "Mike, stay for a few minutes. I have to talk to you about something." Eddie walked his guests up the stairs and out the front door and watched as they proceeded to leave in their cars. "Mike, in order to make this deal happen, I had to give up some of my vig money to make everyone happy. Now I think it's only fair that you contribute some of your new-found cash to me in the sum of twenty bucks for every car that Frankie gives you. And I have someone else who may want to bring cars for you to hide with the same deal as you have with Frankie. Of course, I get twenty for those cars too." Mike had no choice but to say yes. In fact, saying no would screw everything up for all involved. "Yeah, Eddie, I'm ok with that. I guess that's why you got the nickname Money." Eddie smiled, and as, he walked Mike down the end of the driveway to Mike's car, he turned to Mike and said something that Mike never expected from his cousin Eddie. "It's nice to be king," Eddie said smiling. Mike just smiled and entered his car and rolled down the window as he started the engine. "This guy Tommy D, is he a cop or something?" Mike asked looking at Eddie to see his response. "You're a smart man Michael. You said it, not me. As you know, in this profession, the less we say, the better. Good night, cuz."

Mike drove off with a sense of accomplishment. Eddie cut a deal with everybody, and all were committed. Mike drove home with the radio blasting and singing almost all the way home. Yes, he was euphoric to make more money, and his boss was in on it. Perhaps he could afford to go to Gino's restaurant a little more often in the near future.

Several days passed and Frankie was a no-show with cars, and Mike had no idea why. Later that day he called Frankie "Frankie, no cars?" "Be patient Mike, I took some time off and now I'm back, so soon you'll have something." Mike was thinking that he was going to receive cars every day and had no idea how stealing cars worked. Frankie was a master at the game. He had master keys to almost every car on the market, and if he didn't, he would make them on the spot with a key maker he had in his possession when stealing cars. No one wanted a broken car with the ignition assembly ripped out, and Frankie had all the tools to get any car.

That Thursday afternoon Frankie pulled up to the shop in a Mercedes coupe and parked it next to the gate leading to the back lot. He walked into the rat infested shop and was greeted by the shop dog Duke, who was the shops mix breed guard dog. "Nice doggie, don't jump on me, or I'll have to break your fuckin' legs for getting me dirty," Frankie said as he pet the dog's head in an effort to stop him from jumping up. The exterior of the shop was old red brick portico with two gas pumps located in the front of the building while the mechanic shop had three bay doors on the side and a smaller office door. The open car yard was located on the side of the building. Fenced in and covered from street view, it was big enough to hold twenty cars. Finding Mike working under a car on the lift, he shouted "Your first one, Mike. Open the gate so I can put it in the yard." Mike walked out and opened the gate and watched as Frankie drove the car into the lot and parked it behind the front line of cars. "This spot good, Mike?" Frankie asked. "Fine," Mike said nervously. "I'll see you next week with some more. I think I'm going to sell this one, so I need you to change the tag. I'll get you the new tag and have Carmine do the paperwork." Carmine was a master at forging papers of every kind; passports, car registrations, government documents, just about anything you could think of concerning paper documents. Carmine had his own print shop and did a lot of work for the government and civilian sector, so he had all the seals and stamps needed for forging. He was mastering the art of counterfeiting money and was almost perfect. He needed a little more time improving the paper issue. And after that problem was fixed, he was ready to print on demand to the mob for an enormous profit. "Frankie, you gotta let me know if you want me to rip this one apart for the dash tag," Mike said as they walked out of the lot. "Okay. Do it, Mike. I'm sure I can get good cash for this one. I'll bring you the stuff on Monday or Tuesday the latest depends on how busy Carmine is." "You sure?" Mike asked seeing dollar signs in his eyes. Every car Mike had to fix was one-fifty less the twenty to Eddie. He would walk away with one-thirty clean, not bad for an hour of work. Mike walked into the shop as Frankie got into another car driven by Frankie's partner whom Mike did not know and didn't want to know. Mike pulled out a little book that he had hidden in his desk and wrote down the make of the car, year, color and amount he was owed. Anything with a cross next to it was to signify the car was retagged all others would have an X signifying it was being shipped out.

Friday morning Mike took the car into the shop and started to disassemble the dash so he could remove the VIN tag. He was ready for the new VIN tag to install. *Now I can relax and enjoy the weekend,* Mike thought to himself as he locked up the shop and drove home.

When Mike arrived home, Jackie gave him a kiss and an invitation card from his uncle Vincenzo. "What's this?" Mike asked as he opened it. "An invitation to a fourth of July party at the big house," Jackie said with a smile. "We're going, right?" she asked hoping for the answer she wanted to hear. "Well, how can I say no? If we don't show up, I might get whacked," he said jokingly. They both laughed. "I'll tell the kids. They'll be so happy" Jackie said as she put dinner on the table. Mike started to think to himself, *Do I say anything about getting involved with Eddie and Frankie? No, I'll keep my mouth shut and see if Uncle Vincenzo knows first,* he thought to himself as he started to dig into Jackie's famous chicken parmesan made with her mother-in-laws one-hundred-year-old Italian recipe. Aside from going to play cards with the fellas at the local club, everything was relaxing and normal.

The next week, Frankie showed up with four more cars to hide and paid Mike the money owed. Mike took out his little book and marked everything down. When Donny came on that Friday, Mike gave him a copy of the list and Eddie's share of the money. Not a bad week at all. Mike had made four hundred fifty bucks cash, and that was more than a week's salary for working forty hours on cars for Anthony. Mike was excited that for the first time he made extra cash. When he went home, he gave Jackie one hundred for spending money. "This is for you; treat yourself to whatever your heart desires," Mike said with a smile from ear to ear. "Okay, Mike, what's going on here? Suddenly you are giving me money, and it is not for the bills? What's going on honey?" she asked, as she held the money in her hand so tightly while looking directly into his in the eyes. "I'm making some extra money doing extra work at the shop. You have a problem with me making more money?" "No, as long as you don't get into any trouble doing this," she said walking into the living room. "We are still going to your Uncle's house this coming weekend, right?" "Of course, we are. The kids know yet?" "Yes, and they are excited to go." With that, the phone rang, and Mike answered. It was his cousin Eddie on the other end. "Mike, did you get an invitation to Uncle Vincenzo's for the fourth?" Eddie asked. "Yes. Are you going to be there?" Mike replied. "Kat and I will be there a little late, but we will be there" Eddie answered. "Mike, did you say anything to him about this thing of ours?" Eddie asked hoping to get the answer he wanted to hear. "No, he knows nothing about our deal or my involvement." "Why, did you?" "No, and the less he knows, the better, Mike" Eddie said with his voice slightly raised. "Uncle Vincenzo will not hear it from me," Mike assured Eddie on the phone. They both agreed to say nothing, but they both knew that sooner or later Uncle Vincenzo would find out through the grapevine. That was a problem they would deal with when the time came, but for now, all was secret. They only hoped that Frankie wouldn't open his mouth first. Frankie had a tendency to brag, and that worried both Mike and Eddie.

The following week went fast, and during that week, a guy showed up at the shop that Mike knew well. It was Johnny (Dapper). "Dapper, what brings you to this place?" Mike asked as he shook his hand. "Mike, I hear you can hide some cars for me." "Who did you hear that from," Mike asked curiously. "Your cousin, Frankie Ragu mentioned it to me, and I thought I would ask you if could hide some of my cars?" Johnny asked. "Does Eddie know you came to me?" Mike asked Johnny. "How the fuck do I know? Ragu told me, and I'm here asking you." Johnny said with a little anger in his voice. "Wow, don't get pissy John. I got to make sure this is on the up and up with Eddie first. Wait in the office while I call him," Mike said as they started to walk to the back office. "I know Ragu is already storing some cars here," Johnny said as they walked. "Ming-ya, you seem to know a lot" Mike replied. "If Eddie says it's OK, I think I can handle some more business, but you gotta keep it quiet," Mike said as he picked up the phone. After talking with Eddie, he looked at Johnny and said, "Well, it looks like where doing a little business together Johnny. I get one large for each car that goes bye-bye and one fifty for re-reg. You have to go see Carmine for the paper, deal?" Mike was waiting for Johnny to agree. "I got a large crew. You sure you can handle the load?" Johnny asked. "Yeah, that's fine, except you gotta be with these guys who drop, cause I don't know who they are, and they could be cops or Feds. If I don't see you, I'll turn them away. That's the only way this will go down, Johnny. I gotta make sure we don't let the wrong guys get wind of this thing we got, you understand?" "Mike, once you get introduced to my crew you will know they're with me, I can't come to every drop-off, but I will come with the guys so I can introduce you to them and then were good, right?" Johnny said as they walked out to his car. "Yeah, I guess that's good. But you gotta be with them till I know them or no deal, Johnny" They shook hands, and Mike gave him a squeeze a little tighter than normal. That in itself showed Johnny the strength Mike had and the size of his vise grip was without words, a form of pain if he fucked up the deal by not being with his crew for the first few drop-offs. Mike knew Johnny from the neighborhood and the club, but they never did business together. Mike wanted to make sure they got off on the right foot in this thing of theirs. Mike liked Johnny. He was well-known in the neighborhood as a clean cut and up-and-coming guy who was always well dressed. He was a good earner with his own crew, who worked for the Gambono's. Johnny was not a button man, but he was surely on his way to becoming one someday.

That week ended great for Mike. He earned several hundred bucks, and Friday was ending. Frankie didn't show up to pay him for the week, but Johnny, and his guys did. Frankie still owed him for four cars that he drove in that week. Most of Johnny's cars were marked to ship out, so none were changed over to new tags. Mike wasn't too worried about Frankie. He had to show up sooner or later to pay up, or Eddie would hunt him down. Mike would tell Eddie at their uncle's party that Saturday about Frankie owing. On the other hand, Mike did meet some of Johnny's crew who dropped off five cars, and they passed the "who the fuck are you" test. They were OK to drop without Johnny being there.

It was the morning of July fourth, and the kids were already harping about wanting to go to Uncle Vincenzo's house because they wanted to play with the dogs and swim in the pool. "Jackie, calm these kids down. We're not leaving till eleven, and they're breakin' my balls" Mike said as he was eating breakfast. Jackie turned the TV on and told the kids to watch cartoons, and when Daddy was ready, we would go. Mike started reading the paper to see what was going on with the Kennedy rally and how Kennedy was doing in the polls. The people loved him, a nice Catholic boy, good looking, smart and young. He should win with no problems; Mike thought to himself. Mike also knew that the families backed him as well as the unions which the families controlled. The man is a shoe-in, and the mob would make sure he got the vote, no matter what it took. They wanted him in the White House. They already had lawyers, politicians, judges, cops, unions, construction and many more influential individuals on the family payroll and owed favors of all kinds. John Kennedy would be the pinnacle of the connections. Besides, Samatoro Giancolla and the five New York families made a promise to the old man. They were putting Kennedy in the White House.

After breakfast, Mike went into the bedroom to pick out what he was going to wear for the party. He started thinking, *"What do you bring to a man who has almost everything?"* That would be a problem. It had to be special, not just cake or cookies. Mike asked his wife if she thought there was a store that sold knick knacks, figurines of a sort. She told him there was a place on Pitkin Avenue. She didn't remember the name of the store, but they had that kind of stuff. Mike decided to take the ride to see if he could find this store and buy something nice for his uncle, something special, with meaning. He knew in the old days Uncle Vincenzo was nicknamed the Ice Man, because as an immigrant boy, he made a living working the streets selling ice from a horse and carriage, and he collected figurines of ice trucks and such. Uncle Vincenzo had dozens of them in his study, and Mike was on a mission to find the perfect figurine for his uncle. Besides, Pitkin Avenue was not that far from Atlantic Avenue, and he would be back in no time to get ready to go to the party. After searching for a few minutes, he found the store Jackie told him about and walked in to find several dozen figurines of all sorts. He told the lady what he was looking for, and she took him to a section where he had several to choose from. Mike found a horse-drawn cart and asked if she could have something put on it. He wanted it to say "Ice for Sale" on both sides, and she obliged for an extra fee. Mike had no problem with the cost and asked how long it would take. She informed him ten minutes or so, and he waited. It was perfect, and Uncle Vincenzo would love it. He had a collection but none with a cart that said "Ice for Sale." Mike drove back to the house and started getting dressed to leave.

The family arrived at the party on time and were amazed at the number of people gathered. His uncle had many acquaintances, and there had to be one hundred people or more at this party. Greeting his uncle, he gave him the gift and watched him open it. "This is beautiful. How did you ever find one like this, Michael?" he asked. "I had it made for you Uncle, and there is none like it anywhere. One of a kind, like you," Mike replied while hugging his uncle. "That's why you are my favorite, but don't tell your cousins. They will get jealous," Vincenzo said as he put his new figurine center stage on a shelf. "Come, let me introduce you to some of my friends," Vincenzo said as they walked out to the back yard. Uncle Vincenzo introduced Mike to dozens of very important people like lawyers, judges, politicians and even celebrities who had a connection to family members in one way or another. There was a band on the stage by the name of Jay and the Americans who were unknown at the time and made it big in later years. Many of Mike's cousins were there, and they reminisced about things they did when they were young and what they were doing now.

One person Mike had seen many times but didn't know was a skinny man in his thirties, very short but with a loud voice to make up for his size. His name was Richie Russo (aka Shorty). Mike took a liking to him and wanted to know him better so he introduced himself. It turned out that Richie was a made man for the Lucheesa family and did a lot of work for Vincenzo. Mike knew his uncle Vincenzo was a member of the Commission and several members of the five families were at the party. This was a great time to get to know them. Richie was a guy Mike would do business with and become best friends with in later years. Richie told Mike that he should go with him sometime to Vegas where Richie had some business matters he was required to take care of, and Mike liked the idea saying, "Thanks, I'll take you up on that someday." "I can use a thug like you with those claws of yours" Richie replied. Richie inquired what Mike did for a living. Mike felt comfortable telling Richie, who was a made man, that he just started moving cars for his cousin Ragu and Johnny G. Richie laughed saying "Small potatoes, Mike. One trip to Vegas and you could make twice what you make with them guys. Don't get me wrong, they're nice guys, but it's not worth the risk for chicken feed. If your uncle is Vincenzo, why are you working small change like that? He's got plenty of work you can do for big bucks," Richie said as they walked the grounds getting to know each other better. "I never asked him. Besides, he doesn't even know I'm doing this car thing. I just started a couple of weeks ago, and the money is good so far" Mike said. "When you're ready to make some real cash, call me," Richie said as he handed Mike a card with his personal number on it. "I will. I promise," Mike said putting the card in his wallet. "Well, I have to visit some of the boys," Richie said. They shook hands and went their separate ways for the rest of the party. Mike questioned himself about telling Richie about the involvement he had concerning the car deal and shrugged it off saying, *"He's a made guy. It's not like he's a cop or something."* However, he was a little nervous about saying too much.

Mike and the family had a great time and met many people both involved and not, but many would come into his life in later years to come, he just didn't know it then. The party ended with fireworks over the bay, and the kids were tired and ready for bed. It was very late and his uncle Vincenzo told the family to stay over as he had many bedrooms and they were all welcome to stay. Mike asked Jackie, and they decided to stay for the night and leave Sunday afternoon. Around twelve thirty they all retired to their designated bedrooms. The party was over, and all had a wonderful time.

Morning arose with a surprise as uncle Vincenzo greeted Mike with a breakfast sit-down in the kitchen. "Michael, I hear that you met Richie last night, and he tells me you are involved in cars with some of the family. Is this true?" Vincenzo asked as he sipped his morning espresso. "Yeah, It's true Uncle. I need the money, and the offer was too good to say no Besides, Eddie made a deal that I was bound to agree to so I couldn't say no. Are you upset with my actions?" Mike asked hoping his uncle would approve. "You do what you must provide for the family, Michael, and I understand," Vincenzo murmured in Italian. "You do understand the commitment you have made is a lifelong commitment," Vincenzo said. "Yes," Mike replied. "As you well know, I have been a member for many years, and I'm still committed to the needs of the families. And now that you are involved, I may ask of you a favor on behalf of the family which you must agree to follow. You understand this request of mine?" Vincenzo stated with control in his voice. "If you ask of me, I will do whatever you want. You are family, and I respect your honor. We are blood," Mike replied while staring Vincenzo eye to eye.

"Good, Michael, I had hoped you would understand my position in this matter." I am old, and when I was young, I did many things when asked of me. That is why I am in the position I am in and have provided for my family, as well as the Commission. They respect me and my lifelong connections with very powerful people. You understand?" Vincenzo asked with a stern voice as he held Michael's hands. "You need only ask of me, and it will be done," Mike said as he gripped Vincenzo's hand. In Italian Vincenzo said, "This conversation never happened, and you must keep the vow of Amorta always. No one should know what you do, and if you have problems, you come see me first, understand?" Vincenzo said to Mike as he loosened the grip. "Now enjoy the morning with your family. I have to go to New York on business. Call me in a week so we can talk about this thing of ours and if you want to join. Take some time to think about it." Vincenzo proceeded to the front door with his bodyguard and driver. The ride home was quiet, and the summer was ending in two months.

Michael thought long and hard about his getting involved, and knew it was a marriage with no divorce. When his uncle came back home, Michael asked for an audience with him. He wanted to discuss his getting involved. He was greeted, and together they went into great detail about Vincenzo's position and what would be expected of Mike if he chose to join with his uncle's crew. "I know you are street smart, but you know nothing about this business of ours. You will have to learn from some of my crew how to do business our way. If you say yes, I will send you out with one of my trusted enforcers so you can learn how to make people see things your way," "How long will it take before, I make the big money?" Mike asked. "It takes as long as it takes. If you want to be a part of my circle, and maybe someday take over for me, you will have to learn the ropes," Vincenzo replied. "So long as I answer to you and I'm working for you, I will do it. I'm already involved with this car thing anyway" Mike replied. "Fine, I will send you out with Eugene Melvino. We call him Doc. He's known as the pain doctor. He will teach you how to collect money or information from anyone. He's the best at extracting information and cooperation. He works for me and is sometimes on loan to other members, when they need him," Vincenzo replied. "Why do they call him the Doctor?" Mike asked. "He was studying to become a doctor and had to drop out so he could support his mother and siblings after his father died. He studied Chinese healing methods and acupuncture. He has a way of using his knowledge and his fingers for getting answers or money that is owed to me from deadbeat fucks that borrow and don't pay back. We also use him to make people see things our way, like a judge or crooked politician who is not cooperating with the family needs," Vincenzo said with a smile. "If I can learn some of those pressure points with my fat fuckin' fingers, I could be dangerous. Is that what you have in mind for me?" Mike asked. "See, you learn fast, my nephew," Vincenzo replied laughing. "Is that all I have to do?" "Don't be so fucking quick to think this is a few weeks and you're in. It doesn't work like that," Vincenzo said sternly. "After the doctor, you will go out with Richie. He will teach you the other sides of the business that the doctor does not do. "Mama Mia, this is gonna take time. I could see it now," Mike said. "You want in? I want you to be respected and feared by others. Training is a big part of that if you wish to command respect from other members. If they fear and respect you, they will listen to you" Vincenzo said. "Okay, I'll do it," Mike answered. "Good, welcome to the family, Michael. Now go home and someone will be in touch with you in a few days," Vincenzo said as he stood up informing Mike it was time to leave.

After several days, Mike was called to go on a job with the Doctor for extracting information for one of the New York bosses. Mike watched intently as the Doc worked his magic using pressure points on the supposed informer, who during the process, was spilling the information the boss needed to make his decision about one of his soldiers. The Doc was more than delighted to teach Mike his style of inflicting pain, knowing that with Mike's fingers, the apprentice could become the master in a very short time. After several months with the

Doc, Mike learned different pressure points and other forms of pain that could be used on people, leaving few marks. Doc taught him well.

Mike would spend the next two years learning from the Doctor and Richie on how the operation worked and who was who in the organization. When Vincenzo was pleased with his progression, and with approval from his peers, he welcomed Mike into the inner circle of his family operation by throwing an enormous party in his back yard. It was his way of letting it be known that his nephew, Michael Delagatta, was officially a member of the family. Not a Capo, but a high-ranking soldier. Two years had passed, and it was already the end of 1960.

That November 1960, John Kennedy had won the presidency with the help of the families and the unions. January was the official swearing-in of John Kennedy, and the families were in their glory. Parties were everywhere, and the families were strong and expanded into other ventures. Mike was doing fine. All that winter, Frankie, and Johnny G were bringing cars and were paid up with Mike. Everyone was happy, including Eddie (Money). Christmas was good for Mike's kids, and wife and Mike was buying a new home in Lido Beach. It was not a huge mansion, but it was a four-bedroom three-thousand-square-foot home in a beautiful neighborhood. A far cry from an apartment in East New York, Brooklyn. His family moved into the new home in April of 1961. Money was coming in, and Mike paid cash for everything to keep the IRS from seeing the additional income. He also bought one of the Cadillac's that Johnny G. had brought to the yard. It was a 1960 Deville coupe, silver and immaculate.

Mike decided to see if his brothers wanted to get involved with some extra business by supplying Mike with items to sell through their work connections. Harry provided flatbed trucks from the army surplus yard, and Jimmy told Mike, which international containers could be stolen. Jimmy cooked the books to hide the delivery of these international containers, and Mike worked out a deal with some of the club fellas to take the trucks from Harry's deal to steal the entire container from Jimmy's dockyard. Mike always stopped by the secret garage where the containers were emptied and distributed to the soldiers of the various families to sell on the street for cash profit. Truckloads of watches by Bulova, suits from Pierre Cardin, high-end clothing, shoes and other high-end merchandise from around the world were easy to sell and made a shitload of money for everyone involved. Mike was making a name for himself within the close circle of wise guys in the neighborhood. For Mike, it was a shitload of extra cash for him and his brothers and cousins who were involved.

That August Mike received a call from Eddie about a favor that uncle Vincenzo needed to have done. Mike could not say no, as he promised his uncle he would comply with his request when asked. "Mike, uncle Vincenzo has a favor that he needs to be done. Come to the house so we can talk," Eddie said on the phone. Mike dropped everything and drove to Eddie's house. "We have a problem with the Galli boys, and Uncle Vincenzo needs us, you and me, to take care of this person to send a message," Eddie said as he showed Mike a picture of a member of the Galli crew. The person in the photo was Fat Jimmy Randazo, and he was from the old neighborhood. Eddie told Mike that he set up a fishing trip with Fat Jimmy and two of his associates who wanted out and would help Eddie get rid of Fat Jimmy. "You know, they all have to go, and we can't have anyone to finger us, so I asked Tommy D. to come with us to take care of this matter," Eddie said. "So we're going fishing with them?" Mike asked confused. "Yeah, we're all going fishing this Tuesday at Sheepshead Bay. We'll pick them up. It's all set. They told Fat Jimmy they have some friends, and we're all going fishing. Be here at 4:00 am sharp Tuesday," Eddie said sternly to Mike. "OK," Mike replied. That Tuesday they pulled up to the dock at Sheepshead Bay and picked up Fat Jimmy and two of his friends. They drove out to the inlet and went about a mile out to sea. Eddie gave Tommy the nod to shoot Fat Jimmy, and Tommy D. shot Fat Jimmy twice in the head. While the two friends of Jimmy were looking at Jimmy's dead body, Eddie shot the two men with a shotgun he pulled from the boat cabin. Although Mike did not kill these guys, he did have blood on his hands. Whether he wanted to or not, he was now part of the big-boys club. Mike, Tommy, and Eddie tied the bodies of the three men to massive concrete blocks and chains and removed Jimmy's shoes, then dropped them into the ocean.

Eddie was instructed to put a fish in the shoes of Fat Jimmy and leave the shoes in front of the Galli family restaurant to leave a simple message. Fat Jimmy sleeps with the fishes. Little Joey got the message and was now on the run with his crew. They were marked because they were creating publicity the families did not want, and they were marked for elimination by the bosses. The Galli group was exceptionally large with some fifty crew members, but only three were made men, including little Joe Galli and Andy Deangelo (aka Big Andy). Fat Jimmy and two of his associates were now out of the picture, never to be found again. This was the beginning of a war that lasted for several months.

Eddie made his bones, which was a requirement for becoming a made man, and he would be recommended by uncle Vincenzo for membership.

About four months later, Eddie was inducted into the Gambono family with the traditional ceremony performed when a member is promoted to a made man within the family. Eddie threw a huge party at the local Italian club and friends were there to celebrate, including Mike. Uncle Vincenzo and Tommy D. did not show up because they wanted to stay under the radar and not be associated with any connections. In Italian Mike said to Eddie, "Congratulations on your promotion," and they both hugged. "Does Uncle Vincenzo know I was there that day," Mike asked Eddie. "He knows and is very thankful for your devotion to him. You know that he may ask something of you again someday, and you have to do whatever he asks. I have been doing this for quite some time, and we can never say no. If we say no, we get whacked because we betrayed the family," Eddie said as they walked together to mingle with the crowd of people at the party. Mike knew exactly what Eddie meant by his statement. He was deeply involved, and there was no return to the past. What was done was done, and no one could change that.

Michael was running into a different problem that he never saw coming. Hiding money was not easy, and it was all cash that Uncle Sam was not supposed to know about. He decided the best thing was to see his brother Salvatore. He was in the banking business and could advise his brother on how to move the money. Sal told Mike to set up separate accounts under different names to hide some of the money. He also set up offshore accounts to hide the bulk of the cash. Mike was so impressed with his brother's ability to move ill-gotten money, he asked if he would consider doing it for some of Mike's associates. Sal agreed, for a fee of five percent of the amount moved. Mike, seeing an opportunity, would charge his associates seven percent and pocket the extra two percent for himself, sort of what he called a connection fee.

Between his brothers making money and him making money from his brothers, the cars with Frankie and Johnny and their associates, Mike decided to buy out his boss Anthony and made him an offer of one hundred thousand dollars cash for the business. At first, Anthony said no, but after Mike had spoken to Eddie (Money) about his intention, Anthony changed his mind a week later and sold Mike the business. Mike did not know if Eddie had any involvement with Anthony's decision and Eddie never mentioned it either. Mike wanted the business, because it was a great front for storing the cars for the guys, and now it was a legit business for making legal money that he could use as personal income for tax purposes. It was a lucrative income for Mike, so he hired a longtime friend to run the shop for him so he did not have to be there anymore. Mike was now free to do whatever he wanted on a regular basis without having to worry about clocking in and out of work.

Things were moving faster than ever during the early sixties. John Kennedy was president. The construction business was booming, and all the families were making money. The downside was a vacuum of struggle from within families for leadership and control as things got better. Made men wanted to be the boss of their family. Mike stayed under the radar from all of it, and so did Eddie. They both knew that by sticking your head up out of the trench, people would take notice, and that could be trouble. They both learned this lesson from their uncle Vincenzo, who had been a council member for many years, and before that was a made man for close to thirty-five-years. He succeeded all his predecessors before him by laying low and staying out of the public eye and government investigations into the so-called Mafia.

Mike liked to gamble on the horses and was a frequent attendee at both the Belmont and Aqueduct racetracks. Although he was never correct in his choices of winners, he did love the sport and spent a lot of money in what he called "feeding the horses with his greens." One day a friend by the name of Fast Robert told Mike that he could buy a horse that was running in that race. He showed Mike how much it would cost for the horse as it was noted in the race form for that day. Mike was intrigued by the fact that, if he chose, he could buy the horse he liked and then get involved with the horse breeding and training and racing for the purse prize. He became excited about this new possibility and had to think it over and get suggestions from others about a possible new venture in the horse-racing business. He was so impressed with Fast Robert that he offered to take him out to dinner at Gino's Italian Restaurant as a thank you, the same Gino's first introduced to him by his cousin Frankie. Mike had visited several times since then. Robert took him up on the offer, and the outing would be held that Friday night with their wives and children.

It was a family outing for both Mike and Fast Robert's families. The next morning Mike called his uncle Vincenzo and asked if could come over to ask him more about this horse-racing thing. Mike was new to it and not sure how it worked. He knew that his uncle would be able to give him more info about setting up a front business to operate the entire venture. He called Eddie and asked him to go to the meeting too. He wanted a partner he could trust and share both the costs and profits.

The meeting was set for that Wednesday night at Vincenzo's house. Mike decided to go to the club that Tuesday night and see if anyone at the Italian American Club knew about the jockeys and any inside info pertaining to horse racing. He was surprised when a fella by the name of Tony La Roach (aka Sparky), overhearing Mike, asked about the racetrack business. He told Mike that he knew some jockeys who would throw a race for the right price and that he had fixed some races in the past when he was able to get these three jockeys together in a race. Mike's started thinking about a fixed race where one of his horses could win big if a large bet was made, and the odds were high. In fact, it would practically pay for the purchase of the horse. He told Tony Sparky that he would talk to him when the time was right and left it at that for the time being. Mike was excited that a fix could be made and couldn't wait to tell his Uncle and Eddie at the meeting that Wednesday night.

The day came when Michael was ready to pitch his offer to Vincenzo and Eddie and receive vital information in the horse-racing business. His uncle had some experience in this endeavor in his younger years when he worked as a bookie and knew some races were fixed. Mike had high hopes of becoming a racehorse owner and couldn't wait for his uncle's advice. Mike drove up to the sprawling mansion that was his uncle's home and rang the front door bell. To his surprise Richie, opened the door and greeted Mike with a smile and a handshake. "Hello Mike, we meet again." "Hello Richie, didn't expect to see you here." "Your Uncle asked me to come over 'cause he wanted a favor from me, and I think he wants you involved too," Richie said as he walked outside to the yard with Mike in tow. "That's odd, he said nothing to me about this." "Your uncle never discusses business on the phone when he can do it in person. How do you think he has stayed under the radar for so many years?" "You are right about that." Mike said as he saw Eddie and his uncle Vincenzo sitting under the umbrella. There were other people there too, but they were seated in another section of the yard. Greeting each other with the traditional kiss on both cheeks and speaking in Italian, they sat down and Michael started his pitch immediately. "Wow, slow down," Uncle Vincenzo said sternly. "I have some questions to ask you before you start opening your mouth about this horse business shit you want to get involved with." "I'm sorry Uncle, please speak," Mike said as he looked at Eddie and Richie, who both had a smile on their faces. "Michael, are you sure this is something you want to do?" uncle asked. "I mean why buy race horses when you can still make money on the bets? You don't have to own horses to make money at the track, but you can earn money using your brother and the banking business. Insurance on horses and collecting could make a shit-load of money, if you have the right horse and connections" Vincenzo said with the biggest grin on his face. "In the old days, we used to insure horses and then break their leg to collect the insurance policy. Luciano and a couple of us were experts in this lucrative venture until the insurance companies stopped insuring our horses. I must admit, I kind of miss that, but you have to know how to do it right if you want to get involved.

Now you can speak Michael, I am curious to hear what you have to say," Vincenzo said as he lit up a Cuban cigar from his special stash, which he had shipped in special for himself. Mike looked like someone hit him with a brick. His mouth was open and he was not really sure what he had just heard from his uncle. "I never even thought about that. I was thinking of buying horses and fixing the race so they win with crazy odds like fifty-to-one." "But we can do that already without owning the fuckin' horse" Richie said looking at Mike. "Unless you have some new way of making more money, you should listen to your uncle if you want to own a fuckin' stable of race horses." Mike didn't know what to say at this point and looked around the table for answers. Eddie spoke up and said "How much are you willing to invest in this business?" Mike replied "I am not sure, maybe a hundred K, but I am not sure what that will get me as far as horses and boarding and training" "Okay, enough of this bullshit," Vincenzo said, as he stood up, and banged his fist on the table. "I am getting too old for this training bullshit, so here is what I am going to do. I have some friends who are in this type of business. I will send you and Richie to meet with them in Ocala, Florida next week to see what they have for sale in the way of horses. If they have something good to sell, I will invest with Eddie, Richie and you. Together we will form a corporation for the business. We will call it Brooklyn Investment Group for legitimate purposes. However, in return, you and Richie must do something special for me and some of my associates which is extremely important for the families and our future endeavors. If you are willing to do this, then we have a deal with all of us at this table. Am I correct in this, gentlemen?" Vincenzo looked around the table and everyone nodded their heads as a form of acceptance and agreement from the boss. "Then it is done. I will make the arrangements for you and Richie to leave next week. Now, I have to meet a man about some pressing matters. You can all see yourselves out," Vincenzo said as he walked away. "Richie, what the hell is my uncle talking about, and why do I have to go with you on this mission?" Mike asked as he looked straight into Richie's eyes. "And don't bullshit me, or so help me I'll cut your balls off and shove them in your mouth." "I only know what your Uncle told me, and don't fuckin' threaten me ever again. I may be small but I will cut you before you can blink," Richie said in a loud voice as the others looked on. "Hey, knock it off," Eddie screamed as he stood up looking upset and pissed. "We all know an answer of no is unacceptable with Vincenzo, and whatever it is he asks, must be done, family or not. So the two of you need to shut the hell up and make nice, or I will be forced to bitch slap the both of you little fuckin' babies. If Vincenzo is sending his most trusted man Richie and a family relative Mike, then to me it is crucial; otherwise he would have sent two assholes instead. All I can say is, don't fuck it up or I may be going to two funerals in the same day, tu capisce? Now, I have been instructed to arrange for the two of you to meet with Vincenzo and others at Gino's restaurant this Thursday at 8pm sharp. Bring no one with you and no guns. This is imperative. There you will be instructed what you will be going to Florida for in addition to Mike's venture for these fuckin' horses he wants to get involved with. Both of you be on your best behavior at this meeting. There will be members of the families attending, so don't act like shitheads." Eddie shook Mike's and Richie's hands and walked away to the side gate leading out to the driveway. "Richie, I'm sorry for growling at you. I got scared and did not know what to expect. I'm sorry" Mike said hoping Richie would accept his offer. Richie started walking away without saying a word and suddenly he turned around and looked at Mike and said "I have killed men for less, and in this case, I will have to think about it." Mike was not expecting that at all. He knew that Richie could be very dangerous if you got on his wrong side and Mike may have done just that. Only time could heal this wound.

When Michael got home that night, Jackie told him to call his cousin Frank. It was very important, she said. When Mike called Frank, he could tell there was something wrong because Frank was speaking very fast and seemed upset. "Slow down Frankie and tell me what's going on." "Mike, there's some new guy in the neighborhood and he's trying to take over my business. I don't know who he is but someone needs to stop him. I've never seen him before and I need your help." Mike replied, "Do you know where he hangs out, where can I find this prick?" "I'm not sure but I've seen him on Eastern Parkway and he hangs with some other guys." "Frank have you been to the club, and do they know him?" "No I have not" Frank replied. "Okay I'll take care of this. Just make sure you keep paying on time." Mike looked at his watch and decided to go to the club that night. It was only 7:30 pm. Entering the club, Mike saw his friend Onions and asked him if he knew who this person might be. Onions was not sure who Mike was speaking about, so he told Mike "Let's go and see if we can find him now." They both left the club and walked to the corner of Eastern Parkway and waited for this individual to show up. It was about an hour later that this person did show up with two other guys.

Mike went into the candy store and called Frank. "Frank, you need to come over to Eastern Parkway and Atlantic Avenue, and ID these guys before I beat the shit out of an innocent guy." Frank replied, "I'll be right there." Mike and Onions kept an eye on the guys until Frank came. "Yeah, that's the fuck who is stealing on my turf." Mike and Onions walked over to this person and asked him what his name was. He replied in a snotty voice "None of your fuckin' business." Onions spoke out loud "Oh, shit, this is going to get nasty." Mike was not amused as he reached and grabbed the kid by the throat with one hand, lifting him off his feet. "Be a good little boy or I will break you in half" Mike said sternly. "Mike put him down" Onions said, "I don't want you to kill him here." Michael let him go and it was obvious this kid was shaken up. "Now what is your name and who are you working for" Mike asked nicely. "My name is Joey Carbone and I'm working for a shop on Sutter Avenue. I'm just trying to make a living too. I didn't know this was your turf and I'm sorry, I was following orders, that all." Mike explained to him this was a protected area and to tell his boss to stay the hell out of this neighborhood or he will pay the price. Mike leaned over and whispered in his ear "If I find out you have been stealing cars around here, I will personally stuff you in the trunk of a car and drive the car off a bridge. Understand?" The kid understood very well and nodded his head up and down, with a look of fear in his eyes. "Whatever you say, I won't be in this neighborhood again." Michael, Onions and Frankie all walked back to the club. "Thanks Onions. I'm going home. I'm tired and I have a busy day tomorrow. I'll see you around." Mike said. Mike looked at Frankie saying, "Find out who owns this chop shop and see if he's paying up. If he's not, start charging him or tell him he will no longer be in business." Frankie agreed and they parted. Michael went home and had a good night's rest.

The next morning after breakfast Mike went to his shop to see if everything was fine. His man in charge, who was called Bo, said "No problem Mike, everything's good." Mike asked if Johnny and Frankie were paying on time and how many cars were in the lot. "I think there is like twelve cars back there now. Johnny is a week behind, but I don't think that's a problem." Mike was happy with the answer and gave Bo $100 bucks and said "Have dinner on me tonight." Mike knew keeping his workers happy would lead to better results in the shop, and Bo was the right man for the job. Mike knew that he was soon to meet some very important people and he would be out of town for a while.

He decided to take his family out to dinner that next night and explained to Jackie that he would be away for a few days, maybe even a week. His children wanted to go to Nathan's for dinner. They loved the atmosphere and food. In those days, Nathan's in Long Beach was a favorite hangout for a variety of people, including bikers, biker chicks, wise guys and regular folk. Mike explained to Jackie he had to go on a business trip for his uncle Vincenzo and was not sure how long it would take, but he would keep in contact with her every day. Jackie knew what kind of business Mike was in and never asked questions. The less she knew the better.

Mike woke up Thursday morning very nervous wondering what would happen Thursday night at the meeting. Around 11am, he called his cousin Eddie and asked if the meeting was still on. "Yeah the meeting is on. If there was any change, I would have fuckin' called you." Eddie said. "I heard there was some young punk trying to steal Frankie's turf and you and Onions had a talk with him. How did that go?" "Everything was fine. He understood and Frankie is looking into who owns the chop shop. Maybe we'll get some more cash flow" Mike replied in a surprised voice. "Good," we can always use more money. And yes, Mike the meeting is on tonight. Be there sharp at 8." Eddie said. It was obvious that Mike was very nervous and didn't know what to do with himself, so that Thursday during the day he stayed home with Jackie just waiting for the time to leave to go to this meeting.

Around 7:00 pm, Mike started to get dressed nervously fumbling with his tie. "Jackie does this look good or should I change my tie?" he asked. "That looks fine Mike. You look good" Jackie said as she gave him a kiss, and said, "Please be careful and good luck." Mike looked sharp, well dressed, hair done and ready to impress. He gave Jackie a kiss and said he was leaving. He didn't know what time he would be back, but he would be back that night. Mike got in his car and drove to Gino's restaurant. He noticed there were bodyguards outside the restaurant and knew important people were already there. As he walked up to the door, they asked him who he was and why he was there. "I am here for a meeting with my uncle. My name is Michael Delagatta." One of the men opened the door and followed Mike in. The hostess who knew Mike greeted him and said, "They are expecting him. He's okay. I know him. Mike the meeting is in the back room you know how to get there?" Mike gave her a big smile, said "Thanks, doll" and walked to the back room. Entering the room, he was impressed. There were suits and ties everywhere, men with guns and without, standing around chatting with others. Michael saw Richie in the far corner and walked over to say hello. "Rich, how are you? Did you forgive me yet or should I still be on my toes?" Mike said with a smile as he shook Richie's hand. Ritchie replied, "Too soon, Mike, need more time." "Okay, I understand, but I really am sorry." Ritchie smiled, and they both walked to a table where uncle Vincenzo was already sitting and talking to some older man whom Mike did not know. Vincenzo looked up and said "Michael, I want you to meet a good friend of mine. His name is Salvatori, and he is from Miami. He represents the southern families and is here for this meeting. I explained to him you will be going to Florida on business for me and that you are interested in race horses, and you are also going to Ocala, Florida to meet with a mutual friend who owns a horse farm and that you might be interested in getting into the business." Michael put out his hand to greet Salvatori and very politely said, "It is an honor to meet you, and I look forward to knowing you better in the future." Salvatori felt Mike's hand wrapping around his like mild steel caressing a stick of butter. Looking down, he said out loud, "Your hands, they are massive. That is a sign of good stock." He then turned to Vincenzo and said, "Someday I could use a hand like this to persuade some of the deadbeats I need collections from. You're okay with this, yes?" Vincenzo smiled and said, "In this family, we share with the understanding that it is a favor that must be repaid." The two old men smiled and sat down. Vincenzo said to Salvatori, "You know Richie. He has met with you on my behalf many times." Salvatori acknowledged Richie, who said "It's nice to meet you again," as he sat down.

Vincenzo tapped his glass with a fork to make noise and said, "Gentlemen, let's sit down and start this meeting." There were about twenty men who sat at the table and everything got quiet. All of the guys who were standing were asked to leave the room. One member got up from the table to close the double doors and locked them from the inside. "Now we can speak our minds for all to hear in this room and we take an oath these words will never leave this room, upon our death we swear." A short, stocky man from about the middle of the table stood up and said, "You all know who I am. We have a situation that we must address." Mike knew this person to be Sam Giancolla. He had seen his picture in the papers before. He knew Sam was the Chicago boss and was very powerful. "It seems we are getting some heat from those we put in power, and we must rectify this issue as soon as possible. Although I take responsibility for initiating the election of Jack Kennedy, all of us were involved with him winning. It seems that his younger brother is breathing down our throats trying to investigate our business and this we cannot allow. Vincenzo, who some of you know, has been an associate and good friend of the families for many, many years. He is willing to provide two of his top men to intervene on our behalf and speak to our old friend Joe Kennedy. He will explain our situation and request that he speak to his sons and put a stop to this problem of ours before it gets out of hand. We must take further action in an effort to stop this harassment which could cause all of us great problems in the future."

By now there was some chattering amongst those sitting at the table and Vincenzo stood up and said, "We have all heard what has been said, and we all agree this needs our attention. That is why I am sending, with the blessing of those here tonight, two of my most trusted boys. They are exquisite at staying under the radar, and they are relatively unknown in our business. They should have no problem speaking to Joe Kennedy about his sons and conveying our needs and the consequences if his boys do not behave the way they are expected. I trust these men with my life, and if anyone chooses to speak up, now is the time to voice your opinion." Salvatori said, "You should all know that the CIA has contacted me and several others of our friends about this thing with Castro. They now have their hands dirty with the fuckup in the Bay of Pigs situation. Now they have asked us to provide someone to poison Castro with our Cuban contacts. I do not trust them, and I think they are using us to benefit their own goal while breathing down our throats along with the FBI. I have taken their money, and their poison pills, and you can thank them for dinner tonight. It is on the government's dime that we meet, talk and enjoy good food and good friends. I have not provided, nor will I provide, someone to go to Cuba and slip Castro a mickey fin. I say this, so you all know the government, specifically the CIA, is sleeping in our bed with us and is guilty of the same. Use this information to your benefit should you need to negotiate in the future. I personally am backing Vincenzo's decision to provide his personal men to sit and have a conversation with an old friend of ours in an effort to fix this problem we have." He raised his glass of wine and said, "Saluta." Some men clapped, others did not. They all understood this matter had to be addressed, or the snake may lose his head. Carl Gambono stood up and said, "This meeting is adjourned." He turned, unlocked and opened the doors, whispering to someone by the door to tell Gino they are ready for dinner.

Mike was relieved this meeting was over and now could enjoy the company of his uncle and newfound friends. He was still nervous because many of these people were very powerful. He did not know most of them, but he was comfortable with his uncle Vincenzo's position and knew he was truly a very powerful and respected man of honor among his peers. By all accounts, representatives of the five families were there, including ranking members of the Council and associates. If Mike wasn't known before, he was certainly known now. Mike was relieved to know he didn't have to kill anyone on this mission. He only had to bring a message to a very important man about an even more important son. Mike leaned over to Richie and whispered in his ear, "I'm glad that's over, and now I know what we are supposed to do. Do you know when we are supposed to leave to go bring this message to Mr. Kennedy." Richie leaned over and said, "I think we leave Monday morning. I'm not sure, but we will know soon enough." Mike enjoyed the company and, you could see by his demeanor, was much more relaxed and actually enjoying himself. After dinner, the crowd started to thin out as they said their goodbyes and proceeded to leave the restaurant. Michael walked over to his uncle Vincenzo kissed him on both cheeks and said, "Anything for you Uncle. Anything at all. I am leaving. Thank you for dinner, and I'll be ready when you call." Mike said goodbye to Salvatori and Richie. On his way out he eyed the hostess with a great big smile and said, "Till we meet again, doll, goodnight."

CHAPTER 4

ON A MISSION

Friday morning, July 1 1961. Michael woke up relieved and happy. He knew he had only three days left to get stuff straightened out. The first thing he did was check with his cousin Frankie about who owned the chop shop. After breakfast with Jackie, he drove down to the shop to speak with Bo to see if everything was good and if Johnny had paid his bill. Bo explained that all was good except one little problem. Someone was looking at the cars in the lot, and Bo was not sure who it was. "Maybe it was a cop. I don't know" Bo said. "Maybe you can ask your cop friend if he knows anything." "Good idea," Michael said. "Has Johnny paid up?" "Yes." "Took a little talking but he did pay." "I'm going to be gone for a few days, maybe even a week. Hold down the fort and get in touch with me if anything goes wrong," Mike said as he walked into his office and opened the safe. He took out his handgun and put it in the waist of his pants and removed some cash. "Everything okay with you Mike?" Bo asked. "Yeah, no problem. I have to see some guy about a chop shop, and I might need some protection," Mike said as he started to walk out of the office. "You be careful, boss," Bo said as he locked the office door. "I'll be okay. I'll see you in a week," Mike said, walking towards his car. Mike was having lunch with his cousin Eddie T. that afternoon, and he asked him if he knew of a chop shop on Decatur Street. Eddie said, "No why are you asking?" with a curious look on his face. "Frankie tells me there is a chop shop set up, and he does not think they are paying to run their business. I am going to take a ride over there and see who it is, and if he is not one of us we'll charge them a vig," Mike replied. "So you need someone to go with you?" Eddie asked. "Who did you have in mind?" Mike asked. "I can send Frenchy and Tommy D," Eddie said with a smile. "Frenchy will be fine. Speaking of Tommy D, someone was snooping around the lot where we store the cars. We're not sure who it is. Maybe Tommy can find out from his sources if anyone in the PD is on to us," Mike said as he finished his lunch. "I hope Frankie didn't open his fuckin' mouth. You know he can be a pain in the ass with his bragging" Eddie said as he moved out of his chair and stood up. "If he opened his mouth and we are on the hook, he will get a good beating," Mike said as he laid $100 on the table and they both walked out of Gino's. Michael was looking for his cute little hostess on the way out, but she did not work during the day. "So I'll have Frenchy meet you on the corner of Decatur Street next to the bakery around 2:30." "That's fine," Mike said as they parted ways heading to their cars. "Mike, let me know how you make out with this shop and be careful," Eddie. said. Mike did not reply but did acknowledge that he heard him.

Mike decided to go to the club that afternoon after lunch and see who was there. To his surprise, he saw Dapper and several others who were playing cards. He walked over to Johnny, put his hand on his shoulder and asked with a smile "You winning or losing?" "Losing as usual. I hear you're going on a trip with little Richie to talk to a man about a horse," Dapper said, as he turned and looked Mike in the eyes. "Yeah, gotta run and errand for somebody. And yeah, I am going to see a man about a horse. Funny you should ask," Mike said smiling. "Who knows, maybe you'll get lucky betting on some of my horses if I make this deal." "Good, I can use a good-luck streak," Johnny said as he threw down his cards to another losing hand. "See you in a few days, Johnny," Mike said as he walked to the door and left.

As Michael was getting into his car, he couldn't help but wonder, "*How did Dapper know I was leaving town? That meeting was supposed to be secret. No one was supposed to know about what was said except for those in the room. Who was the big mouth and what else did they say?*" He wondered if he should say anything to his uncle about this or say nothing. If he told his uncle, there was a good chance Dapper could get whacked just for asking. After all, Michael liked Dapper and didn't want to see him whacked. In addition, he was bringing in money and money was something Michael was starting to enjoy very much. Michael was at a point in his life where he was making good money, lots of money, and his brothers were also making good money providing Mike merchandise to sell. They were enjoying their cut of the cash. Mike decided to say nothing and keep quiet. He would pretend like it never happened.

Looking at his watch, Mike decided it was time to leave and meet Frenchy on Decatur Street. Driving past the chop shop, Michael noticed the bay doors were open. That was good. He and Frenchy would just walk in. Mike parked the car and walked into the bakery to see Frenchy having coffee. "You ready?" Mike asked as he looked at Frenchy sitting in a booth. "Yeah, I was born ready," Frenchy replied as he put two dollars on the table and stood up. They both walked out of the bakery and down the block to the chop shop. Walking into the chop shop, Frenchy yelled out, "Who's the fuckin' boss here?" Mike was not happy with the way Frenchy introduced himself. He decided to see how tough Frenchy really was. He would let Frenchy handle this, and he would play backup. What Mike did not see was that Frenchy already had his gun out. As Frenchy reached the back of the building, two guys pulled out their guns. "Whoa, don't shoot. We come in peace," Mike yelled out. "Frenchy put that fuckin' gun away. We're here on business." With that, the office door opened and out came a black-haired individual, somewhere in his thirties, stocky build, five foot six, with a handlebar mustache. "What do you guys want?" he asked. "We just want to talk," Mike said. "Come into my office," the stranger said as he looked at his men and nodded his head to say it was okay. Mike let Frenchy go in first and followed cautiously. "Now, what can I do for you guys? You guys don't look like you're here to buy a car." Frenchy spoke first. "Running a chop shop here or you just fixin' cars?" Frenchy asked as he was looking around the room. "What's it to you what kind of business I am running here?" the man asked. "What family you with?" Frenchy asked. "I am with my own family. What do you mean?" the man asked. Mike stepped in and said, "What my friend here means is, to do this kind of business that we know you are doing, you need protection. And if you are not paying for that protection, we need to set up a payment plan so that you become a part of our protection program. You understand, don't you?" "I think I'm going to have to pass on your offer and ask you guys to leave," he said as he reached into his desk drawer for his gun. Frenchy and Mike felt something was wrong by the movements the guy was making behind his desk. Mike was standing next to the desk, and Frenchy was standing near the door. No sooner did the guy bring his gun above the desk, that Mike drew his gun and shot him in the chest. Frenchy pulled his weapon and shot one person who was standing by the door. They expected to hear more gunshots, but there were none. Mike and Frenchy quickly walked out of the office and noticed a man standing alone. He cried out "Please don't shoot me. I didn't see a thing." "What relationship are you to that guy in the office?" Mike asked. "I'm his cousin, and I just work here." Mike responded to the stranger's answer, "Today you got a promotion; you're the new boss here. You came back from lunch and saw these guys already dead. Tell his wife that you can run the business for her and you will just take a salary. If it doesn't go like that, then you go to the Italian club on the corner of Atlantic Avenue and Eastern Parkway and ask for a guy called Onions. Understand what I just said? Otherwise, we're coming back for you. Tu capisce'?" Scared, the kid said with his voice shaking. "Yeah, I understand. I came back from lunch, and they were already dead. I didn't see anything." "Okay," Mike said. "Don't make me come back for you." Mike and Frenchy walked out of the building and down to the corner. Frenchy laughed saying, "I think that guy pissed his pants while you were talkin' to him." "Well, that didn't go as planned. I'll talk to you later, Frenchy." Michael was upset. He had just shot a man and hoped this guy didn't rat him out. He knew he would be gone for a few days. He would hash it out when he came back. That should be enough time to cool things off. Mike went back to his shop office to wait out the rest of the day. Friday was ending on a sour note.

Mike decided to stay local on Saturday and hang low, but Eddie called him early that morning and simply said, "Meet me at the Olympic Diner in East Meadow at 10:30 today. We need to talk." Mike knew why and replied, "See you there." Mike thought to himself, "So much for laying low." He reminded Jackie he was going out of town on Monday and was not sure when he would be back. She acknowledged saying "Well I'll have to go shopping to keep myself busy" as she smiled at Mike. "Yeah, you do that very well now that we have some money. Don't go crazy, okay? He walked behind her and gave her a smack on the ass and a kiss on her neck. "Hey, I have to go see Eddie at the Olympic Diner this morning. You want some of those Greek pastries they have? I know how much you liked them the last time we were there." "Sure. That would be sweet for dessert tonight," she said as she was preparing breakfast for the kids. "I'm leaving. I'll see you later, babe," Mike said as he opened the door to leave. "Bye," she replied from the other room as Mike walked out of the door.

Mike knew the mechanic shop would be on the way to the diner, and he wanted to count the cars in the lot, get some cash and a different gun in case there was a problem at the sit-down. He had enough time to do both. Everything went fine at the shop, and he counted twelve cars. Three were Corvettes with all the bells and whistles.

He went into his office and called his manager "Bo, everything going good with the shop?" he asked expecting to get the typical answer. "Mike, some guy was looking around the shop, and I don't know who he is. He looked like a cop or something, but I'm not sure" "OK, I'll get with Ragu and Dapper and let them know to move the cars out Sunday to the lot on Saxton Avenue, so they disappear by Monday," Mike said to Bo. "Let me know if they are gone by Monday morning 'cause I'll be out of town for a few days on business." "Will do boss," Bo answered. Mike was nervous about the cars in the lot and tying it to him and his business. He started wondering if the cash he was making off the cars was worth the risk. Eddie's advice was needed in his decision since he was also getting a piece of the action. Mike couldn't do it without letting him know anyway. He would ask him at the meeting.

Mike showed up a little early and found a booth in the back next to a window looking out the front of the dinner. He had learned to be cautious and keep an eye on the surroundings and his options in the event something should happen suddenly. Eddie showed up with both Frenchy and Tommy D. They greeted each other and sat down to talk. Eddie started with what Mike knew the conversation would be about. "Frenchy tells me you, and he had no choice cause the guy was armed. Is this true?" Eddie asked as he looked at Tommy D and Mike. "Yeah, he pulled first. I tried to reason with him, and he jumped up from his desk with the gun. We had no choice," Mike answered looking at Frenchy. "Let's hope this bum didn't have backing from some family members and was working alone. I'll hear about it if he was connected. Tommy will snoop around to see what he can find, right Tommy?" Eddie said as he looked at Mike "If he was connected to someone, word will get around at the department, and I'll hear about it," Tommy said looking around the table to see if there was a response from anyone. "You tied up loose ends at this garage and Frenchy tells me you told the nephew he didn't see anything." "Is there anything we should be worried about with this situation that could connect it to us?" Eddie asked Mike looking straight into his eyes. "He doesn't know who we are. But he does know what we are. He was pissing in his pants while I told him what to say, and if he sticks to the story, everything should be fine," Mike said staring back at Eddie. "OK, anything else we need to talk about?" Eddie asked. "We'll, I ain't sure how important this is, but Bo tells me someone was snooping around the shop yesterday, and he thinks it may be a cop or something based on the way he looked. I am going to call the boys and tell them to move the cars to the Saxton Avenue lot 'cause that yard has fencing you can't see through. Other than that, maybe we should talk about the risk involving us directly in this car thing and if it's worth the risk."

Eddie thought for a while and said, "Okay have them move the cars and we will talk about what to do when you come back from your Florida thing. In the meantime, I'll figure out how to get us out of the picture and maybe put it under a dummy corporation, so if they get pinched, it won't come back to us directly." He then turned to Tommy and said, "Look into it and let me know if they are onto us with this car thing." "I'll push them in a different direction and stall the investigation so you can move things around. That should buy you some time," Tommy answered with a smile. Eddie returned the smile saying, "And that's why you are my most trusted insider, eyes, and ears behind the steel wall. We're done here," he said as he picked up the tab for breakfast. "Mike you leave the tip. She was a cute girl, so be generous." Mike slapped down a twenty. "Good luck in Florida and call me when you get back. I want to know how it went with that Kennedy thing." Eddie hugged Mike and gave him a slap on the back. "You'll be the first one I call after the old man gets the news," Mike said as he broke loose of the hug and started to walk away in the direction of his car. "Should I be worried about this meeting?" Mike asked as they walked to the parking lot. "Not that I know of. Should be a piece of cake." Eddie reached his car first. "OK, see you when I get back," Mike said and walked further to his car. Mike drove off feeling somewhat relieved that things were going smooth, short of his earlier confrontation with the chop-shop fiasco. He decided to deal with the chop-shop issue when he got back from his Florida mission.

CHAPTER 5

THE KENNEDY ORDEAL

Mike confirmed with Richie that everything was a go for the Florida meeting and that all was on schedule. Richie had the necessary letter and tickets for the trip, and he was to meet Richie at LaGuardia Airport early so they could go over some things. Mike agreed and went home to get ready by packing his suitcases. Monday morning came, and Mike kissed his wife goodbye and had his friend Onions drive him to the airport. There he met Richie and discussed the plans. "Richie, does Mr. Kennedy know we are coming?" "Everything is set, Mike. The old man will meet us at the Palm Beach Country Club for lunch at 1 pm. He will be accompanied by some Secret Service agents, 'cause of his relationship with the President. But don't worry; they will not be part of the meeting. They are only there to protect the old man. Your uncle wants you to give this letter directly to Joe Kennedy. After he reads it, you are to burn it on the table in front of us, so there is no connection between the families and the Kennedys. After that's done, we are to go to the Fountain Bleau Hotel in Miami Beach and meet with Salvatori and some of the bosses to relay the message we get from Joe Kennedy. We will stay there until we are told we could leave. They will make that decision. This will be a piece of cake. We ain't doin' nothing wrong or illegal, so we can have some fun at the Boom Boom room while we wait." "Boom Boom Room?" Mike asked with a smile. "What the fuck is that?" "The night club at the hotel, asshole" Richie replied. The families have clubs all over the place as well as real estate in probably every fuckin' state except Hawaii," Richie said as he reached into his sports jacket for the flight tickets. "Here is your ticket, Mike. We can get in line to board the plane" Mike was nervous, and even though he was not a drinker, he needed one about this time, even though it was only 11 am. "You never been to Miami, Mike?" Richie asked as they walked down the corridor to the plane entrance. "I have never been out of Brooklyn, let alone to Florida," Mike said chuckling. "I hear that's where everybody goes to retire. That's all I know about Florida." Mike said. Richie replied, "Well, I'll have to show you a good time while you're at the pussy capital of the world. Hot chicks everywhere and willing to put out for a good time and money. You may not want to leave once you get a taste of it."

The trip was slightly more than two hours but to Mike, it seemed like ten. After three drinks he was feeling relaxed. The plane landed in Miami, and they rented a car to drive to Palm Beach. There they checked into a local hotel and relaxed. The meeting was set for the next day with Joe Kennedy at a swanky country club restaurant on premises. Mike and Richie decided to go out after dinner and see some of the local nightlife and enjoy the scenery of Palm Beach. Asking the hotel desk clerk to recommend a hopping night club, they were told to go to the Stork Club, the most famous of all clubs. They entered the club around 10 pm and were greeted by two bouncers at the club door. "Evening gentlemen, come in and enjoy yourself. It is a little early, but the party should get started in an hour or so." "Wow, nice place," Mike said as they both walked into a semi-crowded room. The interior although being dark was well designed with an upper balcony and a stage for live shows. Richie told one of the employees he wanted a table facing the door and close to a corner as he gave the attendant a twenty. "You got a phone I can use?" he asked as he palmed him the twenty. "Yes, sir, at the end of the bar in the hallway are public phones," the attendant replied. They sat down at a table with four chairs around a circular table and Richie ordered a drink and told Mike he was going to call uncle Vincenzo and make sure everything was still set for tomorrow. Mike looked around the room to scope out the ladies and get a feel for the place. Richie walked back and said to Mike, "Everything is a go. Your uncle said to stay out of trouble and follow my lead." Now it was Richie's turn to look around and see the available pussy dancing on the floor as well as his surroundings. They both chatted at the table in an effort to get to know each other better.

Some girls came to the table and asked if they were alone and wanted some company. One was a fiery redhead named Roxanne who liked to be called Foxy Roxi, and the other was petite with jet-black hair who called herself Jenny. They sat and talked for a while, and Roxi asked, "So what do you boys do for a livin'?" Mike stayed quiet, and Richie spoke up saying, "We are investors, and we're here on business. What do you girls do?" Richie replied as he looked at Jenny with a smile." "We are just local girls workin' for a living. We come here to unwind every now and then," Jenny replied as she moved her leg under the table closer to Richie's leg in an effort to let him feel her leg rubbing his. Richie smiled wide and said, "Ladies, tonight is a night you will never forget." "Oh really," Roxi said looking at Richie and Mike, waiting for something special to happen at that moment. "What do you say we have a few more drinks then go back to our place for a little something to eat?" Richie asked as he looked at Roxi. "Something to eat? Well, I hope it's me. You boys look a little hungry. I hope you have a big appetite," Roxi said as she reached for Mike's hand. "Oh my, what big hands you have. I wonder if everything on you is as big as your hands?" Mike laughed saying, "no one has ever complained about my size if that's what you're asking." "I think I'll have one more drink, and then we can go. I can't wait to be surprised by what Mr. big hands has to show us, girls." Jenny blushed as she said looking at Roxi, "If he's too much, call me for help. I'll be happy to hold him down for you." "Okay, this is getting a little too hot here. Perhaps we should skip the drinks and go to a cooler place where we can continue this conversation, ladies," Richie said and motioned the attendant for the check. Mike reached into his pocket and pulled out a wad of cash and said he would take care of the tab. "You could choke a horse with that wad," Jenny said looking at the stack of bills Mike had just revealed. "Can you neigh like a horse?" Mike asked as he looked at Jenny and Roxi. Both girls started neighing and laughing like crazy. Richie and Mike struggled to get out of their cushioned chairs. The crotches of their pants were bulging. "See what you did to me?" Richie said as he looked down at his crotch. "Let's hurry back to the room. We want to ride that pony," Jenny said as she reached down and wrapped her hand around his swollen crotch. "I may need a saddle for Mike's pony," Roxi said looking at his huge bulge. Adrenaline was rushing through Mike's blood. He was not the type to have a one-night affair with a woman. For the most part, he was faithful to his marriage, but not tonight. He had to pound this hot redhead just to allow his blood to calm down. They all piled into the rented Caddy and off they went to the hotel room where Mike and Richie had their way with the ladies they had just met.

That morning Roxi walked out of the bedroom telling Jenny that Mike was so big and endowed she would be walking funny for a few days, and just one hand covered both cheeks of her perfect ass. Jenny replied that Richie was an animal in bed and did her every way possible for an hour. All four got dressed and headed out the room for some morning breakfast in the hotel. They talked, and the girls gave their numbers to Mike and Richie but did not receive one back in return. Richie and Mike did not give that sort of information to strangers. They only told the girls they would be back in town sometime in a month, and they would get together again. They all said goodbye and went their separate ways. It was 10 am. Mike and Richie had to forget about last night and concentrate on their upcoming mission with Mr. Kennedy. Mike and Richie talked and laughed about last night as they were getting dressed in the hotel room. "How bad did you hurt that red-headed horse last night?" Richie yelled out from one of the bedrooms. "I taught her how to trot like a Tennessee walking horse if that's what you mean," Mike replied. "Big hands and, I guess, big dick," Richie said with a smile as he walked into the foyer leading into Mike's bedroom. "You ready? We have to go soon," he said to Mike, who was putting on his tie. "You look good, real sharp Mike." "You too Richie. You got the letter?" Mike asked as they both walked to the room door. "Yeah I got the letter and were not supposed to read it either, just give it to the old man and burn it when he's done reading it." The country club was a distance from the hotel where they were staying, and conversation during the ride was quiet. Few words were said leaving Mike nervous, but he couldn't back out. Richie was so cool. It was like another day at the office for him. As they approached the large doors leading into the eating area of the country club, Richie took the letter from his suit jacket and gave it to Mike who put it in the front pocket of his suit jacket. "Don't say anything. I'll do the talkin'," Richie said as they got closer to the table. Mike replied "Good, my mouth is shut. You do all the talkin." They sat down at the table, but Mr. Kennedy was not there yet. There were already two agents sitting at another table near the one Richie and Mike were seated at. "You don't think this is a setup, do you?" Mike whispered softly to Richie. "No. We'll wait a half hour, and if he's not here by then, we go," Richie said leaning over to Mike. About fifteen minutes went by when a man came in and asked them to follow him into another room. Mike and Richie did as requested. As they entered the room, two men stopped them. One said, "I have to make sure you don't have any weapons on you, okay?" "Sure, Richie said as they stood there being frisked. "You can have a seat at the table over there," one of the men said and pointed. Once they were seated, Joe Kennedy walked into the room and sat in one of the chairs. It was obvious that he was a Kennedy as his facial features were an older version of his son Jack, light skin with rosy red cheeks and in his mid-sixties. "What can I do for you, gentlemen? I know who sent you, but I don't know why?" Joe said as he sipped on his drink. Mike reached into his front suit pocket slowly and gave Mr. Kennedy the letter. Richie said softly, "You are asked to read this letter than allow us to destroy it after you're done. You understand, we can't leave any evidence of this matter, and this meeting never happened." "Of course, I understand," Joe said as he was opening the letter.

The letter;

My dear friend,

It has been many years since we have greeted each other in person and it seems it will be many more due to the company you are forced to tolerate these days. I have asked my nephew and my associate to personally deliver this letter to you so there can be no misunderstandings in the future concerning the matter we are faced with these days. You understand this is simply business for us, and we ask that you keep it our little secret. I thank you in advance for your sincere cooperation in this special request and hope it may not escalate to a more serious matter between your family and us.

Sam sends his regards and always speaks highly of you and reminisces about the old days of prohibition and how you helped keep the product on the shelves for our clubs. I also remember those days, when life was easier than present-day problems. We have all come a long way, and we are men of our word, as you know. It seems that our assistance in your desire to have your boys in politics is causing our families great hardship with investigations and harassment. We kept our promise to get Jack elected to the highest office possible, and this is how he repays us? We are, as expected, very upset and ask that you personally speak to Jack and Bobby concerning our contributions to this country. You understand we are of little patience, but we'll wait and see if anything comes from this meeting. But do not underestimate our tenacity concerning those who trespass against us. It is with the utmost respect that we ask you to straighten out this matter with your boys before someone gets seriously hurt. I leave you with a promise. If they leave the families and our organization alone, your son will see many more years serving the people of America. This comes from all the families, and I speak on their behalf.

Do us all a big favor and have a special talk with your boys. Enjoy your family. Life is short!

Sincerely your friend,
Vincenzo

Joe looked at Mike and Richie with genuine fear in his eyes and crumpled the letter in his hands. Mike asked for the letter and burned it in an empty glass ashtray on the table before him. Both Richie and Mike bid farewell and walked out of the room never to see Joe Kennedy again.

Getting in the car, Richie said, "I wish all my jobs were that easy for your uncle." Mike said nothing and was glad that mission was over. "Where we goin' now?" Mike asked. "Miami Beach," Richie said as he turned up the radio. "Were going to Miami, land of more beautiful women and fancy clubs." "Sounds good to me, Richie" Mike replied with a sigh of relief in his voice. "What do you think was in that letter that scared the shit out of the old man?" "Don't know and don't care to know. We did what we were told, and our job is done. The rest will come, and I'm sure we will be part of whatever it is," Richie said as he focused on the road ahead of him. "So when do we have to call uncle Vincenzo to give him the message that the letter was delivered?" Mike asked. "We don't have to. One of the agents in the room works for us, and I am sure your uncle will know in a few hours, but you can call if you want," Richie said with a smile. "You tellin' me that a special agent in that room works for us?" Mike asked with a surprised look on his face. "Yeah, Mike, he's on the payroll. And we have others too, but they were not there. I knew who he was as soon as I saw him. In fact, he was at your uncle's Fourth of July party. You got a lot to learn, Mike. Stick with me and I'll teach you the ins and outs of this racket." Mike sat deep in his seat and was shocked at what he didn't know about this business he was involved in. It was 7 pm by the time they reached Miami and checked into the hotel under the alias name of John Carmella. Everything was pre-arranged for them, the room at the hotel, the restaurant they were to eat at and a list of instructions on the nightstand by one of the beds in the room. All they had to do was follow the instructions they were given.

That night they were to go to room 741 at the Fountain Bleau Hotel for a sit-down with the bosses and discuss the outcome of the meeting with Joe Kennedy. Even though there was not much to say about the Kennedy thing, the bosses were happy to hear the letter was delivered and that his facial expressions confirmed that Joe knew the meaning of the letter and was visibly shaken up. Salvatori said he was happy that Jack would get the message, and perhaps this will stop Bobby in his tracks. The bosses decided to have a closed-door meeting among themselves and asked Mike and Richie to leave the room, have dinner, and while in Miami, enjoy the nightlife within the hotel walls as they may have a message for them to bring back to Vincenzo concerning this Kennedy problem.

Mike and Richie did as ordered and went back to their room to change. "You think they are going to do anything about the Kennedy boys?" Mike asked. Quickly, Richie replied, "I wouldn't want to be them right now. You know the game. You fuck up and create problems; you disappear. Besides, even the president has skeletons in his closet and Marilyn was just one of them." Mike didn't say much. He knew there was a possibility they could get whacked. Even the president had no shield of armor to hide under if bosses put a contract on him. Dinner and the club were on their agenda for the night, and Richie was looking forward to finding a little Spanish girl to play doctor with. Mike was hesitant to go but knew he couldn't say no.

Mike and Richie did find three girls who were impressed with them, and around 2am, they decided the bosses were not calling on them that early and enticed the girls to go with them to their room for a night of wild sex. As usual, the girls were shocked at the size of Mike's fingers. One of them implied they looked like fat hot dogs with a marble as a finger nail.

The next morning a loud knock on the door woke up one of the girls. She opened the door to a rather large man dressed in a pinstripe suit and let him in. The stranger slapped the girl on the ass and said, "Go tell those bums the family would like to see them for breakfast at 10 am sharp. She stumbled into the bedroom and jumped on Mike's back saying "Some big dick at the door said you bums gotta see your family for breakfast." Mike jumped up and grasped her as he said, "What did he look like? What did he say exactly?" She looking shocked, said "The guy said you and Richie have to see your family for eggs and shit at 10. That's all he said." Mike woke up Richie and said they had a visitor and to get dressed. Richie decided to get rid of his morning stiffy and planted it in one of the two girls he was sleeping with. They got dressed and went to meet the family leaving the girls in the room, only telling them they would see them at the club that night. They didn't realize the girls were about to rob them blind of anything they could get their hands on, including Mike's stolen Rolex that he left on the nightstand. Richie lost some of his shirts and cufflinks which didn't add up to much more than six hundred.

The message was clear at the families' breakfast meeting. Sam Giancolla, Salvatori, and Carl Gambono, along with others of high-ranking, were present when they gave a decree and a large envelope to Richie. Sam said, "You give this letter to Vincenzo and this envelope to Mr. Marcell, who should be at the Ocala horse farm when you get there in three days, Tu capisce." Richie nodded his head and acknowledged the orders. "You have a flight from Miami airport to Orlando at 10 am. tomorrow. Be there," one of the bosses said out loud. Richie and Mike left to go back to the room. It was now 11:30.

When they got to the room, they found their stuff thrown all over the place. Mike laughed, saying, "Well, they were worth the shit they got, even if it was my good watch. I only hope we see them again, so I can get another three-hundred worth of pussy for my watch." Richie smiled "They both owe me a blowjob for the shirts. Those were silk, Armani. Fuck, the cufflinks were my favorite pair." They both had a chuckle and decided to investigate the city of Miami and what it had to offer.

During the day, touring the city, both Mike and Richie made the necessary phone calls to keep in touch. That's when Richie heard about Frankie being caught for stealing a car and was in jail. He decided to tell Mike in Ocala. He didn't want to interfere with the fun he was having with Mike during this trip.

They did go to the club that night, but never saw the girls they were looking for. On the third morning, they went to the airport to go to Ocala. Chit chat on the plane ride was limited to who they knew and what fights were within the family structures. Dapper's name did come up as a guy to watch. "He is moving up too fast," said Richie as Mike nodded his head in agreement. Once in Orlando, they rented a high-end car and drove to Ocala Farms, which was owned by an old time captain by the name of Lefty Rothstine. No one knew his real first name. They always called him Lefty, and he was the king of thoroughbred horse training and studding. In fact, he was the same guy who was involved with Vincenzo in the insurance racket, as well as the fixing of the races in the old days. He was completely off the radar because he retired to Florida many years before and opened a legit horse-farm business as his retirement gift. He was still involved because you never actually retire; you just go into servitude for the rest of your life when called upon.

Lefty greeted both of them and offered to put them up at his home for the length of time they were in Ocala. "Perhaps you guys should stay here for the time being. It would be better off if no one knew you were in Florida. We don't want to leave any crumbs behind if you know what I mean," Lefty said as he showed them their respective bedrooms. "Oh, are we prisoners here?" Richie asked with a smile. "Prison should be so good. You fellas hungry? I'll have my girl cook you up something quick to eat," Lefty said. Mike was starving and responded, "Sure. By the way, I am Michael Delagatta. Pleased to meet you." Lefty snarled, "I know who you are. Your uncle gave me the scoop. You're in luck; I have two perfect ponies for you. We can see them later when one of my trainers is here to run them on the track for you." "Thanks" Mike replied.

After a late lunch and a show of the horses in action, Mike and Richie concluded they both liked two horses. One was named Sargent of Arms and the other was King of Hearts. They were ready to race and were insurable for three hundred thousand dollars each, according to Lefty's experience. "I can hook you up with a broker for the insurance," Lefty said as they walked back to the house. "Now let's talk money," Lefty said sitting on the leather couch. "How much?" Mike asked. "Seeing how your uncle is involved, I can give them to you for sixty K, each and that's a steal. I raised these ponies from colts, and they owe me some feed money for the last three years. It is nonnegotiable on the price, so don't insult me by making offers." Mike agreed, with the understanding that his uncle had to OK the deal, and it was left at that. They met with Mr. Marcell on the farm that evening and handed him the letter as instructed by the bosses. All Mr. Marcell said was, "Thanks, boys, I'll take care of this issue with my associates in New Orleans when I get back home. You never saw me and I was never here, right?" Mike nodded his head replying, "I have no idea who you are, and I am blind. That goes for my buddy, too," while looking at Richie. The next day they were instructed to drive back to New York with a rental car instead of flying. "No paper trail is what your Uncle said," Lefty told Mike. Lefty also gave Mike a suitcase filled with diamonds and jewelry to bring specifically to Vincenzo. Tell him "This is from the Boston heist years ago. Send my share when he fences them in the bowery to his Jewish friends." Mike obliged and accepted the case for delivery to his uncle. They took their time driving home and swapping stories. "There has to be three hundred grand in this fuckin' case, and I don't want to get busted for some freakin' job I didn't have anything to do with," Richie said as he opened the case during a piss break halfway to New York. It was two days before they reached Long Island, and Mike went directly to Vincenzo's. They wanted to get rid of the case containing the goods Lefty gave them. Unannounced, they went to Vincenzo's house. They were not expected. Vincenzo's maid opened the door and escorted them to the kitchen where Vincenzo greeted them. "Welcome back, boys. I'm in a rush and leaving in ten minutes. We will have lunch tomorrow at two and catch up on your trip." Mike gave him the case and told him what Lefty said. Vincenzo gave it to the maid telling her to lock it in the basement desk. She took the case and disappeared. Mike and Richie walked out the front door. Mike dropped off Richie and went home. The trip was over and the day was at an end. Mike was tired from the trip and went to bed early, even though his wife was nagging him to learn about his journey to Florida.

CHAPTER 6

PEOPLE SOMETIMES DISAPPEAR

It was the end of July 1961, and it was steaming hot in New York that year. Mike had returned the rental that morning and was preparing for his meeting with Vincenzo. Richie had told him about Frankie getting popped by the local PD, and it was an issue he had to take care of. He also had that chop-shop thing that he left open before he went to Florida. He had hopes that it was still a mystery as to who had done it and in time it would disappear.

On the way to his uncle, he stopped off at his business office to see what was going on with his mechanic, Bo. Short of getting his gun and some cash, all was fine at the shop. No fuzz were looking around the joint for stolen cars. Bo made an offer to Mike for the purchase of the business with a cash deal where Mike keeps a percentage of the income. Bo was anxious to buy in, but Mike had to carry a loan with vig to allow Bo to purchase the shop and retain a piece of the action. It was just what Mike wanted. For Mike, it was time to move on to bigger and better things.

Mike picked up Eddie on his way to uncles, and they chatted on the short ride. "So, what are we gonna do about Frankie?" Money asked. "What do you think?" Mike said. "He does open his mouth before he thinks, and that could be a problem for us. I say we grill him to death and see how he reacts. We will know if he is lying. He could never keep a straight face even when he was a kid playing with us" Eddie replied. "OK, Mike said wondering in the back of his mind if Frankie was next on the list to disappear for having a big mouth or squealing to the cops. "Yeah, we will know and decide what to do if he's lying," Mike said out loud and turned the radio up higher to change the subject. They arrived an hour early and entered the house. They greeted Vincenzo and the others in the room, including Richie and Tony G, whom Mike had not seen for several months prior to his meeting at his uncle's house. "This is a big surprise, Tony, didn't expect to see you here today," Mike said. "Long time, Mike," he said as he hugged him and kissed his cheek. "At least, you didn't kiss both cheeks, and then I'd have to run" Mike expressed with a laugh.

After mingling for a while with others he knew, Vincenzo came into the room and asked Mike and several others, including Richie, to meet with him in the game room located in the basement. Everyone jockeyed for their seat as they sat around the table. Including Mike, Richie, and Vincenzo, there were four others at the meeting. Vincenzo started by saying, "First, I want to thank you all for coming. As you know, a letter was delivered to Joe Kennedy and he now knows where we sit on this Bobby thing. It's a shame that Jack is involved, however, if you can't take care of those who work for you then you are to blame. It's a shame 'cause I personally like the president, but business is business, right? Now speaking of business and expanding, I've asked Tony G to join Mike, myself and Money in this new interest of ours because he has connections in the race-track unions and can assist us. He will put up his share of the money to be a partner. My attorney has drawn up papers for this little venture of ours, and we are calling it Brooklyn Investment Group. All in favor?" The table responded with an astounding yes, and the deal was done. "OK, if that is all with the horse thing, let's move on to other matters. It seems that little Frankie Ragu has gotten caught stealing cars, and this is a problem for us. Any suggestions here or do I have to make all the decisions?"

Eddie spoke up and said he and Mike had a discussion on the ride over, and they would handle it. Everyone was in agreement because they didn't want any blood on their hands concerning whacking Ragu and getting involved. "This is a family matter," Richie said, "and I'm sorry I didn't tell you sooner, Mike. We were having such a good time; I didn't want to spoil it." Mike acknowledged and said, "Next time tell me and let me decide how I feel Richie. I don't like being left out of the loop." Richie agreed and with that; they all were told to enjoy the house and food. Vincenzo closed the conversation by saying "Mike, you stay here with Eddie and Richie. We have stuff to talk about in private." They remained sitting and waited for the others to leave the room.

Vincenzo informed them that a good friend of his had passed away two days ago whom he grew up with and worked with in the old days. "You may not know, but my childhood friend and partner in crime. Jimmy Profosso, passed away, and I have to set his house in order for the family at the Commission's request. I will be out of town for a few weeks and want you, boys, to handle the cash transaction with Lefty in Ocala. I also want you to look into meeting with Hoffa and his contributions to the Vegas deal. It seems that the Feds or somebody is breaking his balls about this money they are investing.

Richie, you go to Vegas and take Mike with you. Handle it and get back to me. I want them boys in Vegas to know he is part of my family. And make sure he doesn't get into trouble over there. The last time you went, I had to stick my neck out for your shit you stirred up with those celebrity kids. You know what I'm talkin' about" he said as he pointed his finger at Richie with a smirk on his face. "Yeah I know boss. I couldn't help it. I got caught up in the moment, and all that" Richie said and smiled. Mike was confused with the entire conversation and was dying to know what Richie did in Vegas. He would have his chance to ask in time, but for now, it was their secret. "Mike, I know a lot of the people you saw at the Florida meeting you didn't know. Richie can fill you in on the names and shit. You did make an impression on Myer Lansky the Jew boy. He may ask me for a favor one day and wants you to handle it for him. I don't know if that means he likes you or he wants to see what you can do. Either way, he controls Cuba, what's left of it, and along with Salvatori, all of the southeast region of our operations. So if he wants you, I may have to give him my blessing. Don't worry, Richie or someone will go with you." With that Vincenzo got up and told Eddie to handle the collection of B.I.G. investment money to wire to Lefty's account in the Caymans and have the horses insured for their race when the track opens for business in the spring. "I like the names of the ponies you picked, but if they don't make us money in two years, break their legs, Tu, capisce?" With that, they all got up and went upstairs to enjoy

Vincenzo's house girls Mike called Richie to the side and asked him about the Vegas thing. "In time, Mike. In time you'll know" Richie replied. Mike asked Eddie if Frankie made bail or if he was being held. "The longer he stays there, the more likely he may say something," Mike said. "Yeah, you're right. Call Onions from the club and ask him to make sure Ragu gets bailed out, and tell him to instruct Frankie to stay home till we go see him this weekend." Mike agreed and went to the living room to call the club and talk to Onions concerning this matter. Onions answered with two words "No problem" and then hung up. Mike told Eddie it was being taken care of, and he would pick Ragu up to chat with him on Eddie's boat, Liquid Assets. "In case he needs to disappear, he is already on the boat," Mike said sadly. "I really hope this fuck didn't open his mouth. I'd hate to lose a family member and have his wife Annie asking all kinds of questions afterward," Mike mumbled close to Eddie's ear. "Yeah, that would suck" Eddie replied. That evening Mike went home to spend time with his wife and kids.

The next morning Mike drove to Frankie's house. Talking on the phone would connect him to Frankie, and Mike liked staying under the radar, so the Feds and the local cops had no idea who he was and his involvement with family matters. "Ragu, what the fuck happened?" Mike asked as Frankie opened the door. "I got popped, that's all, Mike." "Did you say anything to the cops?" Mike asked. "Did you say anything at all to the cops, Frankie? I gotta know if I need to move these fuckin' cars out," Mike said sternly. "They don't know nothing, Mike. I swear on my kids eyes. I told them nothing about the cars. The only thing they know is I got caught bustin' into a car. I told them it was a joy ride," Frankie said as he lit a cigarette. "So you're tellin' me they know nothing about the cars, and they got no info on anything, right?" Mike asked. "Yeah, they don't know anything. You think I'm a fuckin' idiot and that I'd say something that could get me killed?" Frankie said to Mike. "For your sake, I hope not," Mike replied. Eddie wants to have a talk with you so be at the Apollo Diner tomorrow morning at ten. I'm just passing on the message." Mike said. "Why does he want to see me? I told you everything that happened. You gonna be there too?" Frankie asked. "Not sure if I can make it," Mike replied. With that, Mike left Frankie as he said, "Don't leave the house till you see Money, and he decides what to do." "Great, now I have to get fuckin' approval to go out of my house. This is bullshit, and you know it, Mike," Ragu screamed as Mike was walking down the stairs to the front door. "You're a big boy. You do what you want, but remember there are consequences to what you do," Mike said and closed the door to return to his car.

Mike decided to go to the club to hear the rumors and ask around about what the neighborhood was talking about. As he opened the door, he saw it was crowded more than normal that morning. There was some meeting going on in the back room having to do with who was going to take over as boss of the Joe Profosso crew. It was rumored that his brother-in-law Joey Magi was to be the interim boss. His crew was not happy with this arrangement and wanted a coup to replace him.

Mike knew his uncle was making arrangements for transition but did not know who it would be. After seeing Onions and repaying him the bail money to spring Frankie, he gave him five hundred more saying, "Thanks, Onions, I owe you one." Onions reply was, "Yeah, you owe me one." "Did you hear anything about that garage thing? Did that kid come see you?" Mike asked. Onions replied, "No, not a thing. The kid never came to see me" "Take a ride over there and see if they're closed or if you see the kid" Onions told Mike. "Yeah, I'll do that sometime today," Mike said as he walked out of the back room. He went over to Dapper and asked if he heard anything about Frankie Ragu and what the word was on the street. Dapper said he knew about Ragu getting popped, and it was a problem for him and his crew. They had to lay low for a while. "You know that he has a big mouth, and he is a fuckin' problem," Dapper said to Mike. "Do you think he said anything?" Mike asked Dapper. "I think if the cops come sniffing around, he has to go bye bye. That's what I think. He's your cousin, so you have to take care of it. But if you don't, I will," Dapper said walking away from Mike. "If anything happens, you want his crew?" Mike asked as he walked closer to Dapper. "I'll have to hand pick the ones I want, and the others have to disappear, 'cause they know too much," Dapper said as he moved further away from Mike in an effort to separate himself from Mike's presence.

Mike took the hint and went on his way to mingle with some of the other fellas in the club. In the time he was there, he learned very little and decided to leave. He drove by the garage where he had whacked the owner. It was all closed up and for sale. He had hopes that nothing would come of it and drove around the neighborhood looking for the guy he had threatened during the incident but did not find him either. He spent the rest of the day going to his old shop to see Bo, and then drove to Money's house to talk but he wasn't around. Kat said he went for a ride on his boat to think about things. Mike wanted to know what was on Money's mind but would have to wait until the meeting at the Apollo Diner the next morning.

Everyone met at the diner on time, and Frankie was given the third degree on what he said to the cops and if anyone else knew what was going on. Frankie screwed up when he said that the cops knew he was stealing cars and was having them shipped out of state. "Someone has a big mouth; Money said as he looked at Mike. The question is, who?" Frankie swore it was not him, and he didn't say anything to the cops. "Do they know where the cars are stored?" Mike asked Ragu. "I don't fuckin' know. Am I a mind reader?" Ragu shouted angrily. "Perhaps you need to lay low for a bit while we figure out what to do about this problem," Mike said looking at Money and Ragu. "So what am I supposed to do, stay home and not make any money? I gotta eat too, you know," Ragu said looking around the room. "Ragu, we got a problem, and you're involved with it. We need some time to decide where we go with this freakin' mess," Money said in reply. The meeting ended abruptly as they all got up and said their goodbyes. "Eddie, I'll get with you later," Mike said as they all walked out the door.

Several days passed and it was decided that Frankie Ragu was too much of a problem. He had a court hearing in a month, and the family could not afford him flipping to save jail time. Approval was given by the bosses to whack Frankie in public as a warning to the others in his crew to keep their mouths shut. Frankie was invited to a late dinner meeting at Taccino's Italian Restaurant in Westbury, Long Island, which was owned by a fellow mob member. The meeting was set up in a back room away from the main dining room. Several members showed up for the meeting. Frankie without prior notice entered the room with his girlfriend. Apparently, Frankie was using her as protection as well as a witness if anything happened to him. Eddie and Mike exchanged glances of anger as well as an acknowledgment that the deal was set, and they had no way of stopping it. They had hired outsiders to do the job. Nothing was going to stop the whacking of Ragu, even if his girlfriend had to go down with him. It was planned. On schedule, about one hour into the dinner, two men walked into the room and shot Frankie twice in the head. His girlfriend, now screaming and in shock of what she witnessed, was taken with the shooters where she would later disappear. The family had outside business with Middle Eastern interests. She would be drugged and sold to them, where she would become a prostitute in another country. The action was mostly for runaway girls, but this time, she got caught in the middle of something she should not have been involved with. The family didn't like killing women, but they did have other ways of dealing with problems like this. Although she lived, her life would never be the same again. She became part of the cargo of cars being shipped out on freighters leaving the country from the mob-controlled Brooklyn seaport.

Several days went by and as, Mike predicted, Annie, asked him to stop by the house. She wanted to ask him something about Frankie. Mike stopped at the house a few days later, and she started asking questions. "It's not like Frankie to stay away from home so long, and he always calls me. I haven't heard from him in days, and I am worried about him." Mike absolved himself of any knowledge or involvement. "You know Frankie, Annie, he disappears for days, and no one knows where he goes. I'm sure he will show up sooner or later. Give it some time then kick his ass when he gets home." When Annie asked if Mike knew where Frankie might be, Mike only replied "Haven't heard from him since last week. When he gets home, I might kick his ass myself. Just give it some time, Annie. He always comes back." Annie now crying asked if he could put the word on the street that he needs to call her and come home. Mike agreed to put the word on the street, knowing that Frankie, Ragu would never be home again. Mike stayed away from Annie as much as he could and always gave the same answers when she asked. A few days later, Ragu's body was found floating in a pond outside of Brookville, Long Island and the hit went public in the local papers. This was enough for his crew to break up into little pieces and be absorbed into the other family operations around town. Just as planned, they said nothing and went their separate ways, but still involved in the life of crime. Dapper took some of them into his crew and increased earnings for the family he worked for. Everyone was happy, and Frankie was a memory at that point.

The summer of 1961 was a turbulent time within the five family structures. Underdogs were pushing to get to the top any way they could, killing rivals, cutting ties and re-organizing with other families. Many disappeared under coffin boxes, buried somewhere in the back of member-owned bars and clubs while others were chopped up and used as fishing bait in the Atlantic. Dozens vanished without a trace never to be seen or spoken of again. Loose tongues were a death sentence, and everyone knew that. Some laid low while others accomplished exactly what they wanted.

The Gambono family was virtually untouched, and many of the old bosses stayed the same with only some minor changes to the underdogs. Mike was promoted to underdog for the Vincenzo group, even though Vincenzo's group was not subordinate to any one family. Vincenzo was a chief counsel of the committee for all the bosses, and he had a piece of everything as compensation for his involvement. The closest allegiance Vincenzo's group had was to Carl Gambono because Carl was from the old men of honor. Vincenzo was a childhood friend of his. He was, however, not working for or a part of Carlo's control. Vincenzo and his small group of enforcers and businessmen were independent of the five families, and he wanted it that way. Not being in the limelight of the FBI and the other government organizations was perhaps the best thing Vincenzo accomplished, and it was for a reason. He was, as the silent partner of all the families, and his ties to politicians, judges, union businesses, celebrities and legit corporations would have exploded like an atomic bomb crushing not only the Mafia but the entire government structure if his association with the families were known.

Mike's promotion was merely a means of taking Vincenzo's position in the event anything should happen to him. It was a sign of respect in passing the control to a family member, and Vincenzo's crew was aware of tradition, especially from a man who was part of the original bad boys during the Italian immigration to America. Mike saw it as an undeserved position, but said nothing and accepted it as such. Mike didn't know all of Vincenzo's connections, but in time, he would learn how powerful his uncle really was. If anything happened to his uncle, he was expected to continue the operation through the connections already established over forty years by his uncle, Vincenzo.

The summer was winding down, and things were starting to calm with the 1962 gang wars within the New York area. Mike had decided to start racing his horses after several months of hard training on the farm and securing insurance from two different companies; one from his brother Louie and the other from Lefty's connection (Ocala Farms) totaling close to half a million dollars for each horse. If the horses lost money over time, they could collect the insurance money and still make an enormous profit.

Mike's uncle received a call from one of his CIA contacts and requested a meeting with some of the family bosses. Vincenzo obliged him and set up the meeting in a secluded place on the Jersey shore. Vincenzo informed Mike that he and several other members of his crew were to be at the meeting with Vincenzo. He knew the agent but wanted protection due to the recent summer battles within the families. The meeting was set for September ninth. Vincenzo had heard rumors that John Kennedy was upset with the agency and was planning to break it apart. He also heard from an inside informant that Kennedy was looking into the alleged interaction between the mob and the FBI, as well as the CIA. Both John and Bobby were against them since the botched murder plot jobs on Castro in 1961.

The meeting took place in one of Vincenzo's safe houses off the Jersey shore. All were present that September 9, including several CIA and FBI agents. The proposal brought forward by a high-ranking official of the CIA was known as project North-Woods. It involved the bombing of south Florida cities and blaming it on the Cuban government in an effort to gain public support for retaliation for killing innocent civilians. The family involvement was to get an insider to kill Castro by slipping a pill into his drink. This would be done by his ex-girlfriend, who was part of the Cuban underground still working for the involved families trying to regain a foothold in Cuba after they were pushed out of the casino business. Several members had massive investments in Cuba at the time, and Salvatori, and Myer, were in control of the operations before Castro's overthrow of the government.

The families were more than eager to get involved; however, the killing of civilians was out of the question. Mike was never introduced to the agents, but they did see what he looked like, and Mike saw them too. Vincenzo said, "I will bring this to the council and get their vote on it. However, we are not in the business of killing those who are not involved with our interests, gentlemen. Perhaps you should find another way to solve this matter. We will assist with a pill from our associates in Cuba, but that may be our only involvement in this issue. If there is anything else you wish our services for at this time, please speak now." "Jack is planning to break up our department, and that is a problem for us. It seems he is unhappy with our covert operations and thinks we have become too powerful. We don't want to see that happen," one of the high ranking agents said openly. "This is your problem, not ours, but sometimes you do what you must. Jack and his brother are a thorn in our side, and we all know it. You take care of your problems, and we will take care of ours," Vincenzo replied as he stood up from the chair. "We will get back to you on this matter of yours. However, I fear we will not get involved," Vincenzo said as he ushered the men out to the driveway. The meeting ended and Vincenzo called Mike into another room. He told him who the people were by name and association. Mike was impressed that his uncle was even associated with high-level government officials within the CIA and FBI. "Do you think they are planning something on the president and his brother?" Mike asked his uncle. "They can be ruthless when it comes to power. If they have him in their sites, only God knows for sure," Vincenzo replied.

CHAPTER 7

BUSINESS AS USUAL

September was ending, and October was around the corner. Money had one month before he would land his boat, Liquid Assets and cover it for the winter season. Things were quiet in the neighborhood and a new season was coming in. Time to race the horses Mike and his associates had invested in. Mike called a meeting at his house for those involved with Brooklyn Investment Group. It was time to set things in motion. Vincenzo did not show up. He was still involved with that Kennedy and Castro thing in Miami with some of the bosses. He did convey to Mike that whatever he wanted to do about the horse thing was OK with him. Mike informed the investors that he wanted to rig the first race for one of the horses to win. "King of Hearts is ready to run," he told the others at the meeting. "We have to make sure he wins," Mike said with a smile. "This contact at the club, you sure he can pull it off," Richie asked. "If he fails, we break his fuckin' legs," Money said jokingly. "OK, Mike, you talk to him and set it up. But don't let it look like this freakin' horse is strolling to the finish line, or we will have problems right off the bat," Richie replied. "OK, I'll talk to him this weekend and let you know when the race is on," Mike said. "This fuckin' meeting is over. I need to go fishing for some new pussy; Richie said as he retreated from the lawn chair outside where the meeting took place. "For a little guy, you sure have a big appetite for pussy," Eddie said as he laughed. "When you got it, you got it," Richie answered as they all started walking to the driveway. "Mike, you take care of this horse thing and let us know, but don't tell the fuckin' world 'cause the odds go down when everyone is betting on him," Money said as he entered his car.

During the month of October, Mike was concerned because Cuba and Russia were in the process of moving missiles into Cuba threating the USA, and Jack Kennedy was not standing for it. It was known as the Cuban Missile Crisis. Although it had nothing to do with the mafia, Mike was concerned that it might have something to do with the CIA and the Northwoods project they spoke about the month before. His uncle Vincenzo assured him that the families were not involved. As for the CIA, he was not sure. Kennedy stuck to his guns and forced the Russians to pull the missiles out of Cuba. The CIA wanted Castro dead and would do anything to see it happen. The mob played along but forced the CIA to do all the work, and nothing ever came of it, so they gave up.

Winter came and went, and Mike's horses were coming in the money most of the time in the races that were fixed. The summer had been fruitful with new cargo coming into the New York Airport and cigarettes were at a premium at five dollars a carton. Everybody had their hands in the cookie jar, from suits to shoes, cigarettes, and watches. They were all making a boatload of cash. Mike was stashing money in his backyard under the gazebo because the money coming from different investments was coming faster than he could get to his brother Sal to transfer it to offshore accounts. Mike even had to buy more trucks from his brother Harry just to transport the truck heist merchandise to other family members. With the help of Bo at the shop changing the ID tags to match, he had some twelve trucks running goods all over town. The docks were also producing money with goods from other countries coming in and disappearing with the help of his brother Jimmy. Yes, this summer would be a record breaker for Mike and his uncle's crew. Everybody was happy and fat with cash. Vincenzo's crew laid low to avoid federal investigations involving them.

Mike received a call from Richie telling him that Vincenzo wanted him to go with Richie to Vegas for a job that needed their attention. They were leaving soon and would be there for several days until the job was done. Mike asked, "What is this job we have to do?" Richie answered, "Not on the phone, Mike. Meet me at the club this weekend and we'll talk there." Mike agreed and hung up the phone. That weekend they met, and Richie told him they had to pick up some cash owed to the old man and straighten out some problem they had with a made man from Chicago who worked for Sam's interest in his investment. They also had to see Jimmy Copper for a package that was to be delivered to Vincenzo and no one else. Mike couldn't say no and had to agree to go. That weekend they left from the New York airport to Vegas. Mike had never been to Vegas and Richie informed him that Miami was kids' play compared to Vegas. "Fair warning, Mike, you will never forget Vegas. Anything goes in Vegas." On the flight to Vegas, Mike wanted to know what they were doing in Vegas for the Chicago boss and why them. Richie replied, "Vincenzo and Sam go back a long way. They sometimes do each other favors, and in return, they get a marker. A marker is a promise to do something for the other no matter what it is, and that is paying off the marker. We have to see a guy by the name of Tony Spotini and help him find out who whacked two of Sam's men and take care of it with Tony. We also have to see a guy named Johnny Rosselio and tell him to be at a meeting in Miami concerning this Kennedy thing. Johnny is supposed to introduce us to some Hollywood money guys for a film that your uncle is backing. I know that Carl Gambono's godson is in the movie. Vincenzo wants you to meet some of his Hollywood connections 'cause he wants you to know who his ties are in the event something happens to him; you will keep the contacts alive. Yeah, we might have to whack some punks for taking out Sam's boys, but other than that, we're free to enjoy the strip however we want. We even got a suite at the Sands Casino while we're in Vegas." Mike rolled his eyes and said, "It is what it is, and we do what we gotta do, that's my new motto." Richie laughed and said, "Yeah, this is the life we chose and somebody's got to do it, so why not us. So long as you stay out of jail, it's not such a bad life. I've been workin' for the old man for almost ten years now, and the one thing he taught me was, never leave crumbs behind you 'cause they lead to a place you have been. That means, no business over the phones, no loose ends that can come back to bite you in the ass, and most of all, never get well-known to your enemies or the Feds. Perhaps that's why he has never been caught and the bosses like his loyalty." Mike only agreed saying, "He's a smart man and I don't know if I can fill those shoes as good as him" "Well, he ain't got no intentions of dying anytime soon, so you got some time to learn," Richie replied.

They landed in Vegas, and a car was there to pick them up. A little man jumped out of the passenger seat to greet them saying, "It's about fuckin' time. I had to drive out here with this asshole to make sure he knew where the fuckin' airport was. How you doin'? I'm Tony Spitini, but you can call me Knuckles. Sam told me you guys were coming to help me track down these two fuckin' shmucks who whacked some made men that worked for Sam. Come on, I'll show you Vegas."

The ride to the Sands was interesting, to say the least. Knuckles told them his whole life story and how he was such a big shot in Vegas, watching over Sam's money. Richie, being the person that he was, stopped Knuckles in mid-sentence and said, "You know, you talk too much. You told us your whole life story, and personally, we don't give a fuck. We were sent here to help your sorry ass, and we're not here to make friends. We just want to get some rest and tomorrow you can tell us who these two pricks are and where we can find them, tu capisce." Mike laughed and Knuckles replied, "OK, they sent me two jimbones to rough up some punk hoods. I get it." Mike sat up straight and shouted, "We ain't jimbones. We're not here to rough up anybody. We got orders to make them mummies in the fuckin' desert, you little shit, something we have to do for you and your boss. Now show us some respect before I crush your head like a walnut with my bare hands. We're tired and hungry. Can you, at least, take care of that, little man." "Yeah, I can get you something to eat. How about a fish sandwich?" Knuckles replied with anger in his voice.

Mike tried reaching for Knuckle's neck in the front passenger's seat when Richie stopped him saying, "Wow, stop this shit. Mike's a little uptight, and he's never been to Vegas. You show him a good time and maybe he might like you. Can you do that for us?" Knuckles, although afraid to sit back in his seat, agreed and said "Yeah, I can make that happen. Just keep that fuckin' crazy bastard away from me and I'll see you guys get whatever you fuckin' want." "Give him a fat juicy steak and he'll be happy," Richie said laughing while watching Mike calm down in the back seat. The ride was nearly over, and Mike was ready to eat and relax for the rest of the day. He had enough and was not happy with his first meeting with Sam's boy in charge. "OK, boys, this is the Sands Casino. See the front desk clerk and ask for your room under the name John Brooklyn. He'll know the rest. I'll get you a table at the restaurant and order you a fat steak. Your tab is on the house during your stay. You're on your own for the rest of the day. I'll call on you in the morning so we can get this thing finished and you fellas can leave my happy little paradise. That sound good?" Richie acknowledged him with a nod and Knuckles moved in a different direction. "That little prick has a way of pissing off people, doesn't he?" Mike said to Richie as they walked to the elevator door leading up to their suite. "Yeah, he sure does. I thought you were gonna kill him in that fuckin' car when you went after him like a wild man" Richie replied, "He fuckin' needs a good beating to put him in his place, that little shithead." Mike said as the elevator doors closed. The doors of the elevator opened leading into a large private suite, and both Mike and Richie were quite impressed. "Now this is what I like, built for a king," Richie said as they walked in awe around the rooms. "OK, maybe I can forgive the little dick. After all, he did give us a nice place to stay for free," Mike answered. "Let's put our stuff away and go eat. I want to check this casino out and arrange for us to have some company for this evening, how's that sound to you, Mike?" "That sounds fine. How can I say no," Mike responded with a grin on his face.

After unpacking, Mike sat down to watch TV and Richie went to the lobby to check things out. Richie found Knuckles and asked him to set up dinner and maybe some cute girls to accompany them that night to dinner and a show. Knuckles obliged, and they separated. After some gambling at the tables, Richie went back into the room, and Mike was sleeping on the couch. Richie decided to play a joke, so he shouted loudly, "hands up, you big fuck." Mike opened one eye and punched him right in the balls. "When I'm ready, you skinny bastard." Richie didn't think it was funny, but Mike did. He heard Richie coming in and pretended he was sleeping. "I hope my dick works. After a shot like that, my balls may be swollen. "If it was a stranger, my fist would have come out of his asshole. So that was a love tap. Did you locate that little shithead and arrange for dinner and a show for tonight?" Mike asked Richie. "Yeah, it's all set. Dinner and some babes. All compliments of Knuckles. Tomorrow we have to look into this situation and find out what actually happened. I don't trust this Knuckles guy" Richie said to Mike as they were getting dressed.

The night started with a perfect dinner and two lovely ladies accompanying Richie and Mike. The show was even better than expected. Frankie Vali and the Four Seasons were singing, and some of the doo-wop bands completed the show. Knuckles sat Richie, Mike, and their company in the best front-row table in the house. That evening the girls stayed with the boys all night and the next morning they went for breakfast. During the conversations, Mike asked one of the girls how they knew Knuckles. One of the girls replied that she sometimes fences jewelry for him, and he gives her a commission and house privileges at the Vegas clubs that he runs. "Does he do the break-ins himself or does he have somebody else do it for him?" Mike asked. "No, he doesn't do it. He's got some local guys he deals with, and they do the robberies. "I think his name is Frank. He's the leader of the group." "This Frank got a last name," Mike asked. "I don't know his last name, but they do call him Casper. 'cause his hair is really white. Not blond like mine, but white like old," she replied. "I said too much already. It ain't my business to talk about other people's business with strangers, and you boys are strangers." "Were we strangers when you girls were screaming last night? And now we're strangers. Ok, tonight we'll get some new strangers for dinner, and a show and you girls can go back where you came from," Richie said angrily. "No, that's not what I meant. If Tony knew I was talking business with you guys, he might get mad or something" The other girl replied. "Oh, you two both do the fencing for Tony?" Mike asked curiously. Blondie stepped in saying, "What she means is, we don't want to talk business now. So if you boys want us to see you tonight, let us know now, 'cause she has to get ready for work at the club, and I need to rehearse my dance for the show in the club tonight." "You girls work here for the Casino?" Mike asked. "Yes, we do. That's how we met Tony." "Okay, I think we can meet again. We like your company. But there are gonna be more questions asked once you ladies get to know us a little better," Richie said as he smiled getting out of his chair. "We'll see you girls tonight, same place in the lobby as last night. Don't tell Tony about any of this conversation, okay? It's our little secret." "I may be blond, but I ain't stupid," Blondie replied as her redheaded girlfriend stood up from her chair. "My name is Donna," said the redhead, "and she is Helen." "I'm Mike, and this is Richie. Donna and Helen, would you join us for dinner tonight and perhaps a show afterward?" Donna replied, "I can, but Helen's in the show this evening. But don't worry, we like to share. I don't think she minds if I have the two of you to myself for a while, and she can join us after the show. Right, Helen?" Helen laughed saying, "Don't hurt them too much. I need my fun too." "Fine with us," Richie said as they walked out of the restaurant. Going out to the rental car Richie said, "Where we going with this questioning, Mike? You think they know something?" Mike stopped in his tracks, turned to Richie and said, "How do we know what this little prick is telling us is true. For all, we know he could have done it and is blaming it on somebody else. We were sent here with very little info. All we know is what he told them, that some guys he knows killed Sam's boy. And it is up to us, with his help, to find and finish them for killin' a made man. That's all we have to go on. Now we know that this little prick Knuckles is fencing stuff with these girls as his movers, but we don't know if he's involved or shoving us in the wrong direction on purpose. For some strange reason, I don't trust the little prick and my gut tells me something ain't right." Richie looked puzzled and said, "Maybe you're right, but I don't want to stay any longer than we have to. I got things to do at home and this ain't one of them. I promise less than a week here, and if it's more, we whack them all and say we couldn't help it, they were snitches." Richie smiled saying, "Let's just whack them now and get it over with." Mike replied, "Let's talk to Donna when we got her by herself and see what more we can find out." "Fine," Richie said.

They had a meeting that afternoon with Knuckles and asked him where they could find the guys who were responsible for killing Sam's representative? Knuckles told them that he wanted to be there when they spoke to the guy. They agreed and told Knuckles to set up a meeting for Saturday morning, which was the following day. That gave Mike and Richie enough time to question the girls and pull out what they knew about the killing and Knuckles' involvement if any.

The dinner went great, and Helen left early to dress for the show leaving Donna with the boys. "I'll see you boys later tonight. Donna take good care of these studs and don't wear them out." They all parted, and the boys went on to playing cards at the tables before meeting up. Walking into the club that evening they were amazed at how gorgeous Donna looked with her hair pulled up and in a tight sleeveless dress. Everything about her was perfect, and all eyes were on her as she walked over giving both Richie and Mike a kiss on the lips while the usher moved the chair for her as she sat down. "Doll, you look good enough to eat right on this table," Richie said "Later you can eat me, honey, but you'll have to liquor me up first. Get me too drunk and I might not remember anything afterward." After a few drinks, Donna was relaxed.

Mike started the conversation with "So you know this Casper guy who works for Tony." After complaining for a while about the subject, Donna obliged them with some information. They now knew that Knuckles told Donna and Helen that he thought he was being watched and had to take care of the problem. She also told them that Knuckles said the guy was a big shot, and he had to be careful. After a couple more drinks she also told them that Knuckles and Casper had borrowed her car, and when she got it back, it was full of sand, like they went to a beach or desert. "They didn't even have the fuckin' courtesy to bring it to a car wash and have it cleaned out. I guess they took care of the guy who was watching them," she said. Mike and Richie heard more than they needed to conclude that both Knuckles and this Casper guy were somehow involved with this big shot who Knuckles knew was Sam's man. Who was sent to watch Sam's investment in Vegas? When asked how long ago this was, Donna said "A few weeks, like three or four. You guys friends of this big shot who Tony got shook off his tail?" Donna asked, heavily under the influence of alcohol. "No, we're here on business. That's got nothing to do with us. We don't know nobody except Knuckles, I mean Tony," Mike said and looked at Richie with a smile. "Okay, no more talk let's have fun and enjoy the show," Richie said as he lit up one of his favorite cigars. Donna was pretty much out of it, and the boys decided she had enough to drink and cut her off. She wasn't happy but complied at their insistence.

The show ended, and Helen met them backstage. She saw immediately that Donna was completely out of it. "Well, I guess she won't be any fun tonight, but I'm ready to howl at the moon. What say we have them send drinks to the room, and I play doctor with you boys? These shows always make me horny afterward. I think it's the outfits rubbing against my cookie that does it." Richie and Mike both laughed and agreed to the offer and led the way back to the room. Putting Donna in one of the bedrooms, they all enjoyed themselves in the living room and then the bedroom. It was as expected and there was no conversation with Helen about what they had learned from Donna. They knew they had enough to question Knuckles and this Casper guy when they all were to meet the next afternoon. They kept it silent and to themselves.

Morning with the girls was funny, to say the least. Donna had no idea what happened that night and only remembered waking up alone in a separate bedroom. "I'm so sorry for getting drunk like I did. I tend to get nervous when I'm alone with men. We all have flaws that one is mine," Donna said as she sipped her coffee. "Did you take advantage of me while I was out, and how did I end up in that room with all my clothes on?" Donna asked with an inquisitive smile. "You were out of it, and your girlfriend here saved the night without your help. And I must say, she did an excellent job of it," Richie said with a grin as he touched Helen's inner thigh under the table. "Yeah, she told us all your little secrets," Mike replied laughing as he reached over and brushed the hair out of Donna's eyes. "I will say this; you looked beautiful last night Donna. The men couldn't keep their eyes off you all night, especially when you started dancing on the tables in just your panties. That was something." "What, I was dancing on the tables naked?" Donna asked with a look of embarrassment on her face. "Just kidding, you weren't naked," Mike said looking at her blushing cheeks. Donna slapped Mike's arm saying, "You're playing with my head, aren't you? Taking advantage of a poor innocent girl like me? You owe me a gift for getting me so drunk, Mike." Mike sat back in his chair and said, "Anything you want, it's yours." "So sweet. I could use a good watch or a diamond chain to remember you by." Helen stepped in, "If you can get tickets for Dean Martin tonight, we would do anything you want, and I mean anything at all." Richie sang out, "Dino is my favorite. I'll get tickets for us, even if I have to kill somebody for them. Let me make a few calls and see what I can do. You game for that, Mike?" "Sure, that sounds great," Mike said as they all stood up ready to leave. "OK, you girls meet us here tonight, and I should have tickets for the show," Richie said. They all hugged each other and said goodbye.

Walking out to the car, Richie said to Mike, "I have to go find Knuckles and get these tickets for the show before this meeting if you know what I mean. We might not be able to get them from a dead man, so I gotta get them now. I'll be right out. Wait here. Or better yet, call your uncle and tell him what we know and see what he says." "Yeah, I'll call him and see what he wants us to do," Mike said as they split apart and Richie went looking for Knuckles in the casino.

About an hour later, Richie caught up with Mike and flashed the tickets. "I got them. It was like pulling teeth, but he finally gave in and gave me four tickets and put us at the same table we had last night, nice and close to the stage." Richie was in his glory knowing he had tickets to see his idol. "So, did you talk to the old man about this problem we have here?" Richie asked Mike. "Yeah, he wants me to call him back, something about getting permission from Sam. I think we have to get the car dirty and let them find a replacement here in Vegas. If that happens, we go to the show with the girls and in the morning we get the fuck out of this town, agreed?" Mike said as they got out of the car after driving around seeing the sights. "That's fine with me," Richie replied.

The afternoon came quickly, and they were to meet Knuckles at the lower bar in the casino at one pm. Knuckles showed up a little late and Richie bawled him out for holding them up. "This fuckin' guy better be there, and if he's not, I'm gonna kick your little ass for makin' him get away because you were an hour fuckin' late." "Slow down, cowboy. I just got off the phone with him, and he is there waiting. I had some business to take care of, sorry I'm a little late," Knuckles said as they walked out of the casino. "We'll use the rental car. I'll drive," Mike said sternly. "Fine with me," Knuckles said. The ride to the meeting was quiet except for chit chat about Vegas and girls. They arrived at a warehouse and walked to the office where they met with Frank (Casper). He introduced himself as Frankie Daluca and asked what this meeting was all about. Richie asked straight out, "Do you know the guy you whacked a couple of weeks ago was a made man?" Casper looked over at Knuckles saying, "What the fuck are they talking about, Tony?" Knuckles replied, "You know, that little job I told you not to do. I told you it would come back to haunt you, but you did it anyway." Knuckles started backing up to the door when Mike slid between him and the door "Where the fuck are you goin? You're not leaving us alone. We need more info than just your word." "Now, Frank, why don't you tell us your side of the story, and don't be shy," Richie said as he reached into his pocket. "Wait a minute here.

He's a fuckin' liar. He ordered the hit, and he came with me too. You're tryin' to set me up for this job. You were the one that said he had to go 'cause he knew too much. You fuckin' bastard." Casper started walking over to the desk, and Richie advised him to stop there as he moved his hand in his pocket. Mike saw that Knuckles was agitated and wanted to leave the room. In a split second, Knuckles' pulled a gun out of his pocket and was going to shoot Casper, but Mike grabbed the gun and Knuckles fingers with his massive hand and started to squeeze hard. There were three cracks. Mike had broken Knuckles' fingers which were still wrapped around the gun. The pain forced Knuckles to drop to his knees, and Mike hit him with a left hook that shattered his jaw, as his teeth fell out of the front of his mouth. "Now look what you did," Richie said while watching Casper's every move. "Now tell us what actually happened, Frank, and maybe we will let you go. It seems Knuckles here wanted to whack you before you had a chance to defend yourself." Casper spilled his guts, telling them how Knuckles found out that Sam's boy knew he was skimming more than his share and stashing it in bank deposit boxes. He told them how he was approached by Knuckles to help him get rid of his problem and bury him in the desert. Casper confirmed they used Donna's car to do the job, and they even left the shovels in the trunk. Richie said to Casper, "What's in the desk that you were going for, protection?" Casper said nothing as Richie walked over to the desk. Richie reached into the drawer and pulled out a revolver. Confirming it was loaded, he pointed it at Knuckles and pulled the trigger putting one in his head and one in his throat. Turning the gun on Casper, he said, "You leave me no choice. You seen too much. Now you can't leave." Again Richie pulled the trigger and gave Casper the same beauty marks he just gave Knuckles. Both Knuckles and Casper were lying dead on the floor in pools of blood. Richie looked at Mike saying, "Now, let's clean up this mess and bury these bastards. Mike replied "What a fuckin' mess. Did you have to make such a fuckin' mess?" Mike and Richie cleaned up the room. Mike wiped down the gun and emptied the remaining bullets into his pocket and put the gun back in the desk drawer and closed it. They put both bodies in the trunk of the rented car and drove east to the desert. "Got any better ideas?" Mike asked Richie as he drove out of town and into the scorching desert. It was still daylight and hot when they reached the outskirts of Vegas. Some thirty miles out of town they saw a ridge. Richie said, "There. Maybe we can find some shade by that ridge while we bury these fucks." "We ain't got nothing to bury these fucks with, not even a shovel, and it's too fuckin' hot out," Mike said. Mike drove up to a gorge, and they decided to use the lug wrench and car jack in the trunk to dig a hole. "This is gonna take all afternoon to dig a fuckin' hole big enough for two freakin' bodies," Mike said angrily as he pulled the items out of the trunk. "We don't have a fuckin' choice. If we don't do it right, they'll be found before we even get out of Vegas. Stop bitchin and start digging. You do some, and I'll do some," Richie replied as he dragged the bodies to a shady spot. Neither one wanted to, but they had to get rid of the bodies. So they spent the next four hours digging and then filling the hole. By the time they were done, they had looked like lobsters, all beet red with sunburn and stinking with sweat. "I need a nap after that workout," Richie said laughing. "Maybe next time we can plan it a little better, like bringing a fuckin' shovel," Mike replied. Richie responded, "Like I knew we we're gonna whack these fucks. What am I, a fuckin' psychic or something? Call the old man before dinner and let him know the story, and this problem had to be taken care of the way we did it. If Sam knows that Knuckles was the one who ordered the hit and money was stolen, he would have approved the hit," Richie said to Mike. Mike shook his head in agreement and said nothing the rest of the way to the casino.

After freshening up, Mike called Vincenzo and updated him on the situation and how they handled it. Vincenzo assured Mike that he would take care of passing the info to Sam and that Sam would have to decide who he was going to stay in Vegas to oversee the operation at the casinos they had an interest in. Vincenzo also told Mike that he and Richie were to go to Hollywood and meet a man named Johnny Rossilo (aka Pretty Boy). He had information concerning the Kennedy problem, and this information had to be delivered by mouth only. Mike got the information from Vincenzo on where and when and hung up the phone. "Richie, we gotta go to Hollywood right now and meet some guy for the old man. He's got the information we have to deliver to my uncle and all I know is, it has something to do with Jack and Bobby." "Are you fuckin' kidding me? We gotta run another fuckin' errand now in Tinsel town?" "Yep, let's get something to eat and leave. I want to get out of this town as fast as possible," Mike said as they started packing their suitcases. "Wait, I got tickets to Dean Martin. What the fuck do I do with these tickets? And what about the girls?" Richie asked. "Shove the tickets up your ass or give them to the front desk for the girls. Either way, we gotta go and you ain't gonna see Dino tonight or get laid. Sorry, orders are orders," Mike said as he broke out singing a Dean Martin song. "Cute. Real fuckin' cute. You sound like Dino with his nuts cut off," Richie replied. It wasn't long after eating that they were on their way to Hollywood. They took turns driving and sleeping for several hours and reached their destination that evening and slept the rest of the night. The next morning they met with Pretty Boy, and after introducing themselves, Jimmy gave them the information to pass on to Vincenzo and the Commission. Mike and Richie were shocked to learn that the Mob and several government people were planning to cut off the head of the snake and end the harassment of the families and the businesses they were involved in. "Johnny, are you sure this information is correct, and this is what we are supposed to tell the old man?" Richie said looking confused.

"Look, this is straight from Miami and New Orleans. All I am is a middle man who was asked to set up these meetings and get the information the Commission wanted so they could decide what to do with it. Yeah, the info is correct, and the old man has to pass it on." Mike saw that Johnny was getting upset and stepped in, "OK, we'll pass it on just the way you told us, no problem, Johnny." Johnny relaxed for a moment and said, "If you guys are staying overnight, there's a party at this swanky place for some people you may know. Here is the address, and if you show up, I'll see you boys there and if not, make sure that Vincenzo gets the information."

After a short talk, Mike and Richie decided to go to the party. They were already in Hollywood and had the room for one more day. "Maybe we'll find some horny chicks and get laid or meet some celebrities or something," Richie said. "I guess," Mike answered. That night they went to the location given by Johnny, and there they met some famous people and several unknowns. "Hi, I'm Frank, and this is my party. Do I know you" he said to both Richie and Mike. "Pretty Boy told us about the party, and he invited us," Mike said as he put his hand out "You're Frankie Sinati, the singer. It's a pleasure to meet you," Mike said while shaking Frank's hand. "Yeah, I'm that singer guy. You fellas aren't from around here are you?" he asked. "No, we're here on business," Richie said as he shook Frank's hand. "Well, you must come and enjoy the food. It's something I like to do. Kinda kinky, some say, but why not. I find it interesting to see the faces of newcomers when they see it for the first time. Come with me and see what I mean," Frank said as he led them to the back room where everything was prepared.

Mike and Richie were shocked to see a naked girl lying on a table face up with all sorts of food distributed along the front of her naked body. Cold cuts were on the top side of her breast followed by vegetables in the middle and fruits on the lower section of her waist and legs. "What the fuck is this?" both Mike and Richie asked looking at this odd feast in front of them. Frank laughed saying, "See. I love to see the reaction on people's faces, and you guys looked fuckin' shocked and surprised, like most people. Go ahead, enjoy some food and have fun. I'll see you later. I have to say hello to my other guests." Mike and Richie walked up cautiously, wondering if she was real or made of rubber. There were many people picking food from her body and Mike decided to do the same. Reaching for the bread near the girls shoulder's, he said to the girl, "This is fuckin' crazy. How did you get picked to do this?" She did not reply. Mike looked at Richie saying, "You getting some food? I'm starving." Richie walked over near Mike and laughed as he reached for some food himself. "This is the weirdest fuckin' thing I have ever seen, and Frankie has a sick sense of humor." They both ate their fill and mingled with some of the other guests. They found Johnny and said hello. "Does he do this kinda' party often or is this one of those things?" Mike asked "He does this from time to time, and no one knows why. He likes it, and the company is exciting," Johnny said looking at Mike. "Well, to each his own," Mike said turning to Richie. "Well, I have to make a call. I'll be back," Mike said.

Mike found a phone in a quiet room and called his uncle. He told him what Johnny had said about the Kennedy boys. And wanted to see if there was anything else they had to do before returning to New York. "Michael, call me back in two hours while I make some calls. I have to find out what we're going to do with this information and how the families want to move on this matter." Mike obliged and hung up the phone. Mike called Vincenzo back and was not ready for what he was about to hear. "Michael, my boy, there has been a change of plans. After speaking to the council, it has been decided that Richie should stay in Vegas and watch over the family interests and investments in the casinos. He is now the man in charge for the routine operations and the skim distributions to the other families. You have to go to New Orleans and see a man at the Candy Club. His name is Jimmy Blanks. Call me when you are in his presence so I can talk to him directly on the phone. I have made all the reservations for you. After that, you will come home so we can talk. I'm sorry for the changes, but they must be made, and my hands are tied on this one. It comes from the top." "Richie is not going to be happy with this when I tell him," Mike responded. "You tell him the families feel he is the right person to take care of this until Sam can find a replacement for him. It will only be for a couple of months or so, and he will be well compensated when he returns." Vincenzo said. "Okay Uncle, I will let him know." "Also tell Richie to inform Johnny Rossili that he has an open invitation to the Vegas clubs and anything he needs is on the house. Make sure you tell him exactly that way," Vincenzo said with a commanding voice. "Got it. Johnny gets whatever he wants and it's on the house, when in Vegas," Mike replied. "Call me when you get settled in Orleans Michael. I'll talk to you in a few days," Vincenzo said, then hung up the phone.

CHAPTER 8

CHANGE OF PLANS

Mike was nervous walking back to meet Richie. Should I tell him now or wait till we get in the car Mike thought to himself. *"If I tell him now, there is a good chance he will blow his stack and do something stupid."* Mike decided to wait till they get back in the car to tell him. Mike now knew that little Richie had a short fuse. After seeing what happened in Vegas to Casper and Knuckles.

When he caught up with Richie, he told him that everything was alright, but the old man had some other things that needed to be done. Richie wanted to know what they were, but Mike stood fast telling Richie this was not the place to talk about it, and he would tell him in the car going back to the hotel.

After a while, they decided to leave the party and said their goodbyes. Mike saw Johnny and said, "My uncle said that if you're ever in Vegas, anything you want or need is on the house. All you have to do is arrange it with Richie, and he will take care of anything you need." Richie jumped back saying, "What the fuck do you mean, see me? Don't tell me that I have to stay in Vegas, Mike." Mike grabbed Richie by the shoulder saying, "Richie, it's not a choice. You told me whatever the family wants, we are to do without question. I'll fill you in when we're in the car. Please don't make a scene here." "Johnny, the offer stands for Vegas," Mike said as he shook Johnny's hand. "Ok," Johnny said looking at Richie. "I'm not sure what this is all about but, it is what it is," Richie said, looking both puzzled and pissed at the same time shaking Johnny's hand. Mike and Richie walked out to the car, and Richie wanted to know then and there what the fuck was going on. Mike started explaining to Richie what Vincenzo told him, and he could see that Richie was not happy at all. "I have nothing here except a suitcase of clothes. And if they want me to take over, even for a short time, they are going to buy anything I want, starting with a new fuckin' wardrobe and a place to stay, and it's not inside a fuckin' hotel room, either. I am pissed that I have to run this fuckin' place, and they better find somebody quick. I give them six fuckin' months, Mike, that's it." Mike could only reply that he was sorry that Richie had to stay and that he had to go to New Orleans to meet some guy, and he didn't even know why. "At least, you can go home after that. I have to stay here" Richie said in reply to Mike's concern about the circumstances. "Look at it this way, Richie, you already have Donna and her girlfriend to keep you warm at night," Mike said laughing. "Very fuckin' funny, Mike," Richie replied.

Getting back to the Casino, Richie sought out the assistant manager and informed him that Tony was called back to Chicago on short notice, and he was the new boss while Knuckles was gone. He arranged for an employee meeting for the next morning and left it up to the assistant manager to set it up. "Mike, tonight I have to get fuckin' smashed drunk, and then you can leave in the morning. Now let's upgrade our room to the presidential suite and find some pussy to vent this fuckin' anger and frustration I have built up," Richie said walking to the front desk. He informed the girl that he was the new manager and wanted her to change the rooms. She informed him that she did not know him. Tony was the only one who could authorize a move like that. Richie went crazy. "Call the fuckin' assistant manager and get him here now, you stupid bitch," Richie barked. After a few minutes, the assistant came and informed the girl that Richie was the new boss, and anything he needed was approved. "Make sure you're at the meeting in the morning, you dumb fuckin' bitch. You're lucky I don't fire you right here and now," Richie said slamming his fist on the countertop. The girl apologized saying, "I have never seen you before, and I was just doing my job, sir. I am sorry. I didn't know who you were. Please, I have kids, and I need this job." Mike jumped in saying, "He had a bad night and he needs to unwind. I'll talk to him, and you can keep your job, honey. He's just a little upset right now." "Thank you. Thank you, sir. I was just doing my job. I'm sorry." Mike responded, "Okay, just change the rooms so I can get him out of the lobby." The girl changed the room and again apologized to Richie and Mike as she gave him the key.

Mike got Richie in the elevator and up to the room. "Richie, you can't blow your fuckin' stack like that. You got a job to do, and you can't afford people getting pissed at you for being a fuckin' prick to them," Mike said in the elevator as it opened to the presidential suite. "Look, this is fit for a king, and you are now the fuckin' king of Vegas. Smile and relax, you wild fuck. Look at the luxury you'll be living in. You'll have different pussy and anything else you want every night. That should make you happy; you miserable fuck you." Richie gave a big smile and said, "Yeah, I guess I can get used to this. It's not like I can say no. Anyway, I won't have to suffer while I'm here even though I don't want to be here. I have no choice, do I Mike?" "Now relax and order some room service. I'm starving, I could eat a horse." Mike said looking around at the plush surroundings. "So you want me to order you a horse? I can do that now that I am the boss. How do you expect it cooked?" Richie asked laughing as he opened the doors to the bar room. "Make it look like a T-bone steak and I'll be happy," Mike said in reply. "One T-bone horse steak coming up," Richie said as he poured a three-finger glass of top-shelf whiskey.

After dinner with Donna and Helen, they went to the show, and Richie got drunk as he could. Although Mike was embarrassed, he tolerated Richie's drunkenness and around 3 am took him up to the suite and made sure he was down for the night. Mike apologized to the girls and informed them that Richie had a bad day and invited them back to the room. "The Presidential suite? Okay, what the hell is going on here, Mike?" Helen asked. "We'll ladies, say hello to your new boss," as he pointed his finger at Richie slouched on the circular couch. "It seems that Tony was called to Chicago, and Richie here is in charge till he gets back if he ever gets back at all." The next morning Richie woke up with a hangover and woke Mike up. "I have a staff meeting in two hours, and I feel like shit." "You look like shit too," Mike replied

The meeting went as planned and Richie was introduced as the interim boss. Then it was time for Mike to leave Richie in Vegas and head out to New Orleans. Richie sent him out in style with a stretch limo to the airport and kissed him on both cheeks. "I'm gonna miss ya, you big lug. Make sure you come and see me in this fuckin' hellhole soon." Mike gave Richie a man hug and told him he was looking forward to coming back to see him in Vegas.

Mike relaxed on the flight wondering what he was to do in Orleans and why Vincenzo was sending him there in the first place. Who was this Jimmy Blanks guy (AKA Bang Bang) and what was his involvement with the family or the Kennedy's? Was Johnny, a middleman, setting things up for a hit or was he informing Vincenzo of how deep the Kennedy boys infiltrated the family businesses? Mike had no idea, but he had to do what he was instructed to do without question. The plane landed in New Orleans, and Mike chose a hotel room near the Candy Club. He spent the night sitting on the balcony watching people coming and going from the club, which was half a block down the street from the balcony.

He called Vincenzo in the morning and told him he was in New Orleans near the club and informed him that he would call when he met Jimmy that night. Never having been to New Orleans, Mike went sightseeing for the day. Later that evening he went to the club to meet this Jimmy Blanks. All he had was a brief description and a name. Sitting at a table by himself, Mike kept looking for Jimmy. Just when he was getting frustrated, Jimmy came over and introduced himself. "How do you know who I am?" Mike asked. "They told me to look for a big guy with curly black hair and large hands, and that surely is you," Jimmy replied as he sat down in the chair. "So do you know why I was asked to meet with you? I don't know you, nor do I know why my uncle told me to meet with you. So I hope you have some answers. I only know I am supposed to bring you to a pay phone and call him so you can talk to him directly," Mike said, watching Jimmy's every move. "OK, let's call your uncle," Jimmy said as he stood up.

"Hello, Uncle, here is Jimmy," Mike said, and he handed the phone to Jimmy. After listening to Jimmy respond to the voice on the other end, Mike realized that Jimmy was given the order to make a hit on Jack Kennedy. Jimmy hung up the phone and asked Mike if he wanted a drink before he left. Mike agreed only because he wanted to know more of what was going on and what Jimmy's involvement was in all of this. Jimmy went to a table where several other guys were already sitting and talking among themselves. "Mike, let me introduce you to some associates of mine. This good looking gentleman is Clay

Bertrel. The person next to him is Dave Perry, and this lush is Guy Bantel. They are somewhat involved with the job I was given." Mike sat down cautiously sizing up these strangers. "So, what brings you to New Orleans, Mike?" Clay asked. "Sightseeing" Mike replied with a smile. "What's it to you?" Mike asked. "Nothing, I guess," Clay replied. Mike felt uncomfortable and made it known. He had a funny feeling that these guys were not whom they pretended to be. He started asking questions to figure out what connections they had with Jimmy and this contract. "Nice hair. Do you dye it that color or is it that your natural color?" Mike asked Clay. "I like the color and so do my friends," Clay replied. Mike noticed that these guys were a little weird in the way they looked. Dave Perry had the worst hairpiece anyone had ever seen. Clay had bleached white hair and smoked a cigarette with some sort of ivory holder at the end of it. And Guy Bantel was certainly a drunk, as well as being overweight.

Mike said very little as the conversation started with how much they despised Jack for being a pussy on Castro, Russia, and the Vietnam conflict. "This Kennedy is costing me a ton of fuckin' money holding up this war with Vietnam. He won't commit, even though his generals say strike them now before they turn the whole country over to the communists," Clay said as he puffed on his fancy cigarette. "Yeah, seems like everyone wants him out of the picture. War is money, and we can't make money without a war of some kind," Dave Perry said while pounding his fist on the table. "So, I take it you guys don't like Kennedy 'cause he won't start a fuckin' war?" Mike asked looking around the table. "We need a leader who is not a fuckin' commie" Guy replied. Mike looked at Jimmy (Bang Bang). "What fuckin' involvement do these guys have with this job?" Mike asked, expecting to get answers. "They are the other side and they are setting up this patsy to take the fall. They are not involved with our business, but they are the architects for the insiders who are planning the job," Jimmy said. "So, you guys are government boys?" Mike asked. "Not directly," Guy replied to Mike's question. After a few drinks, Bang Bang told Mike that they were to set up a shooter in Dallas, and he (Bang Bang) was to whack him after the job was done. When Mike asked who the shooter was, Jimmy only said that he was a low-level government agent who hated Jack Kennedy for what he was doing to Castro and Cuba. Jimmy was to let him do his job from the building across the street and then take him, the shooter, out so no one could get information from him. Jimmy also told Mike that the hit on John Kennedy would happen when he was in Dallas. He said that dozens of people wanted Kennedy dead, including government officials, because of Kennedy's intent to break apart the organization they worked for, as well as expose the corruption within the government agencies as being too powerful. He explained that the Russians, the Cubans, the government, the bankers and the Mob all wanted John Kennedy and his brother dead, and it was up to him and others to find the right patsy to take the fall, and then whack him. Mike asked Jimmy, "So who whacks you if you fuck up, and you're the only one left?" Jimmy replied that he would be out of the country in twenty-four hours after the job was done and no one knew where he was going. "I wish I didn't know this shit 'cause it makes me nervous, and the heat is going to come down real hard on us afterward," Mike said taking another shot of Bourbon. "Do like me and lay low for a few months, Mike. Take a vacation out of the country. I only told you this much because you're Vincenzo's nephew, and he sent you here to make this connection." Mike could only smile as he said, "Yeah, which puts me in the middle of this shit. So you guys better do your job right, or they'll whack you for fuckin' up and leaving rats in the nest. I heard enough of this. I don't know who you fuckin' guys really are, so this conversation is over. Good day gentlemen," Mike said as he stood up from his chair.

Mike and Jimmy said their goodbyes and Mike left the Candy Club. Mike surely did not want anything to do with this future hit and certainly didn't want to be involved even by association. But he was deep in the middle of it all, and now strangers knew who he was. Mike had to make plans if this went down because it would bring heat from every direction. He couldn't wait to get home and talk with Vincenzo to see what his plans were if this happened. That night he decided to drive home and not call Vincenzo.

It took Mike two days to get back to Brooklyn. The first thing he did was to go to Money's and see what he knew about this planned hit. It seemed that Money knew very little, or if he did know anything, he wasn't telling. After striking out with Money, he went home, said hello to Jackie and went to bed early. The ride back to Brooklyn from New Orleans had worn him down.

The next morning after chatting with Jackie, he went to the club to see if there was any chit chat about the information he was privy to. No one was talking about anything to do with Kennedys or Texas and New Orleans. It seemed to Mike that he was the only person, except for a few others, who was even aware of what was going to happen sometime in the future. If anyone knew more than he did, it would be uncle Vincenzo. Mike went to the auto mechanic shop to see what was going on and was informed that Bo was having issues with Dapper and the car payments. It seemed that Dapper owed money and was keeping cars there much longer than the agreed to four days. Bo asked Mike if he could do something about it. Mike assured Bo that he would talk to Dapper about the problem. After a short lunch, Mike drove to Vincenzo's to bring him up to date and see what else Vincenzo had in store for him. Vincenzo was not in a good mood when Mike arrived.

Vincenzo instructed Mike to meet him outside on the veranda and wait for him. Mike proceeded as instructed. When Vincenzo came out and sat down, Mike asked, "What's the matter? You look upset." Vincenzo lit a cigar and sat back in his chair. In Italian Vincenzo said, "Michael, the wheels of progress are turning, and I am stuck in the middle of all this shit. Some things I have no control or power over and it affects everyone. If this job does not go perfectly, everything falls apart, and the families are no more." Mike asked, "You want to talk about this problem? Is there anything I can do?" "You're already involved with this problem, Mike. You did as I asked, and when you went to New Orleans, you became a part of this job," Vincenzo said as he handed Mike an envelope. "What is this?" Mike asked. Vincenzo replied, "The envelope contains instructions to be carried out exactly as written. And after the job is done, it is to be destroyed immediately. In the event anything happens to me beforehand, you are to do as the letter says. Do you understand?" "As much as I don't want to be involved, I have no choice, do I," Mike said." "I'll do as you say. But, Uncle, I gotta know, what the fuck is going on? I need more information. I am in the dark about this whole thing. It's like everybody is not saying anything, and if I am involved, I gotta know what's happening."

Vincenzo leaned forward in his lawn chair and said, "You're right, Mike. I'll tell you what I know. But you must remember, I am only a small part of this operation. The council has approved of this hit and is sleeping in the same bed with these government guys even though I disapproved. What I tell you must never be repeated and never spoken of again. Some months back some of the bosses in Chicago and Miami were approached at a sit down by federal agents. They explained that they too were having problems with Jack and that he was going to dismantle the CIA and change the banking system back to government control. They also said that he was still pissed about the Castro thing, how it was their fault for the fuckups and this was his payback. It seems that we got the son of a bitch in office, and his brother wants to tear apart the same people who got his brother in office. Jack has made many enemies, like Castro, the Russians, the world bankers, CIA, FBI, and even the Catholic Church for not kissing the Pope's ring. Now, we ain't got no problem with Jack taking apart the CIA and the FBI. But we do have an issue with the banker thing and his brother breaking our balls. You saw his father and nothing was done with that meeting. In fact, it has gotten worse since then. We lost our investments in Cuba and were ready to kill Castro ourselves, but we were told not to do it as it would cause a problem. A year later they paid us to do it, and we took the money. We have helped them several times in the past to try and wipe out Castro, and it failed because of government involvement and politics. It now seems that Jack has made many enemies besides us, and they all want him out, even if it means the death of a president. We agreed only because we have a small part in this, and we want Bobby to stop harassing us. By cutting off the head, we kill the snake. This is not what we do, but we have to make exceptions, and this is one of those necessary evils that involve all of us. The guy you spoke with at the club in New Orleans is a hired hit man not a part of this thing of ours. He will be taken care of after he does his job. You will be asked to arrange meetings and provide information to people. You will not be involved in any actual rubbing out of anyone. That will be done by others, which I do not know. Any questions Michael?" Mike didn't know what to say. He knew it had something to do with the Kennedys, but not this. "Are you sure this is the only way?" Mike asked. "I'm in the same boat as you. If I said no, they would have a contract out on me just for knowing. This is the life we chose, and we are bound by the code to protect the family at any cost. It has been like this for a hundred years. I have stayed alive for almost fifty years in this business by following orders. Even if I didn't like them, I still did them. I sit high on the council, but I too am expendable. I made my bones and have managed to stay under the radar of those fucks who would love to lock me up for anything they could find, but I always stay three steps ahead. In my life, I have made many influential friends, and I keep them close to the vest 'cause when I need them, they pay back their marker. You do the same, and you will be fine. Do what you're told and stay quiet. Never give the Feds something they want," Vincenzo said as he extinguished his cigar and stood up to leave. "This conversation never happened, and you know nothing. Tu capisce?" Mike nodded his head in acknowledgment as he stood up and walked back to the house with Vincenzo. "When is this supposed to happen?" Mike asked. "I'm not sure. They are still planning it out. I will call on you when the time comes, and we can have another sit-down. In the meantime, it is business as usual. Speaking of business, that fuckin' horse is costing us money, and we need to collect the insurance on him. Go see your brother and take care of it. The boys want to see a return on their investment. See if you can find another runner who can fuckin' win some races this time. Maybe you have to go to Ocala again," Vincenzo said. "Yeah, maybe I have to kick some asses at the track too," Mike said smiling. "You do what you have to, Mike," Vincenzo said as he hugged Mike and led him to the front door.

Mike drove off still dazed about the information he got about the Kennedy boys, but also knew he was very much involved and couldn't get out. For the first time, Mike felt alone in the world and this secret he now knew scared him. He had to think of the future and how he could protect his family and all he accumulated the past few years. He went to the club and found Dapper and told him he was getting out of the car business and told him to pay the money he owed and get the cars he had in the lot out in one week. Johnny wasn't happy but agreed to Mike's demands. Three days later the cars were gone. Mike now had nothing to do with the stolen-car business and concentrated on making bigger money instead of chump change. After spending time with the family and renovating his house, he decided it was time for a change, time to start banking the money in the event he and his family had to leave town in a hurry someday. The Kennedy thing was looming over his head, and he wasn't going to be caught with his pants down.

It was now November and Thanksgiving was just three days away. Mike told Jackie to plan something special and invite the entire family. He wanted to see those he hadn't seen in a while and enjoy their company. Jackie agreed and started planning and calling everyone in her phonebook. He spent the next two days tying up loose ends. That Thursday there were some forty family members, from cousins to aunts and uncles, and some surprise guests like Richie and Onions from the club. Mike was happy and pleased to see so many of his family and friends had come to enjoy the day. Sometime after turkey dinner, the men went into the basement to play cards and chat. Mike called his brother Louie to a section of the room and said, "Louie, I need to put in a claim on a horse. He died, and I need to collect on the insurance." Louie laughed asking "How did the horse die, Mike?" "He fell and broke his leg. We had to put him down. As sad as it was, we had to shoot him. The other horse is fine," Mike replied. "You know I have to do a ton of paperwork to make this happen, and it's time-consuming too," Louie said. Mike said, "Yeah, I know. Take ten percent for your fuckin' efforts and deposit it into the B.I.G. account through Sal so he can account for the funds. Some of the boys want to get a return on the investment. I'll talk to Sal and tell him to put some money in Mama's savings. You put some of yours in there too, little brother." "You gonna get another horse? I guess you'll want me to insure that one, too?" Louie said to Mike. "Don't know yet. Gotta talk to the guys and see what they want to do. That fuckin' kid at the track didn't live up to his part of the deal. Might have to kick his ass a little. So, not sure about another horse yet." "I'll let you know what the payout is on the claim when I get approval, okay?" Louie said as they walked back to the card table. "We insured that pony for 250 thousand, so I better get that, less your cut, or somebody will have to break your fuckin' hand," Mike replied as he slapped Louie on the back of the neck.

While playing cards, Mike overheard Tony G talking to Money about something to do with gas stations and state taxes and how lucrative it was with not paying the quarterly taxes and closing the station after nine months and opening another station under a different corporation and doing it all over again. "What's this gas deal

I'm hearing about? Can we do the same thing?" Mike asked curiously looking at Tony and Money. "Sure, we could do the same thing, so long as we pay up our share. I'll have to talk to some people to get the OK. I hear this is a fuckin' shitload of money. Something like a couple million or more a year" Tony said. "Talk to uncle Vincenzo. He's got the connections to set it up," Money said. "Tony, see Carlo and make it happen." "We'll get the old man in on this so we can use his connections to pass the paperwork through," Mike said looking for the okay from both Money and Tony G. "Yeah, that'll work for us. Just a four-partner deal, right?" Money said confirming it. He looked to Mike and Tony for approval. "Yeah, that's fine," they both said at the same time. "I gotta see Vincenzo Tuesday. I'll give him the lowdown and see what he says, but I'm sure he will be in on it," Mike said. Then he walked away to play some cards with the guys at the table.

The rest of the day went fine, and everyone said their goodbyes. On Tuesday Mike went to see Vincenzo and informed him about the gas station scam deal. Vincenzo suggested that he had a friend in the county building department who could help with getting the paperwork through and activating the licensing. Tony got the OK and negotiated a ten-percent take for the boys who were in charge of the national operation. It took about a month, and just after Christmas, they were ready to open several new gas stations in the New York area, as well as Long Island. Cash was coming in fast, and everyone was happy with the return investment. Mike was making an extra ten grand a week, and in an effort to conceal it from the IRS, he had a bomb shelter built in his basement behind a false wall. There he stacked money and silver along with other valuables to keep them close and safe. It was better than getting involved with drugs. At the time, it was a death sentence for any member who got caught dealing in the drug business. The elders and bosses wanted nothing to do with drugs. Drugs were a magnet for the Feds, and they wanted to keep them as far away as possible. During the early sixties, almost everyone who was involved was being watched or was known in some form to the Feds and drugs were off limits, even for a made man.

During the early months of 1963, Mike visited Richie in Vegas several times and always loved being in his company. Sometime around April of 1963, Richie got word that he was free to go back to New York. The bosses found a replacement for him in Vegas. Richie was more than happy to leave. He had enough of Vegas and the headaches it caused him running the casinos and his desire to be on his home turf. The first place he went was to see Mike at one of the gas stations on Fulton Street where Mike had set up his office. "I want in on this gas gig, Mike," Richie said expecting to get Mike blessings. "Richie, you gotta get the blessing from the other members, but it's OK with me." "You set up a fuckin' meeting, so everyone is there and we can discuss it, okay, Mike?" Richie said in response. "Fine, I'll see what I can do. Let's go out and celebrate your return tonight. I'll get some of the guys together, and we can go to Gino's for dinner, my treat," Mike said to Richie as he was heading out the door to a meeting he was already late for.

That night at Gino's Mike couldn't help notice that little Richie was different in some ways. He was nasty and somewhat sarcastic, edgy and quick to start a fight about anything. When he asked Richie why Richie blamed it on running Vegas. He said it made him nasty, and it would take some time to shake it off. "Well, I hope it's soon, 'cause you're gonna get yourself killed if you piss off these Brooklyn boys," Mike said with a smile. Richie just blew it off and said nothing.

CHAPTER 9

TIME TO EXPAND

Richie waited three months for an answer to getting into the gas deal and was getting restless. He wanted in at any cost, so he went to see Vincenzo for a one-on-one talk. He told no one. "Boss, you are aware that I asked Mike if I could get in on this gas money thing that started back in March, and I ain't heard nothing. I'm here to see you personally for your blessing to be involved. As you know, I have worked for you for almost ten years now, and I think I deserve a piece of the action too." Vincenzo sat back in his chair and smiled at Richie. "What can you contribute as a partner in this endeavor?" "I can do anything you ask of me. You know that. I could police the operation and make sure it's not being watched by the Feds," Richie said in reply to Vincenzo's question. "It is going to cost you to join in on this private venture of ours. I think if you come up with, say, 400K, I might be able to talk them into it. You will be a twenty percent partner. That sound fair to you, Richie?" Vincenzo stated. "Minga, that's a lot of cabbage, boss. Why so much?" Richie asked. "Right now we make about twenty grand each a week for four investors, and we only have three stations. With your cash, we can open more and make twice that a week. That's why. You don't like it, don't join. You want in; that's what it's gonna cost you," Vincenzo sternly said. "I don't have that kind of cash right now, but I can sell my house in Vegas. I have about 200k in cash. I'll take half of my cut until the buy-in is paid off. Is that okay with you?" Richie asked hoping for a yes from Vincenzo. "I guess that could work. But I have to hold a meeting with the boys to see if they're okay with it. Go do what you gotta do. I will hold a meeting this weekend and give you an answer by next week, Richie," Vincenzo said as he stood up indicating that the meeting was over. "Thank you, boss. I'll get on it right away and have the rest of the cash as soon as the house sells in Vegas," Richie said as he was led to the front door.

On Thursday Vincenzo called a meeting with the members involved and stated his case concerning Richie and the buy-in. Vincenzo insisted that the money be used to buy more gas stations. Tony interrupted saying "What if we have Richie go around and buy up stations in high-traffic areas? That way we could get five or ten more high-volume stations." "That's a great idea, Tony. Richie could persuade them into selling. He can be quite intimidating at times as we all know, and lately, he has been a real bitch. Vegas made him nasty," Mike said with a smile on his face. "Yeah, but he can't go overboard 'cause it could explode in our faces. Someone has to control him and make sure he doesn't go too far persuading them to sell out," Money said looking around for responses from the others. "Michael, you make sure he doesn't get outta hand, and if he does, you're on the hook," Vincenzo said with authority. Although Mike didn't like it, he accepted with a nod of his head. "So we are all in agreement with this offer? Yes? Case closed," Vincenzo said looking at the others. Vincenzo was getting up from the table. "Uncle, there is something else we need to discuss while we are here," Money said. Vincenzo sat back down looking at Money. Money started to explain, "It seems that some of the soldiers, with the approval of their captains, are dealing in drugs and it may be getting out of hand." "Drugs are not what we do in the families, and everyone knows the rules," Vincenzo said in anger. "Do you know who they are?" Vincenzo asked looking at Money. "I would have to confirm it, but I do know of a few who are involved in our family. The other families have the same problem. What do we do about them? Do we need permission or do we let them take care of their own problems from within?" Money asked. "Confirm if they are being watched by the Feds by using your cop friend Tommy you got on your payroll. If it's true, clean house in our family until I get the OK from the other families. I'll get Carlo's approval, and you already have mine. We already have enough problems with Bobby Kennedy breaking our balls. The last thing we need is drug dealers in our midst. I will talk to the other families and get them to clean all the houses at the same time, but tell no one of this problem. If they know in advance, they may turn on us, and we can't have that, can we?" Vincenzo said looking around the table for reaction or responses. "I don't know nothing about this shit. I'm just a partner in a trucking business, and all we are involved with is merchandise and it ain't drugs," Tony G said wiping his hands to show he and his crew were clean in dealing drugs. "Eddie, take care of this internal problem and put a crew together if you need to clean this fuckin' shit up and do it quick," Vincenzo said as he stood up. "If that's it, then this meeting is over. Mike, stay for a moment so I can have a word with you," Vincenzo said. Mike obliged and sat back down after saying goodbye to the others.

Vincenzo said his farewells to his guests and went to the kitchen table to speak with Mike. "Mike, I need you to fly to Miami with me next week to see the Commission for their decision on this Kennedy thing, to know if it is still on or off. All conversation on this matter is done in person, no phone calls. If the Feds have tapped our phones, they hear nothing about it, even though some of them are the ones who set this shit up and are involved. Personally, I would like us not to be involved, but it is not my choice to say. I think it's time you meet some of our friends so you can represent me when I need to be at a meeting or something and I can't make it. It's the only way I can introduce you to the movers and shakers in this business. You must be introduced by me as my personal representative." Mike had no choice in the decision and only said, "Whatever you need, I am there." They both walked to the front door and gave each other the traditional kiss on the cheek and parted ways. Mike drove home pissed that he was still involved with the Kennedy problem, but he knew he was committed to doing what he was told.

July 1963 was a bloodbath for many of the organized families. Members involved with drugs were whacked all over NY, Jersey, Philly, Chicago and Vegas, all with the approval of the bosses and underbosses of the controlling families. Soldiers, captains and made men were gunned down, disappeared, or chopped into little pieces and used as chum. It sent a message to all that drugs were not to be involved with any family practices, and they should find other ways to make money for their group. Money did his job and, although the boss was happy, some of the members and their crews were not. Money had to watch his back from now on and make sure he wasn't on someone's personal hit list in retaliation for calling the hit on dozens of crew members and leaders. He was so concerned that he asked Vincenzo to spread the word that he was not to be touched by anyone for his actions, and it was approved at the highest level within the family. Vincenzo sent out the word to the other bosses, and they put it out on the street. Money felt comfortable but still looked behind his back from that point on.

July 15th, Mike, and Vincenzo flew out of La Guardia headed to Miami and the Fountain Bleu Hotel for a sit down with the other leaders to discuss both business and the Kennedy thing. Mike was introduced to several bosses from various parts of the USA. He also met with other high-ranking members and their underbosses. This was the second time Mike had met the boss of Miami and was invited to his home. Vincenzo accepted the offer. "We both grew up on the same street in the old days. He has been a good friend for almost forty years. I want to see what he has to say in a private setting about this Kennedy situation, among other things." It was decided that the Commission would play a part in the assassination of Jack Kennedy by having the patsy shooter whacked by a professional hit man who was a marksman shooter. The intent was that those in government who set it up would take care of the president. The hit man contracted by the family would stop the patsy from opening his mouth by whacking him. That way no one was directly involved, and it would confuse people if something went wrong. It was also agreed that the shooter from the mob side would have to be whacked too so he was unable to point the finger at anyone in the mob. The shooter only knew that a government agency was involved, and the patsy from the government never knew, nor was he told, that the mob was involved.

No one wanted this to go down, but they had to commit if they wanted the crackdown to stop within the family business and day-to-day operations. They also knew that Jack wanted to break up the CIA because he felt they had become too powerful and controlling. Jack made statements about powerful people both in and out of government who, in his mind, were controlling the destiny and direction of the country as well as secret deals that even the president could not control. As President, he intended to expose them and break apart agencies he did have control over. The mob was a part of Jack's problem, thanks to Bobby, and the Commission agreed that it had to be done with inside involvement so everyone would be pointing fingers at each other.

The next day Vincenzo and Mike were picked up by Salvatori's limo and taken to his home on the bay where he greeted them at his mansion overlooking Miami harbor. "Welcome to my home, come in. Would you like something to eat? Vincenzo, we have much to talk about. It has been a long time, my friend, and we see so little of each other these days. I am happy to see you. Come, let's talk on the veranda outside. The servers will bring us lunch and drinks," Salvatori said pointing the way to the outside gardens. Mike thought to himself that it was nice to see these two old men smiling and enjoying each other's company in a social manner and not a business environment. They no sooner sat down than the conversation between them started. "It's a fuckin' shame that we have to meet under such conditions concerning this thing of ours," Vincenzo said. "Yes, it sucks, but what else can we do. We worked our asses off getting this kid elected, and now he has stabbed us in the back," Salvatori said. "To tell you personally, I don't like this at all. Getting involved with the Feds will hold a marker on the families that we can't get out of in the future. You know, I like Jack, but his brother is the problem we have. I would be okay with him leaving instead of Jack, but what can I say, it's been decided by the Commission. You know, I had investments in Cuba and Castro took it all away, and I got nothing in return. I blame that on Jack. He could have stopped the takeover in many ways but didn't do anything about it. I have no love for him at all. Business is business," Salvatori said. "This is true, he could have done more, and I know your losses were a big hit for you. Your investors lost money too, but this is beyond what we do. We are talking about taking down someone who is not involved with us, and the oath will be broken when this thing happens. Much internal conflict and much blood will be shed. I just hope it is not ours, my friend," Vincenzo said as the food was being laid out on the table. "We have no choice in the matter, and it is what it is," Salvatori said as they both got up to pick from the trays of food that were laid out.

Mike waited till they had taken their plates back to the veranda before he got up to pick from the assorted food. Walking back to his seat on the terrace, Salvatori looked up at Mike and said, "Mike could you do me a favor while you are here if Vincenzo does not mind? It is a small favor and should only take you an hour or so. I will send my man with you, and he will drive." Mike, confused, looked at Salvatori and asked openly, "What is this favor you ask? I am here with my uncle." Just then Vincenzo stepped in and asked, "What is this favor you ask of him?" "I have this friend who owes me a large sum of money. I know he has the cash, but I cannot send my men there because he knows them too well. He will not answer the door when they show up. I don't want to kill him or anything like that. I do want him to pay up, and I thought that since you are here, maybe you can persuade him to pay me. You know, maybe shake his hand with those claws of yours and break a few bones in his hand, that's all. If he sees a big guy like you who he doesn't know, perhaps he will get scared. I'll even give you some of the money he owes me for doing this favor for me. It's not the money; it's the principle of paying your debts. I don't want to look soft in the neighborhood's eyes." Looking at Vincenzo, Mike said, "If my uncle says okay, I will do it for you as a favor." Vincenzo laughed and said, "Consider this a gift from my nephew, not me. But if, as you say, it is not about the money, let him keep half. How much are we talking?" Salvatori replied, "One hundred fifty grand. He can keep fifty g's if he can get all the money today." Vincenzo smiled and said, there you go, Mike, some spending cash for an hour of your time. Go ahead and say hello to this guy, but take a sidearm with you just in case." Mike had no choice but to do what was ordered of him. He left and went with two of Salvatori's henchmen to pay a visit to some guy he did not even know.

Two hours later Mike came back with Salvatori's men and threw one hundred grand down on the table. "You could have told me he was the fuckin' mayor. All he had in cash was this. I saw him open the safe, and that's all he had in there," Mike said in an angry voice. "Did you hurt him?" Salvatori said with a smile as he looked at Vincenzo. "No, I shook his hand hard enough to hear his fingers crack, but I don't think I broke them. He got the message and led me to a room where the safe was. I watched him open it, and this is all he had," Mike said as he looked at Vincenzo dissatisfied with what he was asked to do. Vincenzo reached over and split the money into two portions, one slightly larger than the other. "This is his, and the rest is yours.

There, he proved himself to you. Consider this a favor to be paid back in the future. You didn't tell us he was the mayor, Salvatori. I may have changed my mind on this one," Vincenzo said as he gave Mike the smaller portion of the money. "I'm sorry, to me, he is just another person who borrowed money for his election and had an obligation to pay it back. I didn't plan to send someone he didn't know to collect, but since your man was here, I took advantage of the opportunity. Forgive me. I owe you one, Mike. Anytime you need a favor, come to me," Salvatori said. Both Vincenzo and Salvatori got up from their chairs to say goodbye to each other. "If you are ever in New York, you must come and be my guest," Vincenzo said as they hugged each other and said their goodbyes. "My driver will take you back to the hotel. When are you going back home, Vincenzo?" Salvatori asked. "We were going to stay a few more days, but now I think it best we leave in the morning. I don't want to be involved with your problems. I have my own to deal with," Vincenzo replied. The next morning after breakfast, both Vincenzo and Mike boarded a flight back to New York. "That was very unprofessional of Salvatori, and I will see that he pays back his marker when you need it," Vincenzo said on the plane ride back home. Mike said nothing and just smiled.

By the end of July, Richie came up with 300 hundred grand. The group accepted the offer, and his share was cut to pay the rest of the money he owed. He was instructed by Mike that it was agreed that Richie would buy existing gas stations any way possible, with limits, and that Mike was personally responsible for his actions. Richie received the guidelines and proceeded to start buying existing stations to add to the operation. Some owners he sweet-talked into selling and others he played hardball until they changed their minds and sold out. No one was hurt except a few who were slapped around in an effort to convince them that they should sell. The crew was pulling in close to 250 grand a week thanks to Tony G. He was forcing all his truckers to buy gas at the stations they owned and started a new gas transportation company with the help of Vincenzo's connections. It even made it easy for stolen goods the truckers were carrying to be dropped off at some of the stations and later distributed among the crew and their associates to sell on the street in neighborhoods they controlled. Cash was coming in so fast the fellas had a hard time hiding it or reinvesting it into legit operations. It got so bad; they had to call a sit-down at Money's house to discuss the problem and what to do about it. In the middle of August, they all met and went out on the boat (Liquid Asset) in an effort to keep it private and insure no Feds heard the conversations and plans they were making. Vincenzo brought up something that he and others in the old days did that resolved the problem of turning hard cash into good money. "You know, in the old days, we set up a produce company and funded it with ill-gotten money to buy fresh produce for some produce stores we started. That money was pure profit because we never paid the ill-gotten money back to the lender, which was us, and the produce sold was free. We sold it at a premium using a legit business. We practically doubled our money and had a dozen or so legit business to boot." "Yeah, good idea, but I don't want to be in the produce business," Mike said with a grin. "Maybe we can buy bars and clubs and supply them, and we own them as legit businesses. We do the same thing by funding the money for a fake company to buy beer and soda from direct distributors and deliver them to the clubs and give them the bill of which they don't pay. We sell the stuff, and it costs us nothing, and we get pure profit from the sales. It's the same idea as the produce business, but we move the cash in the beer and soda business. As a benefit to us, we own the clubs and set up member meetings in the clubs. We make the companies show a small profit to the IRS, and we split the cream," Mike said with a big smile. "Oh, that's fuckin' great. Now we make more fuckin' money. How the fuck do we hide that?" Richie said laughing his ass off. Everyone at the table started laughing hysterically. "Oh, such a problem, more cash to hide," Money laughed saying. "Calm down wild man. We use Mike's brother Sal to send it offshore to banks out of the country." Money said looking at both Mike and Richie. "He can do that for a small fee, say, three percent. I'll talk him into it" Mike said. "Others should have such problems like us, so much cash we have to hide it everywhere. My fuckin mattress is already full. My yard is a fuckin' treasure map in my head. Who would have thought the money could cause so much fuckin' trouble," Tony G said laughing his ass off. "Yeah, like fuckin' pirates burying treasure all over the place." Mike said. Vincenzo laughed, and everyone started laughing till they cried. "So is there anything else on the agenda we have to talk about while we are out here in the middle of the bay?" Vincenzo asked after everyone stopped laughing. "Mike, my man Tommy tells me some guys in his precinct, have been talking to some guy named Joey Cardello about cars being shipped out of state. If he starts talking, your name might be mentioned 'cause of the time you were involved at the gas station you sold to your friend Bo. I thought you should know in case it gets too far out of hand, and you get pinched." "Maybe you need to confirm and stop anything from going too far," Eddie said in a concerned voice. Vincenzo stepped in, "Michael, take care of this problem as soon as possible. We don't want prying eyes on us, tu capisce." "I'll fix this problem as soon as we get back to shore. If there is any truth to it, he will disappear, like the others. I will pick his brains about how far this has gone?" Mike said as he looked at Vincenzo and the rest of the crew. "Done" Money replied.

Once back on land, Mike drove to the club looking for Joey to talk to him personally. He was told that Joey was in Jersey at a high stakes poker game the night before and to ask Sammie the butcher for Joey's whereabouts as he would know for sure. After giving it some thought, Mike decided it was easier to get rid of Joey and end the problem before it even started. The fact that Joey's name was already on the Fed's radar meant he already was a problem. Joey was a low-level runner working for another family. Mike wanted his boss to know that a hit was going to happen, so as a courtesy, he let Vito, Joey's captain, know that he was losing a runner. Vito had nothing to say except, "You do what you gotta do, Mike." That night Joey was told of a poker game at the club and was personally invited to play. Joey couldn't resist the offer. Everyone knew he was a compulsive gambler. That's how he got the nickname Joey Cards. Mike arranged for Onions to take care of the hit and gave him ten grand for the job. During the game, Onions came up behind Joey and wrapped a plastic tube around his neck and strangled him to death. The others at the table helped Onions get rid of the body by putting it in his own car trunk and parking it in front of the local police department as a sign that talking to the cops was forbidden, and Joey paid the price. Mike wasn't too happy with the decision Onions made about the body and told him so, but what was done was done. It sent out a warning to others within the families about talking about family business. That weekend at one of the regular meetings Money said, "Jesus, Mike, that was quick. You didn't even meet with Tommy about this problem."

"His name was already known, so he was a problem for all of us. Sooner or later he would have sung, so I did us all a favor by clipping his wings before he could sing," Mike said. "In the old days, that's what we would have done too. Once they know your name, you become a problem to others," Vincenzo said. "This is the life we chose, and punishment is harsh and sometimes swift," Richie said as he looked around the table at the others. "Speaking of problems, I got some IRS guy asking questions at some of our stations about back taxes we owe on this gas thing. Any suggestions?" Richie asked looking at Vincenzo. "I will take care of that problem. A friend of mine works for the local agency in charge of them. I'll ask him to look into it. I am sure he will make this problem go away. He has been on the payroll for years just for shit like this, and he is, as we say, in our pocket and can't get out." "It's nice to have friends in high places, Money said with a smile. "From the president to the street sweepers, Vincenzo knows them all on a personal level," Mike said with a grin. "Oh, I like the president. He's a nice guy. So be careful what you say, Michael," Vincenzo replied with a look of warning on his face. Mike knew what he meant and kept quiet. "Mike, you got any horses lined up for some upcoming races this month?" Tony G asked with a curious look. Vincenzo stepped in, "Michael, you must see our friend in Ocala and get some ponies to race. I like horses, and I like money too. We made out good with that last horse even though the poor bastard died. We need to get back in the game. Go see Lefty and tell him I, Vincenzo, want a fuckin' horse that can win races and not just eat my freaking money. In fact, let's get two horses this time. I'll arrange the meeting and talk to Lefty myself." "I guess I'm going to Florida again. Richie, you wanna go for a couple of days? We can fly to Miami and see if we can find the girls we met at the Boom Boom Club. It will be fun. Come on we both need a break from business for a while," Mike said looking at Richie for an answer. "When do we leave?" Richie said with a smile. "Next week, uncle has to make arrangements for us," Mike said as he looked at Vincenzo. "That's fine. You can both watch each other," Vincenzo said as he got up from the dining room table. "Eddie, stay for a while. I need to talk with you alone about something," Vincenzo said as he escorted the others to the front door. The others left, and Vincenzo sat in the living room and had Money follow him. "Sit, I'll have the girls bring us something to eat. I'm thinking of recommending Mike for his button with the family, and I want your opinion on this matter. Do you think Michael is ready to be my underboss? He's made his bones for this family and others, and he has become a good earner. He is under the Fed radar, and he does as he is told. I think he is ready. What is your take on it?" Vincenzo said as the maid brought over some cheesecake and coffee to the table. "I think he is ready too, but I also think it is for you to decide," Eddie said sipping the hot cup of espresso. "If he is hiding something, he is doing a good job, 'cause he hasn't told me anything I should be concerned about except for this issue with Joey Cards, which he acted on before confirming it was true. Joey was being watched by the local cops for this old car-stealing thing and perhaps whacking him quick was the best move. But parking the body in front of the precinct wasn't the best thing to do. I would have buried the snitch," Eddie said as he spooned in a forkful of cheesecake. "I have no problem with that, and perhaps the others will be more careful from now on and keep their fuckin' mouths shut about what they do," Vincenzo said as he lit a fine cigar while offering one to Money. "Only time will tell if they understand the consequences if they get caught. We have had some significant changes in the organization this past year, and this will reset the rules for everyone involved," Money said as he lit the cigar offered by Vincenzo. "Well, that's what I thought too. It can't hurt to put people back in their place from time to time," Vincenzo said with a smile as he laid back in one of the plush chairs he and Money were sitting on. "Someday I will have to introduce you and Michael to some of our constituents who are on our payroll. Someday I won't be around, and it is critical that you and Michael both know about these things to keep this group going. We have judges, lawyers, politicians and tons of cops and government officials on our payroll. We need to use them from time to time, just like this tax thing I have to take care of. Families have to use all the cards in the deck, including the joker." Vincenzo said. "I understand exactly what you are saying, and whenever you are ready to introduce us, we will be ready, I assure you" Money said finishing his last bite of cheesecake and espresso. "Good, I am glad we had this chat. I will make the arrangements for what we just spoke about. First, Michael has to get us some fast horses we can groom for the big races," Vincenzo said as he stood up from the chair to walk Money to the door. "This conversation is between the two of us for now, tu capisce? I need to talk to the other members before I make a decision, you understand. Even I need approval sometimes." Vincenzo said with a smile as he walked Money out of the front door. "Good night Uncle, see you soon," Money said as he walked to his car.

CHAPTER 10

RISE TO POWER

The following week came, and Mike and Richie flew to Orlando. They rented a car for the drive to Ocala. There they met with Lefty and told him they wanted racehorses and not slackers. Lefty showed them two horses that were his best on the farm. "Let me introduce you to your new horses. This one is Mister Magoo and the one running in the field is called Running Bear." Mister Magoo was a jet-black stallion with a braided long mane. Running Bear was chestnut brown with a diamond crest on his forehead and white socks around his hooves. "They are beautiful horses, but can they run?" Mike asked. Lefty replied, "They don't come cheap boys. These thoroughbreds can run fast, and fast costs money." "So the horse I bought from you last time was a loser?" Mike asked. "No, he was not adequately trained for the Belmont races, which is the best of the best," Lefty said. "If these horses don't win races, we will be back, and not to buy horses, either," Rich said sternly. "Is that a threat?" Lefty said looking at both of them. "He didn't mean it that way. What he meant to say was we and my uncle want horses that can run and sometimes win, that's all," Mike said as he put his arm around Lefty. "Let's talk money. How much for both of them?" Mike asked with a smile. "Well, I'll let you have them for 200 thousand each." "That's too much for horses we have no proof can win. To us they are worth 125K each," Mike said. "I'm not selling you glue horses. If you want them, it cost 300K for both, and that is my final price," Lefty said as he looked at both of them. "Under one condition. I want them fully trained and ready for races at the beginning of August. Deal?" Mike said looking at Lefty as he put out his hand to shake on the deal. "Fine, but only because you are Vincenzo's nephew am I agreeing to this deal," Lefty said shaking Mike's hand. Mike added a little extra pressure on the shake as if to show power without speaking a word. Lefty got the message quickly while pulling out of the Mike's grip. "Good. We are on our way to Miami. Anyone there you want us to say hello to?" Mike asked politely. "Not really. They have problems of their own down there, and I prefer to be out of it," Lefty said. "What kind of problems?" Mike asked. "The Feds are watching them because of that Castro thing they didn't do. Come have lunch and then you can leave," Lefty said as he walked towards the house. After lunch, Mike and Richie decided to drive to Miami and get a room at the Fountain Bleu Hotel. There they stayed for three days, hooked up with several different women during that time and had fun. Mike never found the girls he was looking for and put it in the back of his mind.

When Mike and Richie got back to New York, they were summoned to Vincenzo's summer home upstate. "It seems we have a little problem," Vincenzo said as he sat down on a chair in the back yard. "There is a little war going on in New York. Hugh "Apples" Macomo was ambushed and wounded during this Gallo-Profosso War. Ali Waffa is dead, and Apples is in the hospital. The Commission wants something done. I assured them I would have my boys take care of this problem before it gets out of hand. I want you to form a crew and take out those responsible for wounding Apples and try and stop this bullshit fighting within the family. Waffa was not too bright but he was Galli's right-hand man, and more blood will be spilled if we don't stop it. Even though Apples couldn't become a made guy 'cause he ain't Italian, he's still a successful enforcer for the families and is Carmine's personal bodyguard and respected within the community. You guys need to handle this fuckin' war for both sides to make peace," Vincenzo said slamming his fist on the patio table. "You have my permission, as well as the heads of the other families, to stop this shit before we get more heat on our heads." Mike and Richie looked at each other as if to say, "What the fuck is going on with these fuckin' guys whacking each other?" "Let me make some calls and get my crew together," Richie said. "Mike, you call Salvatori from Miami and tell him he owes me one and I'm calling in my marker. Have him send some outsiders to take out these bastards who shot Apples. Make sure you tell him I am personally requesting this and calling in my marker, plus he owes you one for ruffing up that fuckin' mayor who owed him some money," Vincenzo said with a stern voice. "Get in touch with me after the problem is taken care of. I will be staying here for a conference with some other bosses to discuss matters, not of your concern." Mike and Richie acknowledged Vincenzo's orders and left to drive back to Brooklyn to organize their crews. It took a couple of days for Mike to find out who started the war between families and then called for a meeting at his house with several associates including Money, Tony G, Richie, Tommy (Detective) and other soldiers. He explained to them the story on the street that he heard about the Galli crew and their intent to rub out the Perico faction in an effort to raise Joey to a higher power over his and Carmine's group. "The problem is that they never got approval to go against another family group," Mike said. Mike asked for a vote by all present to attack the Galli group and put them back in line. It was agreed that Joey started without permission, and his crew would be cleaned out or diminished considerably. Between Money, Tommy D, Richie and Tony G, they would split into two groups with Tommy D picking up three of Joey's guys on a false arrest and bringing them to one of Vincenzo's clubs off Coney Island. There several of Money's boys would whack them and bury the bodies in the backyard under the bocce ball court. Richie and Frenchy would gun down two known guys who were involved with the attack on Apples, sending a message by leaving them where they lay dead. Mike would use Salvatori's men from Miami and nab two other soldiers from Joey's group and bring them to an abandoned house off Atlantic Avenue to squeeze more information out of them. Their lives would depend on how much they cooperated with squealing on who else was involved. Mike would be waiting at the abandoned house and ask them questions while being hidden by a wall. His reason was that these two soldiers did not know Salvatori's men and Mike didn't want them to know who he was either.

That weekend the plan was hatched and executed as intended. Mike found out that Joey's men had no choice in the matter, and it was Joey and his brothers who hatched the plan in order to regain territory they had lost the year before that was now in control of the

Perico group. Each group on Mike's side completed their mission, and Mike decided to let one of the soldiers he had in the abandoned house go free after a severe beating. The other one would be whacked in front of the one they let go and dumped in the basement. It was Mike's intent to have the survivor send a verbal message to his group that they should stop the war between family bosses. "If your boss doesn't stop, the Commission has given the OK to eliminate everyone, including your showboat boss," Mike said from a hidden section of the room. "Let him go to tell the others this war is over," Mike said to Salvatori's three gorillas.

Mike thanked Salvatori's guys and handed them five hundred each and told them if he was ever back in Miami; he would look them up and treat them to a night on the town. They acknowledged his offer and were on their way back to Miami. Everything went smoothly, and Mike called Vincenzo the next morning. "That job you gave me was taken care of, and I don't think we will have any more problems with that leak," Mike said in code to Vincenzo on a public phone. Vincenzo thanked Mike for his services and told him he would get back to him if it became a problem again.

The remainder of July 1963 was quiet, and the wars between families had stopped. In August, Mike got word that his horses were ready to be delivered and run the races. He and other members of the crew bet heavy on Mister Magoo, who went off at seven-to-one odds. Mister Magoo performed like a champ and came in first by five furlongs ahead of the crowd. That evening Mike threw a party at Gino's restaurant for several of his constituents, including Money and Tony G. "Mike, I made a small fortune on Mister Magoo. I bet him across the board," Tony G, said raising his glass of wine. "A Saluda," Money said with a smile. "We got us a runner. Now let's see how that other horse does in the upcoming race. He runs in Saratoga next week, and I hope the odds are better than seven-to-one," Mike said looking around the room. "I hear on the street that Johnny Dapper is making a name for himself. They say he has potential as a big earner," Money said as he lit a fat cigar. "That's what I hear," Mike answered. "He is someone to watch in the future so long as he doesn't fuck up," Mike stated while calling Gino for the check. Mike paid for the party and left the girls, including the hostess he had met when he first started visiting Gino's with his cousin Frankie (Ragu), a fist full of cash averaging about two hundred each for five girls. They couldn't thank him enough. Mike was almost like royalty at Gino's, and Mike had a crush on the hostess. She felt the same about him.

Running Bear did run and came in second in the race, but those who were smart played him across the board by placing bets on win, place and show, which was first, second and third place. He went off at high odds of fifteen to one so a ten-dollar bet on second place would yield a return of about thirteen dollars for every dollar placed. Mike won about four grand, and Money won about seven grand. "OK, he didn't come in first, but he has potential. We can rest him a few weeks and run him again," Money said. About the middle of August, Vincenzo returned home and called for a meeting which everyone attended. "First things first. The horse thing was good for some of us, so thanks, Michael, for getting good horses this time. Second, I would like to announce that I and others here have recommended Michael for his official membership into the family working directly under me and my little crew. He answers to me, and the other families understand the position I have assigned to him as a made man. He will work in conjunction with the other family bosses' requests through me, but he is not a boss in any one family. He is a right-hand man to me, the underboss counselor to the families. The promotion will be held next week at the Madison Hotel in Manhattan, and it is invitation only. Of course, all of you are invited, and some other big shots will be there too. There has been only one request by some of my associates; no guns will be permitted to the party. This is to insure that there are no vendettas from the recent wars between Profosso and Galli. Don't worry, there will be plenty of protection at the door and inside the hall where the party is to take place. If you boys are good with the terms, then you are welcome. Let it be known on the streets, of his promotion. Michael will be my underboss." Vincenzo said proudly and commandingly.

The last weekend of August 1963, the promotion took place with the traditional initiation into the family hierarchy, and the party commenced as planned. Mike was introduced to members he did not know and reacquainted with those he did know or met before. No political or government people were invited. Only made men and bosses, with the exception of Mike's closest friends like Tony G and Money, to name a few were present. "Congratulations, cousin, you are now officially Un-De-bozza," Money said as he kissed both cheeks while others stood in line to congratulate Mike on his promotion to underboss and right-hand man to Vincenzo.

A few days later Mike was summoned to Vincenzo's house for a meeting. They went to the back patio outside because Vincenzo was sure his house was bugged. "Michael, there are things you need to know now that you are in a position to run my operations in the event I am no longer here." Mike knew this was going be a long meeting, so he sat back in the chair and lit a cigar while the maid brought out some food for them to enjoy. "Where do I start? So much has gone on in the past few months and more will come in the near future. You need to hear what I am about to tell you 'cause it is the most confidential information you may ever hear about this thing of ours." Mike was ready to absorb the information like a sponge. "I had a meeting a few weeks ago with the heads of the families at my home upstate. As you know, I was there for about three weeks because of business and that war thing with Joey and Apples, which you took care of for us. We thank you for that, but there was more I didn't tell you 'cause we didn't want anyone to know at the time. It seems there was a plot to take out some of the bosses. Joe Colobi told us about this plot by Joey Maglio and another boss to wipe out the other bosses to gain control. We called them to my summer house upstate to answer to these accusations against them, and it was confirmed. Joe Colobi will be taking over the Profaco family business and is now the boss. Maglio and Bonanni are now retiring and no longer part of the family. We decided to spare their lives in return for fines we levied because of their involvement. We will take care of this betrayal sometime in the future but for now, they live, and they're out. It seems that Joey Galli was arrested and is serving time, so he should not be a problem like before. His crew is in hiding and punished till we decide what to do with them. We will wait a while, and you will see that Joe Maglio disappears. Make it look like natural death so we don't get any heat on us. I will let you know where he is when he settles down, and you will take care of it for me." "So you want me to take out Joe Maglio, and what about Bonanni, him too?" Mike asked. "No, I will have the new boss Colobi take care of that one," Vincenzo said. "What else should I know, 'cause I think you have more to tell me, like this Kennedy thing and if it is still on,"

Mike said knowing this was the one job he didn't want to get involved with, nor did Vincenzo.

"Our friend, Kennedy, has turned into a thorn which must be taken care of, and yes, we had a talk about this problem upstate. It's still on, although I am against it. The others want this problem to go away. They have sided with insiders on this one." While talking to Mike, as if what he was about to say was so secret that even the outside might be bugged, Vincenzo leaned forward in his chair, "There is a long story you know nothing about, so I will start from the beginning and tell you why it must be done and why we have to team up on this job." Vincenzo looked sort of sad and let Mike see he was not happy with his crew's involvement and that he had no choice but to do as he was told, even if it was just coordinating it. The families selected Vincenzo to handle the arrangements due to his connections within the government and other associates.

"You know we rigged the votes for him to win. It was because his father was working for us in the old days and he became a powerful man in the political field during the war. We all thought that having a man in the White House, we could do whatever we wanted 'cause we had control of the puppet. Well, as you know, he was seeing one of the bosses' girlfriends and then he got involved with Marilyn and some other girls. We knew this was his Achilles heel, so we set him up with anyone he wanted. He was still pissed with the Cuban fuck up that the CIA started. He didn't approve it, but they insisted it would work, so he followed their recommendations. Well, everyone knows what happened there. Castro knew that America and the powerful wanted him dead. So did some of our Miami friends, 'cause they lost everything in the casinos and hotels when Castro threw them out of Cuba. They even came to us for help. You remember the poison plot we were involved with? Well, that was only one of many times they came to us for help. We all thought it was a good relationship until his little fuckin' brother was promoted to Attorney General and started coming down hard on us. Our first intent was to whack him, and it would stop, but then his brother and all his men would come down even harder on us. So we decided to cut the head off the snake and watch the rest of the body die off. We all voted on it. You know my position on this, but they overrode me. Jack made many enemies on all sides, starting with disbanding the CIA 'cause of the embarrassment of the Bay of Pigs fiasco. He vowed never to take the CIA's guidance again. Then there was this girl thing with Sam in Chicago, and that made Sam want him dead for betraying his honor. There are the bankers who are afraid that he is going to change the money system, 'cause the Federal Reserve is not controlled by our government. They don't want him to change the money to what was once backed by silver reserves. In fact, he has already told the Federal Bankers that he intends to abolish their control over America's currency control, by implementing a new the United States backed currency system. Add to that the Russians who would be happy if he was dead 'cause of the ongoing struggle for dominant power of the world. Now we got this Vietnam thing starting, and Jack wants no part of it. But his generals want all in 'cause that's what they live for. War makes money and generals love real war games. So we have the Cubans, Russians, Federal Reserve, CIA, Sam from Chicago and the Florida bosses who all despise him, not counting everyone else like the Teamsters union and many others. So you now see the big picture as who wants him out and why" Vincenzo said.

Mike looked stunned upon hearing how many wanted Jack out of his position. "We can't just pull him out of office, and if we whack his brother, we will all pay the price from the top down. The sad part is I like the son of a bitch, and I don't know why. His brother is the problem for us, not Jack himself. I would rather whack Bobby and see what happens later, but that won't happen," Vincenzo said moving his chair to get more comfortable from the glare of the sun." "Well, it seems we have more problems than I thought. Now I know why he is a marked man," Mike said. "Where do I come in on this and what do you want me to do?" Mike asked Vincenzo now knowing he was in as deep as anyone else involved with no way out. "You must go to Hollywood again to see Johnny (Pretty Boy). He is our connection with the insiders, and they are organizing the hit soon, I think, so you leave this Thursday. Arrangements have been made for you to discuss the deal with Johnny." Vincenzo handed Mike an envelope with money, airline tickets and instructions of where and when the meeting would take place. "When you learn about the details, you will come directly back to me. We will discuss more of the details, and I will share with you more of our business and friends who are on our side," Vincenzo said as he hugged Mike and walked him to his car.

"Perhaps you should consider getting yourself a driver and a bigger car now that you're a boss. You never know when someone may want to hurt you. I wouldn't want to lose you so soon," Vincenzo sad jokingly. "I will have to think about that while I am on this little vacation of mine," Mike replied with a smile. Vincenzo waved goodbye as Mike drove out of the circular driveway.

Thursday afternoon Mike landed in Hollywood and was met with a limo and two girls. The limo was there to drive Mike straight to a club where Pretty Boy was waiting. On the half hour ride, Mike took advantage of the two young ladies in any way he wanted. For that half hour, they were his sex slaves in every way. Mike's thoughts were, *Ah if every meeting went this way, I would be a happy fella.* The car arrived at the Copa Caribe Club and pulled around back. Although Mike was finishing up with the little slaves he had for a while, he had his eyes on the drive and the back alley the driver was taking. Just in case, Mike had his hand on his piece watching carefully. The driver opened the limo door and then the back door to the club. Mike told him to go in first and followed. Once inside Pretty Boy greeted Mike and introduced himself. Mike's first impression was, Pretty Boy was as the name implied. He was a beautiful looking man, well built, clean dressed, and had almost pure white hair with a California tan. "Mike, I've been expecting you, come in." "I was told to see you, and you would fill me in on this upcoming thing," Mike said while they walked to a staging area. "Yeah, I have some updates on that question and will discuss it with you over dinner at a party being held which I am inviting you to," Pretty Boy said smiling. "Who's party?" Mike asked. "Can't tell you that. It would ruin the surprise," Johnny said as they sat down. "Mike, what I can tell you now is that someone from the inside is working on getting Jack to go to Texas to stir up some votes and some others are making connections with guys they can use for this operation. Our job is to eliminate the shooter they have lined up for the hit. As far as I know there is only one right now, maybe two. This is going to be a lot harder with the only one back shooter, Jimmy (Bang Bang) Blanks, but he has to know where they will be if it's two shooters," Johnny told Mike. "More, later. For now, you're my guest. The driver is waiting. He will take you to the hotel where you can do whatever. I'll have someone pick you up around seven." They shook hands and Mike went to the car. The girls were still there waiting. The driver drove him to The Roosevelt Hotel on Hollywood Boulevard. Mike asked the girls if they would like to come up with him and they replied, "Sure. You're not gonna hurt us, right?" Mike laughed and replied, "Maybe spank you, that's all, and then I'll buy you girls some candy." One girl's quick response was, "Yeah, diamonds are my kind of candy." Mike's response was also quick;" I'll have to spank you a little harder for that." They all smiled and took the elevator up to a huge suite where Mike took off his jacket and poured a couple of drinks. "OK, I have about four hours to play doctor with you girls, and then you have to leave. I'll see you again tomorrow morning, the same place, say ten-ish." They undressed and proceeded to have wild sex with Mike on the couch as the radio was playing oldies rather loudly.

Around six, the girls left and promised to return for their candy the following day. Mike got dressed and went down to find the limo driver waiting at the front entrance. The driver drove to the back lot of Century Studios and pulled up to a massive double door. Mike was met by some people outside with a list of names of who to allow in the building. Mike's name was not on the list, so he told one of the men to go inside and find Johnny Rossilo and ask him to come outside. After a while, Mike was greeted by Johnny and told that he forgot to add his name and escorted Mike into the building.

To Mike's surprise, he was at a private party for the movie Cleopatra starring, Elizabeth Taylor, Richard Burton, and Rex Harrison, to name a few, who were all there and mingling with other actors. Johnny introduced Mike to dozens of actors as a good friend from New York here on business. Many were awed when they shook Mike's hand. Burton said, "Is that a deformity of some sort? I mean, your hands are twice the size of mine." Mike smiled and said, "No, I just work out a lot." Someone else Mike was introduced to said, "Your pinky is the size of my thumb. What size is your pinky ring, may I ask?" "Size fourteen, I think" Mike replied. Johnny told Mike to mingle, and he would be back in a while to see how he was doing. Mike felt out of place and sat at one of the many tables arranged like at a wedding. Mike knew only a few of the faces that he had seen on film, but most of the people he didn't know. Two hours passed, and Johnny came over to the table where Mike was sitting alone, and sat next to him closely. "I thought it would be better to talk to you here, so no one is listening, like the Feds. It's noisy, and this is a private party, so it's good to have our conversations here," Johnny said. "Other than a few faces, I don't know anyone here" Mike replied. "What I'm about to tell you goes straight to Vincenzo and the committee and no one else tu capisce?" Johnny said in a whisper. "Just tell me what the fuck is going on, and I will pass it on to those who need to know," Mike replied. "Fine. It seems that an insider will get the Pres' to go to Dallas to rally votes for his re-election. That is where we want Jimmy (Bang Bang) waiting for his orders. As of yet we don't know where the hit will be, but it will be in Dallas. The Feds have a guy they are using as the primary shooter. I only know he is ex-CIA and has a shady past with Russia and Cuba. They are using him 'cause he's a sharpshooter and expendable. I guess the disguise is that a radical loner will be the patsy, and no one is the wiser. Our job is to have Jimmy whack this shooter after he shoots the President, so he can't say anything to anyone. This should get Bobby to stop. That's what I know at this time, and I will get more as it draws closer to the time in Dallas, which I believe is soon, before Christmas," Johnny said to Mike at the table. "So everything is on, and it will be in a few months from now. How does this shooter fella fit in with us?" Mike asked. "He was recruited by the Orleans boss through a Dallas connection who set up the meeting. From what I know, he has been prepped for the job and thinks the CIA is calling the hit along with some insiders. My thought is he is a sympathizer for Cuba, and he is being well rewarded for whacking Jack and intends to leave the country after the hit," Johnny said. "Now I can't be too sure. He thinks he is working for the CIA, and that they will give him protection out of the state." "I fuckin' hate this whole thing. Everything can go wrong. Then we have the Feds and everyone and their mother after us. That's what I think," Mike said disgusted to be a part of this undertaking. "Look, I know that Hoppa and the Florida boys want Jack dead, as well as so many others, and yes, we are in bed with the Feds due to that Castro thing. The fact is, we are in so deep, we have to finish the job. I don't like it either, but Bobby is throwing heat on us, and Jack isn't stopping it. So what else can we do except get involved and end this problem of ours?" Johnny said. "Yeah, I guess you're right, but I still don't like it," Mike replied. "So, we done here? I have some ladies waiting for me in the room and want to enjoy my stay while I am here," Mike said to Johnny. "My driver is outside. Tell him to bring you back to the hotel. I will be in touch with you later, Mike." Mike waited two days for Johnny to get in contact with him, but Johnny never called to give him additional information, so Mike boarded a plane for New York.

After reaching New York, Mike set up a meeting with Vincenzo at the Bayshore Diner to fill him in on the recent meeting with Johnny and to discuss their next move concerning the matter. Vincenzo informed the others of the upcoming job and told Mike he had to go back to Orleans and meet with some people to discuss the matter in detail. He was also told that one of the insiders would be there too. Although Mike was not happy about blowing his cover to this government official, he had no choice and accepted the orders. In the middle of September, 63, Mike found himself in New Orleans meeting with Bang Bang, Tony Marcelli, Mr. Jones, who was the insider, and several other people he did not know. He was very careful not to reveal too much about himself or Vincenzo's involvement in the mission and mostly listened to others at the private meeting discussing the facts and plans to complete the task at hand. Mike did speak up several times concerning the locations and where Jimmy should be during the time it was to happen. "We have only one shooter who is involved, and he is a sympathizer, as well as a rebel, who will be doing the shooting. Others are planning the route the motorcade will be taking. I will let Johnny know the time and place as soon as I get the info," Mr. Jones said. "So one shooter in Dallas and we don't know the rest?" Mike asked Mr. Jones. "Correct, there will be a fundraiser after he travels a specified route, being planned by secret service, and the time and dates have not been set." Mr. Jones said. "I hate the whole fuckin' thing, but I will let the others know where we stand. I wish there was another way to do this job and not have us involved," Mike said openly to the table. "Look, Mike, this is a painful thorn in our side, and we have to get rid of the problem. If you have another way to stop it, we are listening," Tony Marcelli said leaning forward in his chair. "Yeah, we could poison him like those stupid fucks wanted us to do to Castro," Mike said looking at Mr. Jones. "All his food is tasted beforehand so that won't work, and Castro fucked you guys in Cuba. That's why we asked if you wanted revenge and offered the job, which never happened," Mr. Jones replied angrily to Mike. Tempers flared, and the meeting was ended. Mike was not happy and let it be known at the table. He went back home to Brooklyn still digesting the information he received from Orleans. He let Vincenzo know his real thoughts about the involvement they were both getting into concerning this complicated job. Vincenzo told Mike that he would personally try to persuade the others to back out or find a different way to whack the Kennedys. Mike felt relaxed that Vincenzo would try to do something different without the involvement of government people, but deep down Vincenzo knew it was like attempting to baptize a cat in holy water. The Feds were already involved as deep as the Mob. It was a ploy to calm Mike down and stop him from getting upset over the orders and to focus on something else instead. For Mike, it worked, and he was a bit calmer.

The end of September was hectic for many of the family bosses. There was a lot of struggles for power starting up against different groups fighting for power positions and more stolen property coming out of New York Airport and the garment district. Mike's cousin Money was also involved in a power struggle in the Gambono family. Some wanted revenge for his involvement in the Profosso wars that took place several months before. While sitting at a diner on Crossbay Boulevard with some of his associates, Money was shot by other members of his own family, betrayed from within. Two of his associates were killed in an attempt to protect Money from the gunfire coming through the window where they were sitting. Money survived the incident and wanted revenge. Mike was told to stay quiet and not get involved for a while, even though he saw Money in the hospital and wanted immediate revenge for the shooting.

After getting out of the hospital, Money wanted his own revenge and received approval from his boss. This started another war among the Gambono family leaders. After some snooping around, it turned out that one of Money's own right-hand men had started the fight first. When Money learned that Frenchy was the instigator, he summoned his men to take Frenchy to the Butcher (Albert Dicolo)) and torture him before chopping him up and disposing of his remains in Sheepshead Bay by offering the boaters free chum for deep sea fishing, which they took enthusiastically. Now that Frenchy was gone, he had the others shot on sight wherever they were found. There was a total of eight guys, counting Frenchy, who were involved and now gone. Money told Mike about the incident during one of their weekend outings on the Liquid Assets. "Imagine these fucks wanted me dead for this fuckin' job they were told to do, and it was not even sanctioned by me. It was the Boss himself calling the shots to have Galli's crew dismantled and stopped." With the help of Mike and his crew, it was confirmed that Money's own man was the instigator of the attack. It turned out that Frenchy's brother-in-law was one of the guys working for the Galli boys, and he was whacked along with the others. "That's why this fuck wanted me out of the picture. Fuck him and his brother-in-law. Now he sleeps with the fish," Money said angrily to Mike. "He got what he deserved. I hope there are no more attacks on you. Watch your back," Mike replied as they drove back to the dock.

CHAPTER 11

CLEANING HOUSE

Vincenzo called for a special meeting to be held concerning this and other matters that were happening during the same time in September 1963. It was mandatory that everyone attend. Mike arrived first and met with Vincenzo in the back yard. "Mike, we got a problem with Joey "Cargo" Valachi. He is about to sing to the Feds about our business. I have to set up a special meeting with the other bosses to decide what needs to be done. You know he is very involved with our business and knows too much of what we do. This is a big problem for us," Vincenzo said privately to Mike before the others came to the meeting. "What we gonna do about it? You want him whacked?" Mike asked. "No, I gotta get permission first. You just can't go whacking guys anytime you want, especially a boss," Vincenzo answered. "Besides, the stupid fuck is in jail, so whacking him isn't gonna be easy. We have to sit on this one for a while and see if he turns," Vincenzo said. "Does he know anything about this Kennedy thing?" Mike asked. "Not that I am aware of, and that's the problem" Vincenzo replied. With that, some of the others showed up, and the meeting between Mike and Vincenzo ended for now.

"I called this meeting so we can set our house in order. We are scattered all over the place with all this business we got going on and need to restructure it. You agree?" Vincenzo asked the men sitting around the large table. "So what do you want to do, boss?" Richie asked first. "This is what I think we should do," Vincenzo said to the group. "Each captain has to be responsible for his operation of business. First we start with the horses. The corporation is our cover for this. I say we have Mike take care of this one, since he was most involved with the rigging of the tracks and buying the horses, not to mention his brother paying off on the insurance claims we made on that first horse," Vincenzo said, looking to all for approval. "Second, we have Richie take care of the gas deal, control the flow of money and deal with the tax collectors. He is to split the profits with the original investors and take his share," Vincenzo said looking at Richie. "Eddie takes care of the loan sharking, and the clubs getting the beer and soda from our suppliers and splits the proceeds with us. Tony takes control of the docks, the trucking industry and the flow of high jacking so that all of us get first dibs on the goods and the money made is distributed evenly. Now, I have something else I think we should get involved with 'cause it can make additional money for us all," Vincenzo said with a smile. "Fat Andy Ferrara (aka Animal) wants to join our crew. He is unhappy with his boss and has asked permission to switch. He has to pay a fee of ten percent of his take to his boss. Some of us know he is an earner in the sports business. We take a vote. All in favor?" Vincenzo said as he raised his hand. Everyone raised their hand in support except for Tony. "I think we could have a problem with him." "Why?" Richie asked. "He's a showoff, and he's got a big ego to match his size," Tony said. "Let me worry about that, Vincenzo said. "I'll have a talk with him and explain how we stay under the radar by keeping quiet about our business ventures. Besides, he only gets a share of his earnings and none of our existing business," Vincenzo said looking Tony in the eyes. "I still don't like it, but okay, if you say so. I still think he's a Jamook," Tony replied. "You're entitled to your opinion. Col tempo la foglia di gelso diventa seta, (Italian phrase that means "Time and patience change the mulberry leaf to satin)," Mike replied. "I think he's a standup guy," Eddie said in response to Mike's answer. "Good. So it is settled. We are now in the sports business," Vincenzo said. "I'll give you all a tip, a gift from Fat Andy, so to say, bet on this colored boxer called Cassius Clay 'cause he's fixed to win this upcoming fight. That comes straight from the horse's mouth. There, you got your first of many fixed fights, compliments of Animal," Vincenzo said. "And if he doesn't win, we got permission to kick the shit out of Animal, right?" Tony asked. "Yeah, that's fair. I take his word for it, so I'll bet ten large on Clay to win. If he loses, you guys can kick both their asses," Vincenzo said laughing. "What else?" Mike asked looking at Vincenzo and the others. "Wow, you got some place to go? Relax. For the first time in a while, we're all here together. Don't be a mama-luke, Eddie said with a smile, addressing Mike. "Well, boys, I have to go to Italy, the old neighborhood, for a few days on business. It seems there is some in-fighting over there as well, and they have asked for my assistance in the matter. It's a territory dispute, I think, so I leave in two days," Vincenzo said looking around the table. "State attenti, guardate dove mettete i piedi" (Be careful and watch your step) Mike said to Vincenzo. "I will, while I am gone, Michael is in control on my behalf. Tu capisce?" Vincenzo told the crew. All agreed, and Vincenzo stood up saying "Let's go inside. The girls made a beautiful table for us. Non c'è fretta, mangiamo poi ne parliamo. (No rush, let's eat, then talk.) The rest of the day ended with laughter and joking about old times and the things they did as kids. It was more a time to reminisce and jokes without a conversation about business. After a few hours, they all said their goodbyes and went their separate ways. Mike told Vincenzo he would like to sit down and talk about the thing with Kennedy after he gets back home from Italy. Vincenzo agreed and kissed his cheek as he walked Mike to the front door.

Vincenzo went to Italy and assisted in fixing the territory dispute between the families. Some of the instigators were dealt with in the Mob tradition. For his reward, he received a plot of property with a five bedroom house on it. One of the family's way of thanking him for ending a yearlong dispute and stopping an internal war which attracted the local police and some government officials who Vincenzo negotiated with on the family's behalf.

During the time Vincenzo was in Italy, Mike and the boys did business as usual, with the exception of Richie, who was getting somewhat out of control with a local sports bookie to whom he owed money and refused to pay. Mike asked Andy (Animal) to smooth over the problem, but Animal sided with the bookie. "Mike, he bets on fuckin' losers, and he owes the money. What the fuck am I supposed to do, forgive him? I do that, and everybody thinks they got a free ride. That's not fair to me or Marty the bookie. I think he has to pay his dues like everyone else." "You're right, Animal. I will talk to Richie and let him know that part of his money from the gas thing is going to pay back the bookie. I'll also tell him to stop betting on losers too," Mike said with a guttural laugh. "Oh, he won't be happy with that, Mike," Animal said laughing too. "Yeah, well he ain't special, and he wants to play so he has to pay, right?" Mike replied. Animal thanked Mike for handling the problem. After Mike had spoken to Richie at the local club, it was agreed that Richie had to pay up, and Mike negotiated a better payoff price for what Richie owed.

By the second week of September, Mike finally met with Vincenzo at his home. Vincenzo was happy to see Mike and asked if everything went well while he was away. Mike replied that all was fine, but he wanted to meet with Vincenzo to talk about the Kennedy thing. He had some reservations on the part of the families getting involved. Vincenzo agreed, and they set up a meeting with some of the local bosses who were involved with the job. It was to be held at Carlucci's Italian Restaurant on Eastern Parkway in Brownsville, Brooklyn on Saturday night. Saturday night came, and everyone showed up with their bodyguards, just in case. Vincenzo opened the meeting by apologizing for such short notice and reintroduced Mike to the men who were in attendance, which numbered about twelve high-ranking bosses. To the surprise of many, the bosses from Chicago, New Orleans, and Miami were also in attendance. Some were not happy with a surprise meeting on such short notice but were eased by Vincenzo's apologies.

Vincenzo stood up from the long table and spoke. "Gentleman, most of you know Michael is a close family member of mine, and I trust him with my life. As some of you may know, he has been our voice concerning this Kennedy matter in which we are all in agreement. However, it has been brought to my attention that we may have to reconsider our involvement with those we have on our payrolls and our associations within the political world. Now, we don't know who knows what outside of this family's involvement. I am sure that some people in government power are very much informed and making their own plans concerning Jack and his brother Bobby. We all want this problem to go away, but my nephew Michael has told me things that may interest you, so that is why I have requested this meeting, on short notice." Vincenzo looked around the room for reactions and facial expressions from those seated. "With that said, I will ask Michael to state his case to the members of this family of ours." Vincenzo gestured with his hands to Michael to stand and speak.

Mike stood up and walked to the end of the long table so that all could see him. After thanking his uncle for his introduction to the men at the table, Mike spoke to the group. Some was spoken in Italian, but most of it was in English "With our desire to remove the Kennedy boys from office, after meeting with some of those involved, my feeling on this matter is that it may not be in our best interest to get involved. Let me explain why. When I was sent to New Orleans, I met with some guy name Jimmy Blanks. Some of you from there may know him by Bang Bang. He spoke to my uncle and agreed to do his part for partial payment now and the rest later after his job is done. Now, only a very few know his background and what he is connected with in the outside world. I don't question the choice made by a member at this table, however, the people he introduced me to were different. Not only did they look strange, but they acted strangely too. For instance, there was this guy by the name of Clay Bertrel, who almost admitted he's a government agent but is also a fag with this white bleached blonde spiky hair. Something about him leaves an uneasy feeling in a man's gut. I did a little checking up on him and found out he owns an exporting company that moves government contracts out to different parts of the world. The company may be a front. He talked about wanting Jack dead because of his business. He mentioned that wars mean money. He is also supplying guns for CIA operations in different countries through his exporting business. He is either an agent or supply man for the CIA.

There were these two other guys, Guy Bantel, and Dave Perry. It turns out that this Guy person is a private eye and ex-CIA. He's the person responsible for testing this Oswald person and getting the things he needs. Oswald is the one that Jimmy Bang Bang is supposed to whack after he shoots Jack. From what has been in the news recently, we now know that Kennedy is going to Texas on November 22. That's only two months from now. This other whacko, Dave Perry, whom I call Baldy, 'cause he has the worst-looking toupee on earth and eyebrows as wide as a paint brush, was working on some government job training Cubans for another attempt to whack Castro in South Miami. I think the project is called Mongoose. I am sure that Florida can check into that and see if Kennedy broke it up and, in turn, pissed off a lot of Army guys in charge, including the CIA boys. Now that you all know who the players are, I ask that we pool our resources together and investigate these guys we are involved with and what they gain from it if Jack is dead. I said before that war means money and they have decided to start a war from within by killing Kennedy and getting the war they want with the Vietnam thing or the Russians or even Cuba. They want to blame it on Cuba so we can go to war and take it over. Gentlemen, this is all about power and wars that we are not a part of and never have been in the past. They want us to whack the shooter, but they don't say if it is one or two or three shooters. By us shooting this Oswald guy, we kill our only out of being involved with Kennedy's death. Oswald can't talk if he's dead. What if the other guys are setting us up to take the fall by implicating us as being the shooter 'cause this Oswald guy was working for us indirectly through our Orleans or Texas connections or for the CIA or FBI? My gut is telling me there is something fishy about working with these government guys. They have always been our enemy, and they always will be. So why are we working with them to get rid of a problem they are going to take care of anyway? Should we play into their game or set them up to take the fall instead of us? God knows who else wants Jack dead? Take your pick, military, CIA, FBI, Federal Reserve, Castro and Russia. I say, if the government boys are going along with whacking Kennedy, why should we get caught in the middle of it? If we play a part in whacking the one shooter they say is so good with a rifle, no one else will get blamed except us. They have the resources to do anything they choose, and if they blame us, or Bang Bang gets caught, the people will want justice, and we'll be the target, gentlemen. I say let them shoot Kennedy. We tell Jimmy not to shoot, keep the money he got so long as he keeps his mouth shut. If he talks, we eliminate his entire bloodline. I will personally crush his head like a grape if he backs out. The architect expects him to show up as our part of the agreement, so we let him show up."

Martelli from New Orleans asked Mike, "Are you telling me that these guys who were at the meeting between you and Jimmy are agents of some sort?" "Exactly. They are working with or for the agency. Three of the guys at the table were from different interests, but working with the government, and now they know we are involved too. Ask yourself why they were there in the first place? Why did

Jimmy introduce me to them when he thought he was working for us directly? Is he working both sides?" Mike replied. "Perhaps you're right, Michael. Maybe we haven't looked into this person or the others, but I assure you, I will have my people look into it real hard. If what you say is true, then we must do something about it and have a vote before this November, 22 date comes around," Chicago boss Samatoro said looking directly at the Orleans boss and others at the table. "Martelli, how did you get this guy Jimmy?" Vincenzo asked "He was recommended by the PI Guy. Now I'm having second thoughts. Maybe we should whack Jimmy and get another shooter," Martelli replied. "Is anyone else going to look into what Michael has said here besides Chicago and my assets in Miami?" Salvatori said. Several nodded their heads in agreement and disgust but agreed to look into getting more information from their sources in order to make their vote in a meeting in the near future. "Michael, you have given all of us a lot of stuff to digest. We have to decide whether we sleep with these bitches or kick them out of our bed," Santo from Miami said, as he noticed some members agreeing with him. As he stood up from his chair, Vincenzo said, "I will have some of our government pockets look into these characters and pull out some of their dirty laundry to see who they are. Some of you know that I am not comfortable with the decision that was made concerning the Kennedy boys at one of our last meetings. However, my loyalty is with the strength and protection of our families. I think we need to look into the connections between us and the company we keep. Perhaps it is time to clean house and sever ties with those who intend to harm us," Raising his glass of wine, Santo said, "Abbastanza affair, oi siamo qui, quindi godiamoci" (enough business, we're here so let's enjoy). Carlo Gambono from New York, raising another glass of vino said, "Un saluto, as he sipped the glass of wine staring right at Mike. The crowd after a few more drinks went off into little corners to discuss the conversations and make connections with each other's assets in their territories. For all intent and purposes, the heart of the meeting was over, and the other members of the group watching the doors and front entrances were called into the room to eat, drink and mingle amongst the crowd Mike and Vincenzo were driven home by Vincenzo's driver Alberto Pachelli, who had been Vincenzo's personal driver for some twenty years and was about sixty years old. Vincenzo and Mike talked all the way home about the meeting and their part in finding out who the men at the Orleans meeting were working for and why.

The middle of September came and went. It was October before Mike was called to Vincenzo's home to answer some questions the Commission had concerning their investigation. "Michael, my boy, it seems you were right about this Jimmy Blanks person. Our friends have informed us that he may be working with the Feds through the P.I. We told Martelli to take care of the problem in Orleans and substitute someone else to take his place, someone that is with us. This way we are sure it stays in-house. Martelli will be punished for his fuck up at a later time, but for now, Jimmy has to go. Now, I need you and Johnny (Pretty Boy) to meet with a man who will be the contact person in Texas when the time comes. He's the one who will tell us where and when, as well as where the shooter will be. Meet Johnny in Hollywood this Saturday and he will fill you in on the rest. Here are your airline tickets and an address. A car will pick you up at the airport," Vincenzo said while handing Mike his tickets. Mike wasn't happy about such immediate notice but agreed to the arrangements and took the tickets. "Any other surprises?" Mike asked with an unhappy grin of disgust on his face. "You're doing this for the family, so get the fuck over it, Mike," Vincenzo replied knowing Mike was not happy with his orders. "I'll make sure Johnny shows you a good time in Tinsel Town. Some broads and excellent food should make it all better," Vincenzo said laughingly knowing it would break the ice and put a smile on Mike's face. "Oh, that makes it all better. Eat, fuck and sleep, and then I'm out of there, right?" Mike replied as he stood up from the kitchen chair. "Mike, in a couple months this will be all over, and we can go back to business as usual, and I promise you will be rewarded handsomely for what you are doing for us," Vincenzo said walking Mike to the front door.

CHAPTER 12

KEEP IT QUIET

October was already getting cold in New York, and on Saturday morning, Mike boarded the plane for Hollywood. Once in Hollywood, he met at a secluded house with Johnny, and a Mr. Simons, who Mike assumed, was the inside government man. There Johnny brought Mike up to date on what was going on with the Kennedy problem. Mr. Simons told Johnny and Mike about the plans they already had in place for the Dallas shooting. "We have a safe house for the shooter. He has been briefed on his particular assignment and staging location the day the motorcade goes through the town. We'll also have spotters in various places in the event something changes at the last minute. We've arranged for most of the President's security to be out of town that week, so protection will be light. I will give Johnny specific instructions two days before the event as to where to set up your counter shooter. We are still staging the location at this time to make sure he gets off a good shot. We're thinking of putting your shooter on the roof of the Tec building, so he has a clean shot and a bird's eye view of the route. Local PD are not involved, so your guy is on his own with them. We have already provided the rifle through a mail-order firm for our shooter because we did not want to have a gun dealer in Dallas ID the buyer. If your shooter needs a weapon, we can provide it. Just make sure he doesn't buy one in Dallas. Other than that, I think we are all set. Any questions?" Mr. Simon asked Johnny and Mike. Johnny looked at Mike for his opinion. Mike, rubbing his chin, asked, "How many shooters will you have on site? This shooter you have, is he this Oswald person I heard of and is he working for you or with you?" Mr. Simon replied, "Now, you know I'm not going to say whether or not he works for us or with us. All I'll say is, right now we have only one shooter in place." Mike was not satisfied with the answers he was getting and became aggravated by Mr. Simon's blunt responses. His temper and demeanor were changing fast. "If this goes wrong and we get pinned for the shooting of a President, I will see that you and those involved never live to see another day even if you are a government agent. We will track you down. You understand!" Mike barked. Mr. Simon's shook his head saying, "Are we done? I have other things to do besides talking to a couple of thugs." At that point, Mike had enough. "Fuck you, you piece of shit. If we weren't in a public place, I'd put a fuckin' bullet in your fuckin' head right now you fuckin' cunt." Mike stood up pushing the chair half way across the room, ready to kill anything that got in his way. "Johnny, I have to talk with the others about this arrangement for their approval. You keep in close touch with this piece of shit, and let me or the others know about any changes before innocent people get hurt because somebody fucked this one up," Mike said as he turned around and left the room. "I guess I pissed him off," Mr. Simon said looking at Johnny. "Wrong person to piss off like that, my friend. He would relish killing you with his bare hands. Try and stay away from now on Okay" Johnny replied.

Johnny had additional conversations with Mr. Simons and then went to meet Mike outside on the porch where Mike was sitting smoking his cigar. "I'm not satisfied with this operation. Something isn't right. I don't think he's giving us all the information about this. One shooter and they are telling us where to be on some fuckin' building. Something isn't right, and I can't put my finger on it, Johnny," Mike said disgustedly. Johnny asked, "What do you think we should do, Mike?" "How the fuck should I know? I'm just a messenger boy, just like you," Mike replied. "I guess you heard that the Orleans thing is being looked into, and we sent a message to Martelli to take care of Jimmy Blanks 'cause he's working both sides of the fence on this one. Martelli says he needs bait for his shrimping business, and Jimmy looks like the catch of the day," Mike said with a grin on his face. "Glad I'm not Jimmy," Johnny said with a smile. "Mike, I have to go to Miami for a meeting of some sort. Not sure if it involves this matter or something else. Wanna come with me?" Johnny asked. "No, thanks, had my fill of Florida for right now, Johnny. Maybe next time," Mike replied. Now that business was over, Mike and Johnny went out on the town for some food and fun. Johnny knew everybody in Tinsel town and introduced Mike to some of his best hideouts.

The next day, Mike was on a plane back to New York to deliver the message. When Mike got back, he was surprised to hear that in the short time he was gone, the shit was hitting the fan. Seeing Money, he was informed that one of the bosses in NY was plotting with a capo of another family to take over the alcohol delivery of some of their bars and clubs in NY. Vincenzo had to put a stop to it. They were called by the Commission to explain their actions for stepping into another family's turf and strong-arming the businesses to buy from them. They were both fined and put on notice that there would be no next time. In the meantime, they were also finding out that Joe Vallachi was going to testify before Congress about the inner workings of the Mob. It seems that Joe wanted a pardon or lighter sentence if he ratted out the organization and how it operates. Around the same time, BMC (Bally Company) was acquired by Mr. Stien with the understanding that all pinball, vending and slot machines would be under the family control and used exclusively throughout family establishments in all districts. In return, they would receive a cut of the take. This included all of Vincenzo's and his crew's holdings of clubs and establishments.

Mike went to see Vincenzo the week he came back to inform him of the meeting he had with Johnny and Mr. Simons. Vincenzo told Mike he would get back to him at a later date because he had to have a sit-down with the others concerning the matter. Mike left, and for the rest of the week, he spent time with his family, including his mother and brothers. It had been a long time since they all got together and enjoyed each other's company. During conversations with his brother Harry, he was told that something was going on at the base where he was located, and they were doing an inventory of everything they had, including building up for something big, like a war was coming. Harry said it was hard to get stuff out, and he had to stop. While this was going on, Mike agreed that Harry should lay low and wondered if it had anything to do with Vietnam and Kennedy not being able to control or stop it. "It seems to me that you guys are going to war soon," Mike said to his brother. "You know something I don't?" Harry asked. "Do you think if Johnson was president, he would let the dogs bite in this Vietnam thing?" Mike asked Harry. "Not sure," Harry replied. At the same time, Jimmy walked over and asked what the conversation was about, and Mike asked him the same question about the Vietnam War. "Don't know about no war, but I can tell you we are getting a shitload of boats lining up at the docks to unload all kinds of shit," Jimmy said to his brothers. "Well, something is going on," Mike replied to both of them. Mike and his family enjoyed the get-together that day and Mike rested the rest of that week.

It was the third week of October. Money called Mike and asked him to come over as soon as possible. He had to talk to him and some others concerning a personal matter. Mike drove over to see him and was told to meet Money in the backyard, whereupon he saw several of Money's crew sitting around the patio table chatting. "What's up, cuz?" Mike asked. "Mike, you know the boys so no introductions are needed. I'll make this short. A while ago I made an investment with that fuck Joey Magi. He's now the boss of the Profosso family. Well, it seems he double-crossed me and is not paying me back my investment. 'Cause he's now a boss, I have to get approval to do anything, and you know that isn't happening," Money said to Mike. "How much are we talkin here?" Mike asked. "Half a million to buy in on a lucrative business in the window installations on the city projects," Money replied. "Wow, that's a lotta schadaul," Mike said. "Yeah, and I would be happy if I just get the investment back at this point." "Does the old man know about this?" Mike asked. "He said it's my own problem. I should have been more careful about dealing outside our turf, and there was nothing he could do," Money answered. "Let me see what I can do for you. Maybe he can retire early after that deal with setting up a hit on some bosses some time ago. You know he had to pay a fine and Carlo still wants revenge. Maybe we can get the blessings to pay back the fuck, and you get part of his operations as your compensation. I know for a fact that Little Joe Colomboni is being eyed to take his place, and that comes from the old man himself. He says he heard it in a closed meeting about what to do with Magi's involvement, and there may be a shift change in the works. If you do it for them, you get the rewards, but you also get another target on your back, too," Mike said to Money while looking at his crew. "I'm in," Money said. "Ok, I'll talk to the old man and see what happens. But in the meantime, keep it quiet," Mike said. "Stay. I'll ask the wife to make lunch for us, Mike" "Lunch sounds good. I'm starving,'" Mike said with a laugh. The meeting was over, and they finished the afternoon bullshitting in the lavishly decorated yard.

During that week, Mike had a chat with Vincenzo and discussed the idea of getting the Commission's nod of approval to put Little Joe C in power for a while, to find a suitable replacement. For the time being, they said wait a few months, and then they would approve the hit. Mike asked his uncle Vincenzo, "Do we know anyone in Dallas that can oversee this Kennedy thing?" "I'll have to make a call to the Dallas boss and ask him to find a guy who can look out for our best interests for that day. That may mean you are going to Dallas soon to check things out. You know, see if he's kosher, not like the other fuck up, from that asshole Martelli and his guy, who by now should be crabmeat," Vincenzo replied. "If we're involved, I have no choice. Now that I put my head on the chopping block with my fuckin' ideas of something wrong, if I don't get it right, I'm a dead man, and we both know how it works, family or no family. Right?" Mike replied to Vincenzo. Vincenzo only shook his head in agreement. "I guess you heard about that rat Valachi trying to work a deal with the Feds by giving them info on our organization and how it operates," Vincenzo said. "We should have had him whacked in his fuckin' jail cell months ago. This is going to cause us trouble," Mike replied. "I can't wait till this Kennedy thing is over and Bobby gets off our fuckin' back," Vincenzo said as he stood up saying goodbye to Mike. Vincenzo, while walking Mike to his car said, "Pack your bags. You may be going to Texas for a few days. Probably New Orleans, too."

At the end of October, Mike was told by Vincenzo to pack up. He was to leave for Dallas in two days. "You will meet with Joe Civelli (aka Piano Man). Joe is a made man with the Pirano family stationed in the south territory and is originally from Orleans. He is a good friend of Martelli, and you know if Martelli is involved, we could have the same problems again. That's why you need to make sure about these guys. See if they are connected with the Feds in any way. I hope not, 'cause I'll call a hit on all of them and start all over with this fuckin' thing. I'm so tired of this shit. I should retire," Vincenzo told Mike. Mike smiled and replied, "I will make sure uncle. I have more to lose than you with this shit."

Mike arrived in Dallas and was picked up at the airport and driven to a fancy hotel where he met with Piano Man on the rear patio overlooking the lake. Mike was expecting to see a mob looking, well-dressed man. Instead, he was looking at a small skinny, scrawny, short man, who looked more Jewish than Italian. After greeting each other and ordering drinks, Mike was told that they would be going to a place called the Crazy Horse Club that evening to meet up with several men who Piano Man wanted Mike to meet. In conversation with Piano Man, Mike learned that he was involved in running guns for the CIA and other clandestine operations. The men Mike was to meet with were involved with both the Mob and the CIA They were working together on this gun-running deal because the CIA could not do it directly due to legal issues. They needed the Mob's involvement to supplying guns and money to a covert group of Cubans working on a second operation to invade Cuba and kill Castro. Mike was stunned that no one knew this was going on, and Piano Man had no blessings to deal directly with the CIA or any other government group. "Are you telling me that you are in bed with the Feds in a secret operation to supply guns and money to another group of freedom fighters in order to take over Cuba? Does the President know this? Names, I want names of these guys involved," Mike said with a stern voice and a pissed-off look on his face. Piano Man realized he said too much and now fearing the consequences quickly replied "First, I got permission from Martelli and Chicago to deal with them. The guys you met in Orleans are the same guys. We are meeting them tonight at the club, plus a few more. I thought you knew, and that was why you were here, to meet the others involved," Piano Man said defensively. "Do you realize that these fucks are getting us involved with moving guns for them which ties us to them? They also have us involved with killing the President. They are setting us up to take the fall for killing the President, and if I get my way, we are not even going to send a shooter to the fuckin' party. They are telling us where, when and how we are to be involved. We don't work like that, Joe. You know that" Mike said grabbing him by the shirt. "The only reason I will meet with these guys is to know who the others are and the part they play," Mike said as he let him loose. "You just introduce them. Then shut your fuckin' mouth. Let me do the talking. So help me, if you open your fuckin' mouth to yawn, I'll break your fuckin' neck like a chicken at slaughter," Mike said pissed. "I'm confused. Do you know something that I don't?" Piano Man asked with a tremble in his voice. "Yeah, I do," Mike said. "These government guys are using us to whack their shooter, which they say there is only the one. I say there are more. They're telling us where our man is supposed to be on a rooftop on the Tec building. Think about it for a minute. If we have a shooter on a rooftop to shoot this Oswald guy, and he does, we become the patsies and take the blame, 'cause with Oswald dead, there is no one to implicate them. And don't forget the fact that Oswald is working for them and not us. The American public will want us all dead. We gain little by Jack being killed 'cause we want Bobby out of our hair. So who stands to gain the most from this? They do 'cause they get to start the war they want with Cuba and Vietnam, and war is money; not for us, but for them and the companies who make the war machines. That doesn't even include those crazy fuckin' Russians who can push the fuckin' button at any time, and no one wins when everyone's dead. Johnson will give them the war they want and they all win except us. We will be crucified on the fuckin' cross for killing Kennedy. Kennedy said in a speech a few weeks ago that in no uncertain terms he was tearing apart the CIA and his military bosses 'cause they have become too powerful and didn't listen to orders from him. This second attempt to invade Cuba is a perfect example. The fuckin' President doesn't even know what these guys are doing behind his back. That's why he wants the whole thing broken up," Mike said to Piano Man whose eyes fluttered and opened wide learning more about how involved he really was with his gun-running operation and working with these inside guys and the Cubans in both New Orleans and Texas. "Jesus Mike, I had no idea how involved this really was and our connection," he said with a shaking voice. "What should I do? I'm way too involved with this shit and just can't walk out. They'll know something is up," Joe pleaded with Mike. "Nothing at all. We have to keep this quiet, 'cause if they know we pulled out, we'll have even more problems. It's not like we can take on the FBI and the CIA and win. We have to play along with it 'cause we are now in too deep," Mike said as he stood up from the table they were sitting at in the hotel room. "I'm fuckin' starving. Take me someplace nice for lunch so we can discuss our plan of action for this meeting tonight," Mike said. "Sure, Mike. I know this great steakhouse a friend of mine owns. We can go there," Joe said walking to the car where Joe's driver was waiting.

At the steakhouse, Mike had many questions and wanted to learn as much as he could about the connections between Joe and the Orleans group. "So tell me how you got involved with these guys from New Orleans," Mike said. Joe told Mike, "It goes back a couple of years ago when Clay asked me if I knew anyone who had a connection with guns that he could buy. I told him I was interested and could get him guns through one of my businesses. We sold him guns, and he was shipping them out to rebel groups all around the world. I didn't know he was in the CIA or associated with them at the time. Last year he introduced me to this private eye named Guy, and Perry, who worked with him on his operations." "Do you know a Mr. Simons? I think he is a fed working for the CIA or FBI," Mike asked. "Never heard of him. Why?" Joe asked. "He is the point man for this Kennedy setup in Dallas," Mike said. "So why are you here in Dallas, Mike?" Joe asked Mike. "We need to replace Jimmy Blanks (Bang Bang), the shooter we had. It seems he was working both sides and may have been setting us up, but Martelli already took care of that problem" Mike said. "So you want me to find someone here in Dallas to take his place?" Joe asked. "Yeah, we have to make it look like we're sticking to our agreement with our shooter, but he will not shoot this Oswald guy," Mike said. "Wait, we supply a shooter, and he does not shoot? What the fuck? That makes no sense Mike. Why even get another shooter if we ain't gonna use him?" Joe asked. "We made a deal with those agents through the bosses that we were going to provide a shooter to kill the real shooter of Kennedy so he couldn't rat anybody out. The problem now is, I think they are setting us up for the killing of the President by pointing the finger at us. We have no one to tell the real story if Oswald is dead. So I told the Commission to go along with the plot, but don't shoot the real killer. If he gets caught, he will tell the public that he was ordered by the group he worked for, and he doesn't work for us or any family. That takes us out of the picture altogether, and Jack is gone. Exactly what we wanted to happen, so Bobby gets off our backs," Mike told Joe. "You really put your neck out there. What if he says that he was contracted by the Mob to kill

Kennedy as a cover-up for who he actually worked for?" Joe asked. "Then I'm dead, and they will find a way to shut him up. But I have an ace up my sleeve, just in case," Mike replied. I had a P.I. from New York investigate this Oswald, and I have proof that Oswald went to Mexico and was also in Russia undercover for the CIA to infiltrate what the Russians were doing. That ties him to the CIA. In addition, he was in the military and was recruited to play a Cuban sympathizer in order to get into Fidel's company, again, to get information about the Russians and Cuba's plans. My P.I. has documents proving all this information, including dates and records proving it, and copies are in a safe-deposit box at a bank in New York. If Oswald claims he worked for us, I will leak the info to some of our news reporters," Mike said with a smile. "Holy shit, Mike, does anyone else know this?" Joe asked. "Me, you and Vincenzo, so far," Mike said in reply. "See, my thought is to do what they do and cover your ass. I think I have with this information, and if I need it, I use it," Mike said. "So, why do you want to meet these other guys at the Club tonight? Joe asked. "To know more about how they are tied into this. We'll have a local photographer take pictures of them with us at the club, as backup proof of who was there. I need you to provide a photographer to take the job," Mike said to Joe. "You are one sly son of a bitch, Mike. Covering your ass like this is genius," Joe said with a grin. "When your life is on the line, you do whatever it takes and more," Mike replied. With lunch over, Joe showed Mike around town and dropped him off at the hotel to get ready for the meeting that night. Joe made all the arrangements to have a photographer secretly take pictures of the meeting.

That night Mike and Piano Man met with several individuals at the Club, which was really a titty joint owned by Jacob Rubinstien, who was a wannabe mobster. Mike pressed for info on how they were involved with gun running; who they were supplying the arms to; how they were involved with Piano Man; and their connections with the Feds. He also got a chance to meet Lee Oswald for the first time at this meeting and asked him tons of questions. He learned that those at the meeting used to work for or were still involved with government agencies. Guy Bantel was still a private eye and an ex-CIA. Dave Perry was an ex-CIA informer and militia trainer. Lee Oswald was ex-military and an ex-CIA trained spy. He also had a connection to this Wallace person in Dallas. Clay Bertrel was an international arms dealer and owned an import-export business in Orleans.

Piano Man got up from the table when he saw the photographer come in the club and told him to hide while he was taking pictures of those at the table. He then went back to the table to continue with the conversation at hand. After several hours of talking and drinking, Mike stood up and called it a night, saying goodbye to all and telling Joe he would need a ride to the airport in the morning. When Mike met Joe in the morning, he instructed him to find a replacement shooter and to have the pictures and negatives mailed overnight to his home address. Several days later Mike got the pictures and gave them to his brother Sal to put in Mike's bank vault for safe keeping. He told Vincenzo that another meeting of the council was needed to update the families on his progress, which Vincenzo said would be done soon.

The first week of November 1963, Mike had his meeting at Randazzo's Clam Bar in Coney Island, which was owned by Vincenzo's family group. It had several party rooms, which made the meeting secure and private. All the bosses were present. They wanted to hear what Mike had to say and to share the information they had found about the men involved. They also wanted to take a vote on whether to go ahead with the job or back out. After an hour of greetings and drinking, the meeting started. Mike stood up. "Gentlemen, thank you for allowing me to make my case concerning the matter at hand which affects all of us and our future endeavors. As you all know, it has been a few weeks since our last meeting on this issue. I have been busy collecting evidence and information about the people I have personally met during my travels to New Orleans and Texas. I have inside information that several of the people involved are working for either the CIA or FBI. I also have learned they are involved with gun running operations that include some of our own family members who are providing the weapons to some of the same people involved with this Kennedy thing. That in itself ties us into this plot that is planned to take place in Dallas on the 22nd of this month. It has been confirmed that Kennedy will travel to Dallas on that day, and his security team will be at a minimum. It seems that someone inside has sent most of Jack's boys to different places for that week, so Secret Service will not be heavy that day. I have also learned that this Oswald person is ex-CIA with a military background and was trained to speak Russian in order to infiltrate the Russian government. He spent two years there and came back to the U.S. without any problems through special operations being done by the CIA. I have heard he was working for the FBI at one time and was handpicked by the CIA for particular intel jobs abroad which included Cuba, Mexico, and Russia. He is either the real shooter or he is part of a bigger plan that we do not know of. I am not sure which, but he'll be there that day in the book depository building, either by himself or with someone else. He's a shitty marksman shooter with a rifle. Personally, I don't see how he can pull it off alone, and I think there may be more backup shooters at the scene just in case Oswald misses his shot. They want us to kill Oswald, but we still don't know if he is the only one. Our man may have to shoot more than this Oswald guy, and we don't even know where they will be. This makes it impossible for our man to find the other shooters and take them out too. That leaves us with a problem. If we are being set up, and there is more than one shooter, and he gets caught or speaks out, we will be blamed. Don't forget that all these shooters, except ours, work for or with the agency and not for us. They will blame someone, and it won't be themselves. That's what I have found about Oswald. The others are different. I'll start with Guy Bantel, who is a private investigator in Orleans. He used to work for the CIA. I don't know what he did for them, but I do know he is a recruiter for them, as well as the coordinator for this gun-smuggling thing. He sets up the connections for the CIA to provide guns for different operations they are involved with around the world, including another attack on Cuba, which I think is called Operation Freedom. The first one was called Operation Mongoose and was stopped by Jack Kennedy and the FBI. We all know that the two hate each other and do not share information. That's a fact. Now, I know if I am wrong, and nothing happens, I have a price on my head, and many would be happy to do the job. Therefore, I leave you with these questions: Do we have the means, the motive and the opportunity to kill the President of the United States and get away with it? Some will say yes, we have a motive. We need Bobby to stop breaking our balls, and killing his brother can do that. We certainly are motivated, and so are others, to remove Jack from office, but I don't believe the opportunity is there for us to pull off such a complicated job. We don't have the assets or power to control the police, CIA, FBI, or any other country wanting Kennedy dead, to cover it up. And finally, this is not our style of killing. Only those in a higher power, greater than ours, are capable of pulling this off, and even they will leave breadcrumbs behind. Gentleman, the decision is now yours, and whatever you decide today, I will follow."

The room went dead silent as the men at the table looked around at each other waiting for someone to speak up. Salvatorio addressed the crowd. "I think Mike is right. This is far above our control. How do we control the police and agents involved? We don't do this kind of shit, and you all know that. It's no secret that I have been against this all along, and this fuckin' bickering about shooters only proves we shouldn't get involved with this. Let someone else do the dirty work for us. We can send fuckin' flowers." Mike replied, "I have arranged for a shooter through our Dallas connections, just in case you all vote to continue with this hit." "Enough! Let's take a vote," Giancolla (Chicago boss) said stomping his fist on the table. "Each man put his vote on a piece of paper. This way no one knows how anyone voted. We throw it in the middle of the table and tally them up." It was agreed, and each person wrote his vote on a piece of paper and threw it in the middle of the table. Then they stood up and walked around the room to stretch their legs while watching Sam count the ballots. Mike sat nervously watching the pieces of paper being opened and tallied for a final vote. His heart was racing and beating out of his chest. Under his breath, he was praying for a no to be the final count. Sam took his time counting, and, after all, the votes had been tallied, he announced the results were in and asked for everyone to please be seated. Sam stood up and read the decision. "Gentlemen, the decision to have a shooter in place in the event someone else does not shoot the President during his trip to Dallas is yes." At that moment, Michael's heart stopped beating, and Vincenzo only shook his head while covering his face with his hands. "Big mistake," Vincenzo murmured to Mike, who was sitting next to him. "I will continue with the plans to have a shooter in place in Dallas as instructed by this committee," Mike said as he looked at the others. The meeting ended and the members retreated to different corners of the room to chat

146

and discuss business. Mike followed Vincenzo around the room as Vincenzo mingled with some of the others. After about an hour they all departed, heading back to their areas of operations, knowing that November 22nd was the day of reckoning for their ongoing problems with the Kennedy boys.

CHAPTER 13

THE SECRET MEETING

The first week of November 1963 started out with internal problems as Richie was investigated by the IRS and the New York division of State taxation for tax evasion. He called Mike for advice on what to do with the gas business. Mike instructed him to separate himself from the business by filing bankruptcy, and Vincenzo would see to it that he rigged the attorney and the judge to rule in his favor. What they did not realize was that the IRS and State Department were immune from bankruptcy proceedings, and Richie would still owe the money. Mike told Richie, "The best thing for you is not to claim income. If you had no job or income, they could not find you. Sell the house you're in. Take the cash and live off the grid." Richie met with Vincenzo to start the ball rolling. He started a new business off the books in the fish market on the docks in Brooklyn. Selling tuna to exporters in the Asian market. He relinquished his control of the gas business, and Vincenzo gave it to his old friend Pat Bruno (aka Papa Bear). Papa Bear had run gas stations and repair shops in the past and was connected with the family in the past. Although he was in his sixties, he was a big man to be reckoned with. Heavy built, when he greeted people, he would give them a body-wrap bear hug that could break a man's back if he chose to do so. If he liked you, he would try to kiss you on the lips. Some say he was gay, but no one would ever say it to his face. He was the man for the job with experience. It was agreed that he would receive one thousand per week plus two percent of the take which would come from the pool of men involved. He would report to either Vincenzo or Mike with the take which was divided among those holding ownership of the operation.

At the same time during that week, Money got the okay to eliminate Joe Maglio, who organized a crew to take out the other bosses some months ago. He was hiding upstate New York and was found to be in a hospital bed for a mild heart attack he had suffered. Money had a friend in Florida send him a bunch of Oleander leaves in the mail, which he had crushed and squeezed to extract the liquid and oils. He then sent one of his boys, who was once part of Maglio's crew in the past, to see him in the hospital and secretly inject Joe's IV bottle with the potent liquid. Once in Joe's system, the poison liquid would cause a massive heart attack that Joe would never survive. Because Joe was already in the hospital for such a cause, the doctors would never know the toxic mix was in his system, therefore, killing him within a half hour. It worked like a charm. Joe died less than an hour later, confirmed by the messenger of death who was visiting Joe by his hospital bedside.

Money conveyed his sympathy to the others and Joe's family and quietly took over his turf until he received his investment and more back. He called it his vig money, which at the time was twenty-five percent. However, in Joe's case, Money felt he was owed forty percent for waiting and being screwed by Joe.

The Commission informed Money his control of the Profosso family was only temporary until they voted to let Little Joe Colomboni take control of the family operations. Joe Colomboni was the informer who told the Commission about Joe Maglio and Bonanni's plot to whack the bosses and become the ultimate bosses of all the families. Although they allowed Bonanni to retire to Arizona, they wanted Joe Maglio dead for conceiving the plot. It wasn't known then, but Money would get to control the Profosso family for less than a year before the Commission gave it to Little Joe Colomboni, who changed the Profosso family name to Colomboni family. Joey Galli was pissed that he was overlooked for the promotion to boss since he worked for the Profosso family since he was a kid running numbers in the early days.

When Mike found out that Money had Joe Maglio whacked by using an Oleander plant extract, he had a captain's hat made with the design of Oleander leaves on it and the words under Captain saying, "It's nice to be king." Mike remembered that at the beginning of his career in the family business, during one of his meetings, Money said to him, "It's nice to be king." Mike never forgot anything he heard during his life and remembered everything like it was yesterday. Eddie laughed when he received the hat in the mail and wore it several times while skippering his boat Liquid Assets. Only Mike and Eddie knew what the hat really meant and kept it their own little secret. At some later point Eddie told Mike he liked the little touches of having the Oleander leaves inscribed on the front of the captain's hat. "That was fuckin' cute Mike. I like the personal touches you had made on my hat," Eddie told him.

In the second week of November, Mike was perplexed about the Kennedy thing and wanted to know who Piano Man and his Texas connection had gotten as the shooter. He told Vincenzo he was going to Dallas to meet with Piano Man to have a sit-down. Mike asked Vincenzo to set up a meeting for him and to let him know he was appointed by the Commission to follow up on the Kennedy problem. At first, Vincenzo told Mike that it was Piano Man's problem and to let it go, but Mike convinced Vincenzo to let him go anyway. "Just to make sure there are no more fuck ups," Mike told him. Vincenzo agreed, but without the approval of the other bosses. "If you go, you go on your own, Mike. I can't back you up on this one, but I will set up the meeting if you insist," Vincenzo told Mike.

November 10th, Mike flew to the Dallas airport and was met by Piano Man's driver who was instructed to drive him to a home outside of Dallas. There Mike would meet with Piano Man and two other men Mike did not know. "Hi, I am Thomas Walker, and this is Jimmy Hillermin. We are aware of your involvement in the Kennedy thing and would be more than happy to answer any questions you have." Mike looked at Piano Man and asked, "How much do these guys know about the Kennedy thing and what do they know about me?" Piano Man explained that all the information would be revealed at a special meeting that was set up for the evening. "Don't worry, Mike. There are some people who you have to meet and everything will be discussed." "Somehow, I don't feel comfortable about this shit. I better get some answers, or I walk out of this. I do not know these guys, and yet they know me and the Kennedy problem. You need to explain it to me before I go anywhere with you and these jimbone's here," Mike said with his guard up. "Mike, I assure you everything is safe, and you don't have to worry. I know these people well, and they are working with us, and not against us," Piano Man said in an effort to calm Mike's nerves. "If anything happens to me, you are a dead man and so are your friends, you capisce? People know I am here, and if I don't come back, they have orders to hunt you down," Mike said. "Wow, you are uptight about nothing, Mike," Mr. Walker said. "Let's understand each other here. I don't know you or your friend, and that makes me nervous. I am told that I'm to meet with more people I don't know. As far as I am concerned, Joe here may have already said too much and that makes me uneasy. I don't know what involvement you guys have in this matter. And being on someone else's turf makes me cautious. I'll go to this meeting, however, if anything happens, you boys have new problems. Tu capisce?"

That evening Mike and the others went to a home owned by Anthony Edwards, who was a prominent lawyer in Texas. He was the go-to man for the big oil companies and other successful members of the Texas big boys. Well-known to the judicial system, he used big oil money to get whatever was needed by those who controlled the oil business in and out of Texas. After being introduced to several people in the parlor, Mr. Edwards told the men that "Soon our problems will be solved, and we will be once again on top." He proceeded to explain that the wheels were in motion and pointed to Mike saying, "Our friends from New York are helping take care of the President while he is traveling in Dallas." They all supported his speech by erupting into loud applause. Mike had a feeling that somehow too many people knew too much already. Turning to Piano Man, he asked, "How much does he know? And don't bullshit me. You told me that you had shooters lined up for this job. This guy is pointing the finger at me as if I am providing the shooter. I want a meeting with this prick and you." "Mike, we will have the meeting after he schmoozes his guests, I promise," Piano Man said to him. Mike was antsy, and he let Piano Man know it.

About an hour later, Mike had a sit down with Mr. Edwards, Tom Walker, Mr. Hillermin and Piano Man. "In two weeks our problems will be over, and the New Republic will live again," Mr. Edwards said with a smile. "Mike, we will provide the shooters needed to take care of this problem. You already know Tom Walker and Jim Hillermin, and I understand you met Oswald in New Orleans several weeks back.

In fact, you met with several people who will be directly involved in taking care of this problem of ours. The only one you have not met with is J.R., and he doesn't want to meet you or anyone else for that matter. These are your shooters for the job. We have everything set from the Secret Service badges to a cop uniform. You see Mike, we have people in very high places. You might say they are second in charge, literally, if you know what I mean" Mr. Edwards said with a smile as he pointed to pictures on the wall. Several pictures were of the most powerful men in the world. Among them were James Rockafella, (owner of the oil industry and a member of the Federal Reserve board) Dave Rothchilder, (leader of the World Bank and Federal Reserve Bank) as well as the owner of dozens of major banks within the U.S. and the world.

One that stood out the most was Johnson (Vice President, under John Kennedy) and the acting director of the Federal Bureau of Investigations, who was in the oil business with the Saudis. "Are you telling me the Vice President is in on this?" Mike asked. "He was a partner in my law firm, and we have oil businesses, among other venues, here in Texas. Hell, we've been partners for many years along with most of these oil barons that were in this room tonight. We have connections all over the world, and if Johnson gets Kennedys job because he is dead, then so be it. He will open the war, and we can sell oil again. Because it would be best that he knows almost nothing about this, we have decided to keep him out of the loop. I requested some inside info about the Secret Service and asked for some badges to hang on the wall in the office next to mine, and that's about all of his involvement in this situation. Total anonymity is the key here. The less he knows, the better. You see Mike yours is not the only group that wants Jack dead. We have lost millions in the oil industry because his taxing the shit out of us and not giving up land for us to drill on. Are you aware of an executive order Jack put into effect back in June of this year? It is executive order 111110, which forces the making of a new currency backed by silver and printed by the United States government. He authorized the department to print four billion new bills to circulate into the economy, backed by silver. It will force the Federal Reserve Bank to go out of business. And if you didn't know it, most of all the banks are owned by seven of the most powerful men in the world, who are also on the board of the Federal Reserve. Hell, they control countries, governments, and the economy, by controlling the printing of money for dozens of countries, including America. They also control the interest rates. So you see, Jack has to go so Lyndon can fix the problems we all have, and we here in Texas have his promise," Mr. Edwards told Mike while smiling with confidence through the entire conversation.

"Well, here is my problem. I have been ordered to have a shooter in place to take out this patsy Oswald so he can't point the finger at anyone. Now I find out that there are several shooters involved. None are from me, and you have your own plan for this whole thing. If I tell the families that I did not have a shooter in place, and Jack leaves Dallas alive, I am a dead man. So I want you to tell me what the fuck I am supposed to do here" Mike said to all those present in the room. "Tom Walker can be your man. We can say that you handpicked him for the job. We can still play it out with the others and still make Oswald the patsy. And Tom can take care of him while they are set up in the book depository. After Oswald takes his shot, Tom will make sure he doesn't leave the building alive. We let Tom take the credit for killing the man who shot the President, and he will be seen as a hero.

"If I go along with this, and somehow it gets out that I did not do what I was told to do, I will know that one of you four guys ratted me out, and I promise swift revenge on you and your family. So long as we all understand each other and this stays our secret forever, tu capisce? You guys better make it happen, or everyone is dead, including me. I will go ahead with your plan. I will let the Commission know that shooters are contracted to do the hit in Dallas as ordered and we'll leave it at that for now. I will also let Johnny from Hollywood know that it's taken care of with the help of our Dallas connections. My life is at stake here, and no matter what happens, Jack cannot leave Texas alive," Mike said as he stood up and looked at the pictures of head shots on the walls of the room, studying the names of each one into memory.

Mike and Piano Man drove back to the hotel. After seeing Piano Man off, Mike called his private eye in New York and gave him the names of the faces he saw on the wall at Mr. Edward's home and instructed him to find out as much as he could about them and their connections. He wanted to confirm the statements made to him at the meeting. "Mike, do you know what you are asking me to do here?

These men are billionaires with long reaching arms. This is very dangerous. If you want me to check them out, it's going to cost you big time. My life could be in danger just for snooping into these guys." Mike's reply was, "Ten grand for this job alone, Phil. That's what I'll pay you for the info I need. Do we have a deal?" "It'll take some time, Mike. I want to be paid up front so I can spend it before I'm dead," Phil replied.

The next morning Mike left for New York and went directly to Vincenzo's home to discuss the ordeal and information that was vital to the organization's involvement. He explained the connections between the Federal Reserve bankers; the executive order Kennedy put into effect in June, the gun running for the CIA and how the family was involved in Chicago and Orleans, the FBI director's involvement in the oil business and his connections to both Johnson and Mr. Edwards. Vincenzo's jaw dropped when he realized how many people wanted Jack dead and how high it went up the ladder and beyond. "So, my only question is, did you arrange for someone to take out this Oswald guy as instructed by the Commission?" Vincenzo asked. "Yeah, there are several shooters in place for the hit. We don't need to hand-pick one. This Mr. Edwards and several others have already hand-picked the shooters, so I didn't have to." "Michael, you did not just tell me that you disobeyed the order to make sure we have a person in place to take out this Oswald guy. If he gets away and the Commission finds out that you let someone we don't know pick the shooters, I cannot help you or protect you. You may have just signed your own death warrant, Michael. Let me think about what I have to do with this information and decide how to handle the Commission if they ask me. Perhaps it is best you leave now, and for the next two weeks, lay low and keep out of sight for your own safety. You should know that I will not lie for you if they ask me," Vincenzo said angrily shaking his head in disgust.

Before Mike was ready to take Vincenzo's advice and hide, he decided to see his cousin Money. He was visibly upset that he was in a position that could jeopardize his life, as well as his uncle. He stopped at a pay phone and called to get the okay to come over and talk. Money's wife explained that he was not home, but she would let him know that he called and wanted to meet with him. Mike went to the old shop to see Bo and touch base with him about what the word was on the streets. According to Bo, everything was fine except for some local kids who broke into the shop and stole some tools and small shit. Mike called Money again and was told that he would be home in about an hour. Kat told Mike it was okay for him to come over and wait for Money. After making a few calls in the shop office, he drove over to see Money. "I hear you just got back from the old man's house, and now you're here wanting to talk to me. Something wrong?" "Yeah, I need your advice on something very important. Can we talk on the boat?" "Sure, Mike, we can do that. This must be real important if you came here and want to take a boat ride," Money said as they walked to the boat dock. After taking the boat into the bay, Money anchored the boat and shut off the engine. "Now, what's so fucking important that requires this secrecy? I've never seen you like this before." Mike asked Money if he knew anything about the Kennedy hit. Money replied "I know they have been wanting him and his brother dead for some time now, and they tried in Miami, but Santos called it off when the Feds got wind of it. I may have also heard Vincenzo talking about some new shit about the Kennedy boys. But short of that, nothing so important that you want to speak to me in private. What the fuck is going on? Are you involved in any way?"

Mike proceeded to tell Money everything and how he was ordered by Vincenzo to set it up, from the secret meeting with Joe Kennedy in Florida to the faces he saw on the wall at the Texas meeting. Money couldn't believe what he was hearing. "Are you telling me that outsiders are going to hit the President of the fucking United States in less than two weeks in Dallas? You got yourself in a world of shit, my friend, and you know the rules of the game, Mike. Now I'm sorry you even told me this fuckin' shit 'cause it puts me in the know. Jesus Christ, Mike, what are you going to do?" "The truth is, I don't fucking know what to do at this point. If the Commission finds out that I didn't hand-pick a shooter to take out Oswald, I'm dead. I have been against this whole fucking thing with the Kennedy family and just wanted to make a good living making money. I never wanted to be involved as much as I am, and I'm not even sure if I am being set up by all those involved, including my uncle Vincenzo and the Commission," Mike replied. "So, what do you want me to do?" Money asked with a puzzled look on his face. "There is something else you should know. For some time now, I have had a P.I. compiling information on all these guys in the event I need to use it in the future, you know, insurance," Mike said. "Oh my God, more fucking people who know about this shit," Money replied. "The P.I. only knows that he is checking out the names I have given him, nothing more," Mike said in a nervous tone. "Don't you think he is going to tie all these leads together and know that it had something to do with Kennedy and the clowns you have him checking out? This just gets worse by the fucking minute, and you have to do something about it right after Kennedy is dead. I'm glad I'm not in your fuckin' shoes, Mike," Money said in an angered tone. "I may need your help with some of this stuff after Jack is dead. You might have to help me get rid of some of the people who know and can point a finger at me. Can I count on you to help me when the time comes, Eddie?" Mike pleaded. "I'll do what I can if the time comes," Money replied as he started up the boat and told Mike he was done with the conversation." Mike said nothing more and they were quiet on the short ride back to the dock. Mike thanked Money and left to hide till the job was done.

CHAPTER 14

THE KILL SHOT

Three days before the trip to Dallas by the president, Mike was getting very nervous about the upcoming events. Was everything going as planned? Were there any changes that he did not know of? What would he do if the President got away? He couldn't sleep, and he had an upset stomach that lasted for days just thinking about it. He thought it best to find out what his P.I. guy had found out about the men involved. Calling to make an appointment for a sit-down in a public place, he arranged for them to meet one last time to touch base. The meeting was to take place at the Rockaway Diner on November 20th at 10 am. Mike asked Money to go with him as both protection and advisor to the information he was to receive from the private eye. At the diner, Mike introduced Money to his informer, and they sat in a booth at the end away from windows. "So, what do you have for me?" Mike asked. "There's a lot of stuff that doesn't make sense here. Let's start with the guys you had me check out in Orleans. It seems that none of them work for the Government, meaning, not the FBI, CIA or any other agency that I know of. Two of them did work for the CIA some years ago and went their own ways. This Clay guy owns an import-export company and may be a gunrunner, and is probably involved in clandestine operations with the CIA 'cause he is selling guns to different factions that the CIA is involved with. Oswald is a strange one. He was military. He was recruited by the CIA to infiltrate the Russians. I think he got nothing from the Russians, so they sent him to Mexico where again he got nothing. Now he is rallying for Castro, which may be another front to infiltrate the Cuban government. The truth is, I'm not sure, but I think the CIA dumped him, or he's working undercover. He is not a sharpshooter or, at least, he is not a perfect shooter, as claimed by some. He came back to the U.S. with no visa, and a few months ago went to Mexico and had since returned. He is not CIA, but may be involved with them. Perhaps he is some offshoot of the CIA or someone involved with them like this Clay guy or Bantel the P.I. guy in Orleans? He's seen as a radical and is connected with several of the men I checked out for you. He is now working in a book building in Dallas and got the job from a friend of this Edwards guy in Dallas. Now, this Edwards guy is for real and did work with Johnson till Johnson went into politics. He still campaigns and helps him any way he can through donations by big oil and bankers. He is who he says he is. This Walker guy from Texas was a special ops guy in the military along with this Hillermin guy, so they are legit. Neither of them was involved with the CIA or FBI that I could find. What I don't understand is why they are associated with Edwards, 'cause Edwards is whiskey clean and doesn't associate with guys like them. His type is political, oil and the justice system. Why he is associated with them beats the shit out of me. There has to be more to the story, and I am still working on it. Oh, by the way, that Simons guy who claims to be CIA? Well, I checked, and no one knows him, and he doesn't show up on their payroll either. He is a complete mystery to me. I have some people checking into it and will get back to you on that one." "So, this Simons guy is not CIA? I need to know who he is 'cause he's supposed to be the go-to guy from the CIA," Mike said as he looked at Money for his input. "Keep searching to find out who this guy is and who he's working for," Money said looking back at Mike with a confused look on his face. "Okay, thanks for the info. I'll get back to you in a couple of weeks for anything you have on this Simons guy" Mike said as they stood up and said goodbye.

November 22, the final hours. Mike, who was at home, got a call from Vincenzo and was told to come to his home, because the Commission wanted to make sure everything was going according to plan, and Vincenzo was supposed to keep Mike in his sights until the campaign in Dallas was over. He was also informed that several other family members were in town to watch the live broadcast on TV at Vincenzo's home. "Michael, come alone, and no protection, please,"

Vincenzo instructed. Mike agreed and drove over to his home where he met with several high-ranking family members. Represented was Santos from Miami, Murry Lanski from South Florida, Gambonno from New York, Sam Martelli from the southern district of New Orleans and Sam Giancolla from Chicago. Mike knew that if he was going to be whacked, it would not be at Vincenzo's because the bosses never do the killings themselves once they are bosses. They have the underboss put out a contract on them. Besides, Vincenzo wouldn't have a murder at his home, especially his favorite nephew Michael. Scared, but safe for the moment, is how Mike felt, but anything could happen if Kennedy was not killed in Dallas. Once a person came in, the doors were locked, and two gorilla bodyguards stood guard at the front door.

Vincenzo had a full house, and all his staff provided anything needed, from drinks to girls giving blowjobs. Conversations were everywhere until the time came to sit and watch the parade of the presidential motorcade down the streets of Dallas. "Okay everyone, please, the show is about to start," Vincenzo shouted out above the loud chatter. All eye's focused on the TV. Everyone was quiet and excited at the same time. Mike's heart was pounding, and he felt sick, but showed no weakness in front of the bosses. His life was on the line, and he knew it thinking to himself, "When will this be over? Will it happen at all?

The clock seemed to be taking forever to move. Time appeared to be standing still. The limo driving the President was turning onto Elm Street. Less than half way down the block, suddenly shots rang out. The television news reporters only said that something happened in the motorcade. The limo with the President started moving faster and faster as a Secret Service man jumped on the back of the speeding limo. Pure pandemonium was viewed by every American watching the live broadcast. "Did they get him? Is he dead?" shouted someone in the room. Everyone was glued to the live broadcast waiting for the answers.

About fifteen minutes later, the question everyone wanted to know was answered. "The President of the United States is dead," Walter Cronkite said tearfully as he sat in the newsroom. Everyone in the room started cheering and yelling. "The son of a bitch is dead" someone shouted out loud. Mike only addressed the excitement with sadness and a frown saying nothing. Vincenzo was visibly upset and only smiled when addressed by the others in the room. Vincenzo and Mike did not want Kennedy dead like this. They all knew that they both were against the whole idea from the beginning. "You guys knew that this had to be done, and now we can get back to business. This should get that fuck Bobby off our backs," Martelli said as he raised his glass of wine. "Per il nostro futuro," (To our future) Sam Giancolla said as he too raised his glass. Out of respect, Vincenzo and Mike raised their glasses in unison with the others.

For Mike, the ordeal was over, and he was redeemed for doing his job as directed. Some were still watching the television and pointed saying, "Oh, now a cop has been shot. What the fuck? Look, they are searching for some guy that may have been the shooter." Mike's heart went into overdrive. No one knew what was happening, not even Mike. As the day went on, the story was changing from hour to hour. Later in the afternoon, the reporters said that a person of interest was being questioned for being involved in the shootings. "Mike, you need to find out from your connection in Dallas what the fuck is going on. Is it that Oswald guy? Wasn't he supposed to be dead by now?" Santos said as he looked around the room. "I know as much as all of you guys about what is going on at this point. I'll have to get a morning flight out to Dallas and find out what the fuck is happening. I'll take care of it, on my word," Mike said. "You better finish this mess, Mike, 'cause we can't have some loose lips opening their fuckin' mouth about this, tu capisce?" Mike snapped back, "Look, I said I would take care of loose ends. What more do you want from me?" Suddenly, Vincenzo jumped in saying, "Michael, a little respect, please. I know everyone is on edge right now, and we all need to keep our cool. I think Santos deserves an apology from you for being rash with him. Remember, he's a boss who commands respect." Mike replied before Vincenzo could say another word. "I'm sorry for raising my voice. I'm under a lot of pressure right now, and a million things are running through my brain. I understand your concerns. They are even more important to me since it is my life on the line, and I'm well aware of that. I'm sorry. It will never happen again." Santo accepted and gave him a hug and whispered in his ear, "I have had men killed for less disrespect. You are forgiven, this time, Michael." Mike said nothing in return and walked away as fast as he could to another part of the room. Vincenzo cornered Mike and said softly, "Tomorrow go see the Piano Man and that lawyer person in Dallas. Find out what happened and finish this fucking job so we can get on with our lives and put it behind us. I didn't tell anyone about that shooter thing we spoke of." Mike could only thank him and say he was ready to go home and pack. With that, Mike said his goodbyes and left as fast as he could from Vincenzo's.

The next morning Mike called ahead to have a sit-down with Piano Man and then boarded a plane back to Dallas. Landing in Dallas, he was met by Piano Man and Tom Walker and together they went to Edward's office in downtown Dallas for a sit-down. There Mike was briefed on what took place the day before. "What happened to Hillerman and Oswald?" Mike asked. "Hillerman got caught up in traffic and was late to the location. He stayed at the back of the book depository in a Secret Service suit guarding the entrance. Oswald got away, leaving his rifle behind some boxes. Walker had to clean up the room and stage the boxes and bullet casings, so it looked like only one shooter was there. He still got away safe and is hiding in Orleans right now waiting to get paid so he can leave for Mexico. "So you guys had three shooters and not four? Hillermin was late and did not take part in the shooting like he as suppose to?" Mike asked. "What does it matter? Kennedy is still dead," Piano Man said. "What does it matter? Hillermin can be a loose cannon, and something has to be done so he keeps his fuckin' mouth shut, that's what's the matter. He fucked up," Mike replied looking angry. "Set up a meeting with Hillermin tonight at your place and let me take care of this problem myself. I'm not asking, I'm telling you to do it, today," Mike said pounding his fist on the table.

After the meeting was over, Mike went to the scene and watched as the Feds were combing the area of the crime looking for anything they could find. He decided it best to leave and go to a local hotel and observe from a window overlooking the plaza. Around six-thirty, that evening he was picked up by Piano Man and they went back to a house that Piano Man used for business. Jimmy Hillermin was led to believe that he was receiving payment for his part in the operation and was eager to come and get his money. Jimmy showed up around eight, excited and cautious. He sat down. "So, you have something for me?" he said. "Before you get your money, I have a question.

Why were you late?" Mike asked as he walked around the room. "Fucking traffic was terrible that morning. The Secret Service had everything blocked off," Jimmy replied. "Hmm, they were there early in the morning blocking off the main roads? Strange, 'cause they only blocked off the plaza area, and that was around eleven. You were supposed to be at the plaza at ten in the morning, like everyone else," Piano Man said with a confused look. "Hey, traffic was bad, and I was stuck in it. That's all I can say," Jimmy said in return. As he was saying it, Mike had positioned himself behind Jimmy. Without hesitation, Mike put Jimmy in a headlock. With his other hand, he covered his face and nose. Mike's huge hands wrapped around his face like a baseball glove covering a hard ball. Mike held him tight until he stopped struggling and flailing his legs. Once Mike was sure he was not breathing, he let loose. "You know he was fucking lying," Mike said to Piano Man, who looked like he just shit his pants. "Now, you have to clean up this fuckin' mess 'cause I can't take him with me. Do a clean job and let Edwards know that this is one problem we don't have to deal with anymore. Tell him to clean house on his side or I will kill him myself. No fuckin' mistakes. I have enough to deal with now that they have Oswald alive. You call Martelli in Orleans and make this Oswald problem go away before he talks. At first, I thought if Oswald stayed alive he would point the finger at those who set him up for this job. Now I ain't so sure 'cause there are too many involved. Now please drive me to the airport so I can report to the fucking bosses and put my fuckin' head on a silver platter to see if they want to chop it off." Mike said as he walked to the door. "What about him?" Piano Man asked looking at the dead body on the floor. "What? Lock the fuckin' door and finish it after you drop me off," Mike replied motioning his hand and saying "Andiamo, sbrigati, Come on, hurry up. Within five hours, Mike was back in New York and headed home. Before the end of the day, the news of the day was that Ruby shot Oswald, and now Oswald was dead. Piano Man had to call Martelli for his okay to force Ruby, who was a wannabe mobster and owned the Go Go club where loan sharking and drugs were part of the Dallas family operations, to whack Oswald and take the wrap. Ruby catered to the local police boys at his club and had free access to the police department, and they all knew him well. He got close enough to shoot Oswald in the stomach and keep him from spilling the beans to anyone. They promised that they would get Ruby off with the help of their connections with the Edwards Law firm and his team. Mike called Piano Man that night and thanked him for his quick action. Mike finished the conversation with, "I owe you one."

Days later Mike would find out more as the media and videos added to the mystery. Piecing together the info he knew from the Dallas connection and the news, he surmised the events that took place in great detail:

It was 12:28 pm when the presidential limo turned the corner of Elm Street. Both Oswald and Walker were in place in the sixth-floor window of the book depository building. They both had the same type of rifle and bullets. J.R. was behind the fence on the grassy hill with the same rifle and bullets. Oswald jumped the gun and fired first missing Kennedy and hitting the sign post which deflected the bullet causing it to veer low to the right of the limo and hitting the sidewalk. Walker now pissed at Oswald's jump to shoot, aimed and fired the second shot hitting Kennedy in the right shoulder blade. This caused the bullet to deflect upward, exiting through the neck, fragmenting the slug as part of the bullet hit the front right side of the windshield and door frame of the limo. A part of the slug hit the sidewalk hitting the concrete, tearing a small flesh wound on a male bystander's face. Oswald took another shot, which was high, hitting Governor Connally, who was in the front passenger seat. J.R., seeing the bullet did not kill Kennedy, took his shot hitting Kennedy in the right side of the head, splitting open his skull and fragmenting the bullet causing massive damage, killing Kennedy instantly. Walker and Oswald got out of the building and left the scene quickly. Oswald was accosted by a local police officer who thought he matched the description of a person of interest. Oswald shot the officer, killing him, and left the scene. He was later found in a movie house by local police officers working on a tip. Oswald had in his possession a handgun matching the one that shot officer Tippits and was held for questioning. Within forty-eight hours, Oswald would be killed by Jack Ruby, who was pressured into it by Piano Man and the far-reaching arm of the New Orleans boss. Ruby knew a threat from the mob was more than a death sentence for him; it was his entire family he was worried about. The only way he could protect them was to take the rap and keep quiet.

CHAPTER 15

RUN FAST – RUN FAR

1964 was one of the toughest years for anyone in the Mob. The FBI, CIA, Dallas PD and several other government agencies were hunting down any leads leading up to the death of Kennedy. Families and the Commission itself were under scrutiny by the government arm. Mike's name was part of the leads that caused the feds to follow him on a constant basis, hoping for one mistake. Mike knew it and laid low by staying home with the family and acting like a family man. He went back to working as a mechanic for his friend Bo at the gas station. Only there could he conduct business, all the while knowing the phones would be tapped. The bars, clubs, horse stable, gas stations and any other business that looked legit was spoken of on the phone, but in coded messages. He did this for eight months, never speaking to any of his crew or anyone involved with Kennedy or the families. No contact, no association.

Only after the feds gave up and got off his back was he able to start finishing up family business using extreme caution and in code only those involved would know. To throw off the heat, Mike spent the rest of the year at the stables he now owned. He made Lefty Rothstine an offer he couldn't refuse with the help of his uncle's persuasive connections. Mike had several horses, but his favorites were Mr. Magoo, the money maker, and Running Bear, who sired offspring that sold for a premium price. Mike, and sometimes his family, would stay for weeks at Ocala Horse Farms. It was not until April of 1965 that he felt it was safe to expand his influence and status as a boss by investing in legal businesses, stocks, and sports bets with the help of Fat Jimmy's tips from the inside. Belmont Race Track became his favorite place to do business with associates and play the ponies, both his and others.

The next seven years he stayed under the wire, with the exception of whacking David Perry in his apartment in New Orleans on the night of February 22, 1967. He knew that Perry was being pressured by the New Orleans D.A. and was summoned to a court hearing. He became a liability to the families and those involved. With orders from the commission, Mike killed Dave Perry with his bare hands by shoving his stiff massive thumbs deep into the back of his skull causing a cerebral hemorrhage in Perry's brain.

By 1973, Mike wanted out of the Mob and its lifestyle. The gang wars within and the government cracking down on the so-called Mafia were taking its toll on Mike's association with the other bosses. It seemed like every other day they wanted someone whacked, or a judge bribed because they had been pinched, and Mike had enough of the pressure providing for the needs of others. After thirteen years of devotion to the families and accumulating over seven million dollars in off-shore accounts with the help of his brother's banking position, plus his tangible assets like homes and investments, Mike wanted out. He knew that once you marry the Mob, there is no divorce. His only way out was to be dead.

He devised a plan to make the bosses want a contract on him for not following orders. He could only implement his plan if he could convince Money and Little Richie to go along with it. He knew that if he made it profitable for his cousin Money, not only would he help, but he had to keep it a family secret forever because of his involvement. Money would receive in return most of uncle Vincenzo's assets, which Mike inherited after Vincenzo's passing from a massive heart attack in 1969. Total value was around 1.2 million in tangible assets. Richie was offered Mike's percentage of the gas scam and some clubs, which made about fifty grand a week. Richie jumped on it. Mike knew that his cousin would be committed to their secret or be whacked for lying to his boss. Richie and Mike became best friends and helped each other over the thirteen-year span of being involved. It meant everything to both of them, and if Richie became a witness to the murder and snitched, he too would be on the Mob's hit list. Money and Richie loved Mike and feared him, as Mike had become

Vincenzo's double when it came to business. They all agreed with the oath of blood to each other, and the plan was set.

Pissing off the bosses was the easy part. Any hint of a rat was dealt with swiftly by the Commission. Getting away with murder was another story for Mike. It had to be perfectly planned out and executed flawlessly. It took several weeks to design, but together, Mike, Money, and Richie decided the best way to whack him was to show proof that the contract was done. Along with Richie and his connections with other family members at local Italian clubs in the tri-state area, they would both start rumors about Mike and the possibility that he may turn state's evidence to avoid jail time if he got pinched. Mike made sure the bosses found out that he was being watched by the feds. With everyone saying the best man for the job would be those closest to him, the Commission ordered his cousin Eddie to make the hit along with Richie.

The plan was acted out.

Money would lure Mike onto his boat and have Richie as a witness to the killing. Once out to sea, Money had to chop off one of Mike's pinky fingers with the ring still attached to it and hand deliver it to his boss as proof. After a while of heavy drinking, Money said, "You drunk enough, Mike? Which pinky do you want to say goodbye to?" Mike chose the left as it was the symbolic finger when becoming a made man. Axe down and it was gone. Money put it on ice to preserve it. Mike had another boat waiting for him. After saying his goodbyes, he boarded it for a trip to the Florida Keys where he would fly to Nassau. Later the next day Money and Richie presented the chopped-off finger of Michael Delagatta to Carl Gambono, who was pleased, and informed the Commission that the problem was taken care of.

Once Mike made it to the safe house in Nassau, he transferred all his money to an Italian bank, making sure there were branches close to the home he was in the process of buying under an alias, in the little town of Parma, Italy.

Mike had made prior arrangements with Money to assist his wife in liquidating the New York and Florida homes and other assets and send Western Union money orders to particular banks in Italy. After several months, Jackie had sold everything, and she and the kids were on their way to Italy. To everyone watching, she needed to downsize since Mike was dead. There they lived a peaceful life for twenty-six years running a tomato and olive tree farm on 100 acres of land. His four children grew up and the boys Vincent, Michael junior and Giovanni went on to marry. His daughter Donna stayed with her father after the death of Jackie, who died of cancer in 1998.

During a regular visit to his doctor, Mike was given a diagnosis of lung cancer from asbestos. Working his younger years as a grease monkey in the repair shops was the cause. His doctor told him it was severe, and he may have one year or less to live.

Knowing he had a short time to live and was dying, he summoned his children to his home. Within several months, his health quickly deteriorated. Summoning his oldest son Giovanni, he told him of his deeds and family secrets that he'd kept from 1960 to 2001. Giovanni knew he was with the Mob when he was younger. He did not, however, know about his father's involvement dealing with John Kennedy and his assassination.

During the next three months, he told Giovanni in great detail his secret participations concerning John Kennedy and his brother Bobby who was also killed years later when Bobby announced his candidacy for president. Mike's personal confessions to his eldest son of what happened laid heavy on his conscience and the proof he had hidden for so many years had to be handed to his next generation, for them to decide what to do with it. "Why are you telling me this? It's old news, and there is no proof," Giovanni said. "Listen to me. In the basement of this house is a safe room behind the glass mirror on the west wall beside the bar locked by magnets. The magnet release is hanging on the wall and looks like a cross. Use it to open the room and there you will find a box in the corner of the room with papers and pictures in it. Those papers are about the Kennedy thing I spoke of with you. After my death, either release them or destroy them. It's your choice. If you decide to release them, be careful, 'cause people will come after you, putting you and others in danger." "Fine, I will look at them and decide what to do with them. If there is something important, maybe I will pass it on," Giovanni said to his father. Three weeks later, Mike died.

The funeral service was held at Mike's home in the usual Italian tradition. Immediate family and local friends came to pay their respects. Money and Richie, who were now in their seventies, flew in on short notice to pay their respects. Giovanni asked Money and

Richie about the Kennedy thing. They denied any involvement or knowledge of it. While at the house days later, Giovanni decided to investigate the information his father had told him about the secret room and what was hidden from view. Using the cross magnet, he managed to open the glass door leading into a hidden room. There he found a large fortified room with a free-standing six-foot tall safe, which was open, holding several guns and several metal boxes. Looking around the room, he located the boxes exactly where he was told they would be, in the corner of the room. Sitting in the room, he opened one of the boxes and started reading the papers that included names, places, and dates. He noticed there were over sixty pages from the private investigator Mike had hired, as they all contained his business logo on the top of each page. Hundreds of pictures were in one of the other boxes, showing Mike at meetings in public places such as the New Orleans club and other places, which Giovanni did not recognize. He did notice that every picture was marked on the back with names, dates and brief description of its purpose. Shocked by what he was in possession of and how it affected the future of many lives, he realized he was now holding information that was undeniable proof of an elaborate scheme to assassinate John Kennedy for the purpose of preserving the status and control of the elite establishment who controlled the flow of money and politics around the world. After several hour of sifting through the material, he felt the presence of his father leaning over him and whispering in his ear "I lived with this secret for almost forty years, and it haunted me all my life." At that moment, Giovanni became emotionally upset and cried uncontrollably knowing his father had concealed both a burden to himself and information that could take down countries, especially America.

Two weeks later the family lawyer summoned the family to read the will and distribute the estate, which was now mostly in Italy. The house was willed to his daughter Donna, and the rest was shared among the boys, with the exception of the Ocala Farms Training Center. It stayed in the family and was to be run by all the children. Before his death at the hands of his cousin Eddie in 1973, Mike had instructed his wife and Richie to reach out to his friend Onions to help run the Ocala Farms for her after Mike was presumed dead. Onions was compensated handsomely by becoming part owner.

Mike's favorite horse Mr. Magoo sired several offspring, and those offspring sired more offspring. The last one was named Big Mike, in honor of Michael Delagatta.

Mikes last wish was to be cremated and have his ashes spread over the finish line at Belmont Race Track in Queens, New York. It was a wish his cousin Eddie, friends Little Richie and Onions made sure would be fulfilled. Using their connections, they managed to have an escort with the Pinkerton guards to the finish line with a small family group, through the Belmont Track to the finish line and commenced his last wishes on April 18, 2002.

Months later, Giovanni, after having nightmares of what would happen if he released the Kennedy information to the press and how it would affect his family, made the decision to destroy everything. The judges and names of all the crooked agencies were part of the documents. *The world can never know how the elite and powerful, whom shall have no names, wanted John Kennedy dead much more than the Mafia;* he thought to himself.

The means, the motive and the opportunity were all there for others. The Mafia had no opportunity to whack Kennedy, nor did they have to. John Kennedy was already a marked man by other powerful people. Over a ten-year period after Kennedy's death, more than fifty-six people involved with the Kennedy case died in mysterious ways or disappeared altogether. The decision for Giovanni was painful but necessary.

Giovanni, knowing of his father's decision to hide the information from the public by never speaking of it and locking the proof in a secret room for over thirty-five years, made a conscious decision to burn them in the fireplace on Christmas Eve of 2002 thinking to himself, *I cannot divulge the truth in fear of my family's safety and the repercussions' it would cause. It regrettably will always be America and the world's deepest mystery.*

The surviving family still lives in a little town outside of Parma, Italy running the family farm of olive trees and tomatoes. On occasion, they get together at Ocala Horse Farms and Training Center to celebrate their father's gift and memory.

Giovanni now lives with the tormenting burden of knowing and hiding the family secret of who killed John Kennedy and why Kennedy had to go.

Mr. Magoo

ABOUT THE AUTHOR

Growing up in Brooklyn, I was quite aware of the Italian connection and what they meant to the neighborhood. My father was a member of the Italian American Club and part of the "Family." Only when he was in his 70's and dying of cancer, did I find out what he did in his younger days and decided to write this story. That is where the idea and concept of Family Secrets came from. Fact or fiction? I cannot confirm nor deny the content within this <u>fictional</u> novel.

I was raised Catholic and was an altar boy at the age of 10. At age of 55, I became a minister and at age 60, wrote my first book God and the Gods.

I am a Brooklyn, New York boy at heart, and still have the New York accent, and will never lose it. I have one sister and one brother still alive.

This is my 2nd book, based on my childhood memories and neighborhood environment of which I grew up in during the old ways of life in Brooklyn. Most of the fellas and friends from the old neighborhood are now gone, but a few are still alive.

To them I say: "Vivere orgogliosa e forte".

Printed in the United States
By Bookmasters